ARCHIMEDES SLAKED

VOLUME 2

by

H. SCOTT STURM

AUTHOR'S
FOREWORD

I dislike lengthy forwards. A novel should speak for itself. But a few short words might be helpful. Archimedes Slaked is ultimately about technology and the complex generational shift and change in consciousness resulting from it. Although I hope it particularly speaks strongly to the young and might even be a rallying cry of sorts, it is for everyone trying to understand how the extraordinary, almost unimaginable, technological promise of our world can exist alongside the divisiveness, extremism, ideology and ignorance potentially tearing it apart. It is in many ways the story of the reluctant passing of the banner of responsibility for the future to the millennial generation by the boomers who are convinced that they and they alone know what is best for everyone, either by brains or by brawn. It is, I hope, a guide in a way, for the young on how to navigate that extremism and ignorance. And a warning to the rest that their days are numbered and their passions and fears are not only out of control but increasingly irrelevant. The solitary power of Atlas bearing the world and its future upon his shoulders is old and stale and will soon be rendered obsolete by the collaboration and technology of Archimedes. It is not an issue of if, but when. After reading these three volumes, my hope is that the young with their remarkable technology in hand, will perhaps be a little better prepared, and the rest, if unable to welcome them, will take their misguided passions and prejudices and narcissism and get out of their way.

I must express my gratitude to many people for their assistance, services and support. Most of you know who you are. If you know me, you know my appreciation. But special thanks to David Osborne, an extraordinarily talented author and publisher, for his thoughtful comprehensive editing and numerous other publishing and presentation services. A special thanks to Dyer Wilk for his visionary work on the covers for Vols. 1 & 2.

H. Scott Sturm
Louisville, KY
April, 2015

CHAPTER 1

"The empires of the future are the empires of the mind."
—*Winston Churchill*

"The future? Give me a second. I've got it right here."
—*Anonymous Internet Post*

"My god, you've actually done it," Nathan Broadwell said, looking down at New Eden. He struggled to properly register his microphone over the roar of the helicopter engine. The camera panned widely to show the new landscape extending beyond the horizon.

"We have a long way to go, as you can see," Abriado Centeri said. "Less than ten percent is at the optimal altitude of eighty feet above sea level. Probably sixty percent is still unreinforced aside from being below the critical level necessary to survive a hurricane or major storm. If the weather were to turn bad now, we would have very serious problems and could lose months of progress."

"But I see vegetation down there. Did you bring that in?"

"That was one of the wonderful surprises. Nature seems to be approving of what we are doing. It is all natural. The botanists have been examining it. It appears to have come from many sources: birds, the wind, our equipment, even from the sea itself."

"Remarkable," Broadwell said, the camera closing in on him alone. "Remarkable progress, remarkable vision. Aptly identified as potentially the most extraordinary, innovative and complex project in the history of mankind. And the complexity is not just attributable to the sheer scope alone, creating a new island the size of Connecticut and Rhode Island combined. But the technology to do so, to literally change the face of the planet, is almost beyond comprehension and has the potential to benefit mankind for generations to come. And that, I believe, is the real purpose of New Eden and the goal of its visionary, the enigmatic Abriado Centeri. While society is destroying itself in partisan, ideological warfare, this remarkable man quietly builds a New Eden with the help of tens of thousands of young technological minds from every corner of the globe."

As the dean of American broadcast journalists, Broadwell had recently retired from regular reporting and broadcasting and now focused on special investigations and documentaries. The press which had long revered him turned savagely against him when he spoke out against bias and the shift away from journalism towards entertainment and the inevitable loss of journalistic integrity. Unlike most of his colleagues in the press who were blatantly partisan, Broadwell's political leanings were a closely guarded secret and had never been disclosed or even implied.

It was a distinction lost on both the press and the public, who seemed to be enthralled by self-proclaimed neutral journalists losing all objectivity and mercilessly attacking their opponents with overt ideological rhetoric. Worse, Broadwell lamented the growing loss of even direct reporting of the news, which was being substituted instead by panel discussions and unrestrained opinion and the proliferation of human interest and soft news. "Merely reporting the news just didn't sell with advertisers anymore, and frankly the viewers were bored to tears," went the response he received from the networks as he explained to deaf ears the loss of an essential constitutional safeguard.

When he approached Centeri through his intermediaries and asked to do a report on the progress of New Eden, he expected no response, as was common for the reclusive and mainstream-media-suspicious Centeri. He was shocked when Centeri emailed him and immediately agreed, requiring only that he be accompanied by New Eden personnel and that Broadwell agree to broadcast the piece heavily on the internet and social media as well. The only topics he could not address were the power sources rumored to be revolutionary and virtually self-generating, and there could be no mention whatsoever of the super hacker now attacking and extorting companies worldwide. Aside from that, there would be no restrictions or limitations. Broadwell recognized that by being escorted by local personnel, he simply would not be shown what they did not want him to see, but he nevertheless was ecstatic. He would confront those limitations at the correct time and felt certain he could push his way in. He was literally the first journalist to be granted relatively unlimited access to what was already being recognized as the next wonder of the world.

"We are standing on what just six months ago was the ocean floor covered by hundreds of feet of raging surf," Broadwell said to his viewers.

The camera shifted to Centeri. "Perhaps more like fifty feet of soft, sandy sea bottom. And the sea is actually quite tranquil most of the time. You see, the reason we chose this location is the entire area was the source of an ancient volcanic eruption and is essentially a relatively shallow shelf. The depth rarely exceeded two hundred feet and was often, like here, very shallow. People do not realize the Caribbean basin is still quite active geologically, as evidenced by recent earthquakes and several active volcanoes. It made our job a little less daunting."

"How do you respond to critics who allege that you have raped eight thousand square miles of sea floor and destroyed the natural habitat forever and irrevocably interfered with the ecological balance?"

Centeri stared briefly at Broadwell. "You do not pull any punches do you? Again, this entire area was geologically mundane, being an ancient volcanic shelf. There was little variation on the sea floor. A very long time ago, the rocks were covered by hundreds of feet of sand. Scuba divers and snorkelers could tell you there was very little to see here. No coral reefs whatsoever and very few rock formations. Fisherman from the nearby islands rarely came here because the waters did not host much in the way of sea life. Certainly it was here, but there are much more fertile areas elsewhere. You must also remember the power of nature and the ecological balance you mentioned. All of the sand and seafloor we are moving here, as huge as it seems, is probably only a small percentage of what nature itself moves every time a hurricane hits this area. You do not see it but beneath the surface, especially on shallow shelves like this, vast amounts of sand and ocean floor are moved by the storms and tidal forces. What we are doing is something nature does not. We are seeding the ocean floor as we shift the sand to New Eden. As we move it, we carefully leave behind countless formations of rocks and other materials and at times artificial structures to create the foundation for active reefs and coral formations. We are creating the infrastructure for vast marine life in an area that was relatively devoid of it. And it is happening fast. There are already thriving communities of sea life building on the reef structures we created in almost every area we have touched. It has happened much more quickly than we ever thought. The technology all of these wonderful young people are employing as they work with us is literally changing the face of the earth and expanding life, not destroying it. That, I hope, adequately responds to the critics you mentioned. As is common in most walks of life, many people attack and criticize based upon their emotions and not the facts. They do not take the time to investigate and learn and use their minds."

"The power and responsibility of the mind and the integration with technology seem to be recurring themes with this powerful man, as he reminds us on virtually every opportunity. And note that he seems to be making an important distinction. He always speaks of technology and mind separately, rarely together interchangeably. To him they are separate but complimentary," Broadwell said, now directly facing the camera. "Every extraordinary development, every innovation is presented in these terms. Perhaps we should all learn more about this unique perspective."

Turning to Centeri, he asked, "How do you respond to the critique that New Eden is nothing but an immense expansion of your own ego, renamed New Ego, and a colossal waste of resources at a time when people are suffering across the globe?"

"Let me show you more of New Eden and its technology and allow you and your viewers to make up their own minds," Centeri answered.

"Technology and mind. You never miss an opportunity do you?"

Centeri did not respond to the seemingly rhetorical question.

With that the camera now showed a broad sweep of what could have been desert landscape in the Arabian peninsula. Instead of sand and sporadic patches of green or small rocks, immense earth moving vehicles and equipment dotted the landscape as far as the eye could see.

Centeri narrated. "The sand has been funneled in twenty-four-seven for over two years now by a massive delivery system, originating with the undersea-modified boring and tunneling equipment we call crawlers on the sea bottom, in some cases sixty miles away. There are over five hundred working at all times. All of these are controlled by a new technology system that permits us to effectively monitor virtually every square inch of their structures. This technology will have virtually endless applications not only here but worldwide. The vehicles you can see, over five thousand of them, which are similarly monitored, are spreading and leveling the sand in accordance with the geographical plans, to result in a highly diverse terrain. Right now, the majority of them are still working to raise the minimum altitude to over forty feet, with most areas to be much higher than that. The plans call for several dozen hills and plateaus to be at over two hundred feet. There will also be lakes, rivers, streams, canyons and all the other geological variety one would expect to find. Our scientists worked for years to develop plants, algae and other biological agents to secure and condense the sand. The original plans anticipated literally tens of millions of foundational beams to be implanted in the sand up to one hundred feet deep. Although it was done throughout the perimeter and often into the surf for a few hundred yards or so to greatly strengthen and support the shores, inland very little was needed to be done due to the success of the natural binding agents we developed and that are actually thriving under the sand. This is just one example of a technology that was developed for New Eden but will have wide applications in construction all over the planet. When the terrain work is done, most of the heavy equipment will be drained of its chemicals and toxic materials and deposited into the ocean to assist the reef building. Nothing is wasted in New Eden."

"What we see now is relatively featureless except for the sloping terrain, which is obviously in process," Broadwell said, now taking over the narration. "One can, with the mind's eye, see what the variety of the terrain may look like when completed. But it still appears barren and desert-like. What can we expect to see regarding trees and tropical vegetation and all the man-made infrastructure?"

"Expect to see the most beautiful, awe inspiring environment on the planet," Centeri answered. "And the most useful, efficient and environmentally integrated infrastructure. You do not see it from here, but many of the earth moving vehicles including modified crawlers are also hollowing out huge underground caverns that will honeycomb the island for the facilities ranging from irrigation, desalinization, water processing and sewage to power generation, communication technology, production of essential materials and supplies, warehousing, and virtually anything else you can imagine. Much of what is unattractive but essential for mankind everywhere else, will be below ground in New Eden. The result is there may be an exotic luxury resort being enjoyed by its guests, but thirty feet below it is a production and water processing facility, out of sight and not blighting the visual environment. Not everything will be beneath the service because we worried about the psychological effects of a subterranean world on the people maintaining the infrastructure, but much of it will be. In a way, we are constructing two worlds, one to enjoy and one to support the experience."

"Remarkable. Yet, this is a tropical climate and no one thinks of the tropics without rain forests and streams and waterfalls and lush tropical vegetation. How are you planning for that?" Broadwell asked.

"Good question," Centeri responded. "Vegetation is far more than the aesthetics. It is absolutely essential for the micro climate to be certain we don't end up with a sunbaked rock. If you have ever been on a tropical island, you probably have noticed that clouds often seem to move from the island out to sea. That is because the vegetation accumulates and traps water, which eventually evaporates and rises, creating clouds which create rain, the whole cycle hopefully repeating itself endlessly. So virtually every inch of New Eden will be covered with beautiful vegetation. Obviously, we cannot create trees overnight, but hundreds of millions of all varieties will be carefully and almost artistically planted, and in this environment should grow quickly. In the interim, we will substitute fast growing undergrowth, shrubs, small trees, and native plants. From day one it will be beautiful to see, with more and more mature plants and trees developing over time. Initially, we expect to rely heavily on irrigation, as the rainfall in this area coming off the sea is not as significant as you might expect, but development of the micro climate should come quickly. We are also planning untouched rain forests on probably twenty percent of the island to help with that."

"My next question is how and why are you doing this, Mr. Centeri?"

"First of all, I am not doing this," Centeri said, looking directly into the camera and emphasizing the word "I." "I am just one of eleven hundred founders and fifty five thousand personnel now, and eventually many times that, who are doing this, as you put it. As founders, we arranged for the funding and then sought out the brightest technological minds available from virtually every discipline imaginable, and the most skilled artisans and engineers to be followed by the most committed and talented operational personnel. As to why, that should be obvious. To demonstrate that mankind can change and enhance the face of the earth positively and take a giant leap forward technologically and to create a venue and attraction that will be enormously profitable not only through visitors and residents but through licensing the extraordinary technologies we are developing."

"So it is ultimately the bottom line that justifies everything," Broadwell said.

"I would not put it quite that way," Centeri answered, "but without that bottom line, there could be no New Eden. That is economics, that is capitalism."

"Do you find it ironic that opposition to New Eden is virtually unanimous even among factions that disagree upon everything else imaginable? Topher Blue called you insane and accused you of wasting capital that could have been applied to far more practical projects. Mercy Green effectively called you a murderer for committing trillions of dollars that could have fed and helped support hundreds of millions of people."

"No," Centeri responded. "Such comments are irrelevant to us."

"Does it bother you when the attacks are so personal, again questioning your sanity and accusing you of murder?"

"Again, I am one of many founders. But I am a spokesman of sorts. Nothing more. Such statements are rooted in profound ignorance. Their mindsets are hopelessly out of date and relate back to a period which they now mindlessly romanticize when either ruthless opportunists or demagogues ruled the world. Rapidly developing and changing technology makes such solitary influence and power in the hands of a few people impossible. No individual mind can grasp the scope or complexities of technology. Collaboration and collective vision are essential. The individuals you mentioned do not understand that and still try to wield influence personally in a manner better suited to a hundred years ago and in doing so, tear society apart. They are in no position to criticize us."

"Harsh words, Mr. Centeri," Broadwell said.

"Far less harsh than accusations of insanity and murder," Centeri immediately responded. "Enough of this, though. Let's meet the extraordinary people who actually are doing this, as you put it."

The next scene was in what appeared to be a massive command center not unlike the control room of a utility or power station. Numerous technicians sat at their consoles while Centeri and Broadwell and perhaps a dozen others observed.

"This is the brain central for the construction of New Eden," Broadwell said to the camera. "Our host asked that we not share with you exactly where we are but I can say we are in New Eden and we are underground. It is a massive, fascinating facility with over two thousand technicians at work monitoring and controlling the never ending process of building this brave new world."

The camera briefly switched to Centeri who, upon hearing Broadwell's overly dramatic narrative, briefly rolled his eyes. "This complex," he said, "is roughly organized by crawler and equipment operation, terrain development, facilities design and development, water management, terraforming, power generation, construction, procurement, communications, planning, administration, and technology support. We have already shown you above the extraordinary equipment and physical operations. Just as impressive, I believe, is the technology development, monitoring and support which effectively drives everything we do. I've mentioned a few of the inventions and innovations generated by the operations on the surface and sea bottom that we believe will have applications worldwide. We believe the truly profound developments are the computer and technology systems that enable all of this to even happen. The people you see here are actually only a small part of the technological minds at work. They are linked at all times to hundreds of other locations worldwide and tens of thousands of some of the very best minds on the planet. The physical scope of New Eden as you have seen is overwhelming. The technological and intellectual scope dwarfs even that. New Eden represents the greatest collaboration of intelligence in the history of humanity. Never before have so many brilliant minds been linked together and immediately accessible not just for the overall vision but the detailed development and operation. Our people are finding that no matter what the problem, no matter what the challenge, they can, within a very short time, find themselves talking to one of the world's leading experts on that very topic or have access by computer to their research. This has never happened before and may well be the greatest achievement of New Tech," Centeri suddenly stopped and corrected himself, "Excuse me, New Eden."

The focus of the camera then shifted to Centeri and Broadwell walking throughout the facility and speaking to nearly twenty New Eden personnel, most well under the age of forty, many in their twenties, about their areas of expertise and responsibilities. With each impromptu discussion, the passion of the participants and the enormity of the project and the technological innovation became more and more clear, enticing the viewer and seducing them with an almost otherworldly, science fiction feeling. Here, anything could be done. Here, anything was possible. Here, the chaos and waste and destruction of ideological warfare did not exist and was replaced by a technological environment of unparalleled unlimited human potential. Here young minds could collaborate and flourish and dedicate themselves to a new world of unprecedented technology and ignore the insanity of an older generation gone mad.

"My god," Neera Solai said, as she listened to Nathan Broadwell's closing commentary and finished viewing the documentary. "It's a goddamn recruitment film."

CHAPTER 2

"I'm sick to death of your whining! Just work goddammit. Stop crying like a baby. Work five jobs if you have to. Pull yourself up by your own bootstraps and don't look for help from anyone else. I did it. Every winner did it. You can too. Giving everything you have opens doors and creates possibilities you never even thought of. But if you chose not to, or if you're lazy or feel sorry for yourself, then don't blame anyone but yourself."

—*Christopher Blue*

"Politically persecuted family seeks asylum in US. Seems like the whole country is an asylum."

—*Anonymous Internet Post*

It was the first worldwide collapse of the electronic funds transfer system used by national and international commercial banks and financial institutions since the adoption of the automatic, internet-based network seventeen years earlier. It lasted for nine minutes and thirteen seconds. But during that brief time, an estimated five hundred eighty billion dollars of credit and monetary transfer transactions were interrupted and delayed, in some cases for hours and even days. The intangible impact was even greater. Systems and procedures taken for granted to be invulnerable were now questioned, and confidence was shaken. The delayed impact reminded observers of an almost global post traumatic stress disorder where countless institutions and companies now delayed payment and transfer transactions until the problem was identified, remedied, and assurances were given that another event would be impossible. The analysts warned that the indirect economic effect of this subsequent epidemic of caution and lack of confidence would be measured in the trillions.

The initial fear was an attack by A10. Within minutes, technicians were scouring every major application for the telltale signs of the defined systems paralysis and shutdown. No such signs were evident. When the global system suddenly sprang back to life, hundreds of thousands of systems experts across the globe went to work trying to understand what had just happened and whether there was any permanent damage. The internet was inundated with countless communications among the often young technological minds speculating on the causes and future safeguards. More cautious observers noted that many of these exchanges were being expressed in a type of restrained euphoria, almost as if it were a plot in a massive video game. A senior systems analyst in the Federal Reserve Bank in New York had even been disciplined for tweeting that "nothing this cool has ever happened before."

Eventually the cause would be traced to a national bank in Switzerland and attributed to its poor systems maintenance procedures, that an opportunistic and entirely implausible sequence of seemingly unrelated events triggered a cascade failure that spread in a system-wide chain reaction. Those subsequent failures were also caused by numerous examples of inadequate systems maintenance.

It was quickly recognized that the breakdown in proper maintenance protocols was the direct result of the technology strike and the intentional withholding of technological expertise. Governments and financial empires across the globe who had dealt with what had only been the inconveniences of isolated system problems previously, now took careful notice of the potential impact of the strike and what just nine minutes and thirteen seconds could do.

The warring political and ideological factions in the United States would once again demonstrate shocking unanimity on their solution to the problem, but for completely opposite reasons. A movement to restore the American Technology Initiative and its call for mandatory technology service by companies with more than twenty employees began in earnest, despite its being struck down by the Solai Systems' successful injunction. President Shank, as he had during the litigation, once again justified the drafting of technological minds as a constitutional imperative under the guise of national security and the preservation of free unobstructed markets and prosperity. He was not at all troubled by the seeming hypocrisy of the program which the Mercy Collective simultaneously celebrated as an historic populist and collectivist call to the service of mankind and the rejection of profit motivated self-interest.

It was not surprising. It was foolish to expect reason and logic where reason was no longer valued. It was equally foolish to expect careful purpose from men and women whose morality was conditional, whose true motivations were unspecified, perhaps even to themselves, and whose thoughts were undefined and reactive, held captive by their emotions and ideologies. The world was slowly learning that extremism was a process, ultimately indifferent to whatever principles laid beneath it, and that eventually those principles would merge into unrecognizable, incoherent rage.

It was estimated that over five thousand companies were now experiencing strike-related effects either overtly or through the interference of service relationships. Some of the strikers remained emboldened, threatening resignation unless sizeable payment and compensation packages were delivered, justifying their demands as consistent with the principles of self-interest and unrestrained free enterprise that had become the mantra for so many. And many employers had paid, in some cases extraordinary amounts. Others were less direct, especially in light of the recent legislation attacking the strikers and threatened police reprisals. They materially decreased the speed and efficiencies of their efforts, motivating their employers to increase their compensation without ever demanding the same. And still others had lost interest in the strike as Topher Blue, the government and many others were urging CEOs to share the enormous wealth they were accumulating to appease their employees and contractors with modest increases still far below prior levels that would lessen the likelihood of more aggressive actions. And finally, there were the youngest of these technical minds, the generation entering the work force within the past ten years. They continued working and seemed intent on doing so to the consternation and frustration of their older colleagues.

The effect was interrupted services, endless unmet deadlines, system failures, late deliveries, company shutdowns, confusion, and a lack of confidence on a slowly but steadily increasing scale. And all within an economy that was experiencing unprecedented unemployment rates teetering near twenty percent, commodity shortages, social unrest, mass demonstrations, widespread homelessness, outbreaks of previously eradicated diseases and dramatic upsurges in violent crime. Yet the wealthiest one percent of America prospered and continued to accumulate wealth at levels never before seen and scarcely imagined. Of the remaining ninety nine percent, half believed in a god-given right to join the one percent and were convinced that only the remnants of dependency, entitlement and government interference with free markets prevented them from doing so while the other half saw the only solution as a collective cleansing and re-education of all those who disagreed with them and were still seeking individual wealth.

The first food riot occurred on a hot summer afternoon in southern Texas, when four major food distribution centers were not restocked fast enough due to a week-long series of strike-impacted system failures that interrupted on a massive scale normally routine shipments of thousands of food items. Although the shortages affected less than twenty percent of the available goods, the public, fueled by internet and social media doomsayers and reckless broadcast commentators, panicked and converged on the stores, wiping the shelves clean. Those who did not found themselves with nothing but uncertainty as to when, if ever, the shelves might be restocked. In the small town of Fetzer, hysterical customers, convinced that their families would starve, beat to death the store manager and head cashier of the town's super grocery store and deposited their bodies in the store's large walk-in freezer. The corpses had avoided being frozen solid only by the quick thinking of their colleagues, who had sought shelter in the same unit and removed their remains after the crowd had moved across town. Similar crazed mobs followed, seriously or fatally injuring forty-three other store personnel in sixteen other towns and small cities.

Cletus Mooz, the governor of Texas, who had been hand picked by Red Shank as his successor, declared a state of emergency and called out the fully armed national guard to restore the peace, which promptly did so by killing fifty seven rioters and injuring over two hundred. President Shank labeled the rioters as "mad dog communists and collectivists who advocate theft and murder over gainful employment" while the Green Collective and numerous other commentators and organizations accused the government of mass murder and genocide and demanded the immediate arrest and impeachment of Shank and his entire cabinet.

Images of the unrest and attacks consumed the broadcast media around the clock while the anchors screamed at one another, asserting their own biases, implausible explanations, and conspiracy theories. The viewing public watched carefully, with increasing anxiety, assured of the authenticity and intelligence of these commentators and purported journalists, unable to distinguish between facts and hyperbole, becoming convinced that an already fractured society was on the brink of collapse. Similar riots broke out in seven more states where the governors quickly restored order, showing more restraint than Mooz had, resulting in less than fifteen deaths and injuries. The traumatized and overloaded viewing public, looking for any relief, deemed this as totally acceptable and agreed with the pundits who considered it a small price to pay for order. A popular social media website called DudesTechRead.com, used for posting commentary, opinion and whatever else was on the minds of its nineteen million young users, received nearly four million posts during the several days of the riots. Eighty three percent focused solely on speculation and heated debate about the technology giving rise to the original food distribution infrastructure system failures. The social unrest, injuries and deaths, though acknowledged and deplored, were considered not nearly as interesting.

It was seventeen days after the end of the last food riot when Governor Cletus Mooz called a press conference. It was ten o'clock in the morning and already the Texas sun was baking the state in eighty-five degree heat. The twenty two reporters present, most of them from the

Texas press, but several hailing from the national news networks, appeared mildly annoyed and eager to attend to other matters.

Mooz walked up to the podium, his shirt unbuttoned above his belt line, partially exposing his pot belly. His hair was parted only two inches above his left ear, the thin stringy hair pulled all the way over to the right in a vain, ineffective attempt to cover his heavily-receded hair line.

"Good morning ladies and gentlemen. I've asked you here this morning to make what I believe is a historical announcement to the great people of Texas. Beginning tomorrow morning, I have appointed a committee, with the full support of the legislature, to investigate, advise, and plan for the secession of Texas from the United States and to establish our great, god-fearing, freedom-loving homeland as an independent, sovereign, and powerful nation."

Near chaos erupted as Mooz's words jolted the press, who had expected a mind-numbing announcement of budget deficits or other fiscal matters.

"Now quiet, everyone. Settle down now, boys. Good gracious, you're acting like a bunch of damn reprobates. Got a lot more to tell you about." Mooz paused and waited for a few moments. "The America we grew up in and sacrificed for and loved with all our hearts is gone, never to return. We owe no duty to any nation that has been irrevocably corrupted by liberal, communist and socialist collectivist values and teaches its citizens to take, not make, and grow fat on the labors of good, productive, God-fearing people. We will no longer permit our boundless natural resources to be consumed by a corrupt nation. We will no longer allow our pre-eminent economic resources and infrastructure to subsidize the lazy and the incompetent. We were encouraged when our former governor Red Shank was elected president, and had high hopes he could turn the tides of collectivism, dependency and entitlement and restore this nation to his heartfelt ideals of individual responsibility, self-interest, small government, and prosperity. But I am afraid to say, doing so is beyond even his formidable powers and we have no choice but to take matters into our own hands and forge our own path as a sovereign nation with the help of god almighty. I am here to tell you that this is not an issue of if. It is a question only of how and when. What we have started here today will only conclude when the bells of liberty and prosperity ring across the new nation of Texas."

Mooz paused to take a sip of coffee and smiled. "Man, that's good Texan coffee, like a lot of other good Texan products." It was unclear to those present whether Mooz was aware that Texas did not cultivate coffee or if he was only bantering with the audience. "We recognize that this will be a formidable process. We recognize it may be unpopular with many outsiders who may attempt to stop us. But I assure you, we will not be deterred. We are not seceding from America because of political or social or religious differences. We celebrate and share the values of President Shank and his administration and applaud his noble efforts but, sadly, it is too late. Seventy years of liberal, socialist, collectivist policies have corrupted the soul of this once great nation beyond repair. Now mind you, we will not be constructing a wall and isolating ourselves. And this will all take a good few years. We want it to go smoothly and not interrupt business. I want to stress that we want the best of relationships with our neighbors and friends and are certain that commerce and cooperation between us will flourish."

He paused again and smiled broadly at the audience while pulling up his pants that had creeped down below his bloated stomach. "That's it, everyone. No questions I'm afraid. Need to give everybody a little time to let this all soak in. Check our website where we've posted all the information you will need. God bless America gentlemen. And god bless the prosperous, sovereign nation of Texas."

Three days later, the states of Oklahoma and Mississippi announced their intentions to join Texas in its secession movement to create an even larger Texan motherland. That same afternoon, the state of Alaska announced its own secession plan. The next day, seven southern states announced plans to begin investigating in earnest the establishment of a new Confederacy. Even New Hampshire hinted of an interest in independence.

President Red Shank refused to respond to the massive barrage of reporters' questions and even inquiries from Congress, responding that the matter was under investigation and that such sentiments were obviously the work of collectivist influence. Insiders responded that there was plenty of time and plenty of options to change the minds of the secession leaders, as if they were children preparing to run away from home. Topher Blue was strangely silent as well.

Mercy Green called a press conference and then promptly cancelled it. Her office released a statement saying that the whole secessionist movement was nothing but a feeding frenzy by the pirates devouring America and now tearing it apart at the seams and that it was too early to give it much credence. She advised her followers to wait for the next presidential election, where the principles of compassion, brotherhood and the sharing of wealth would be restored to government-derailing separatist selfishness and greed.

Four days later, A10 permanently disabled the internal communications systems of both the Texas governor's office and the legislature. It would take nearly one week to design and install an entirely new system. It was estimated that nearly twenty percent of all archival files were irretrievably corrupted and could not be restored. Mooz advisers were evenly split upon whether the attack would be viewed as underscoring the need for a separate independent Texan nation or if it exposed the state as an isolated, vulnerable target.

Shank and Blue continued to remain quiet while observers noticed what appeared to be substantially increased activity in both the White House and the Pentagon.

CHAPTER 3

"An alliance with a powerful person is never safe."

—Phaedrus

"If I could somehow merge with all this technology, if I could become a living computer like an android, even if part of my so called humanity was lost, it would be worth it."

—Anonymous Internet Post

"Adriana, please!" Abriado Centeri called out. "Please don't go. We need to talk."

Neera Solai was stunned. Centeri was almost panic-stricken by the rebuff of the great actress. She had never seen this man of extraordinary control and detachment demonstrate such anxiety and emotion.

"Talk? Talk? We do not need to talk, young man. You need to save lives," Adrianna replied angrily. "You need to take your obscene wealth and stop with all of this nonsense of technology and saboteurs and islands where you are playing god and save lives instead. Do you understand me? Those are the only words I wish to consider."

"We have been through this before Adrianna. I have explained."

"You did not hear a word I said and you never do," she responded.

Neera listened intently to her words, spoken in a calm but dismissive tone. She also noted something she had never heard before. Adrianna Snow was renowned for masterfully adopting dialect and accents in her many roles. In this conversational tone, presumably her normal speech, there was a very subtle hint of an accent. Neera could not make it out but it hinted of a Spanish or Italian dialect.

"Abriado," she continued, now in a more impassioned tone, "You could take ten percent of your money, just ten percent, and you would still have a ridiculous nine hundred billion left, and literally feed one hundred million people in Africa for nearly two years. That is the work of the gods, young man."

"You do not understand," he pleaded. "My wealth is not in cash sitting in a bank account somewhere. Virtually all of it is invested in people and companies. It cannot be converted into cash. I employ directly over three million people and indirectly, with other investors, another five million at least. Most of those people have families. So my efforts alone and with others provide salaries and careers and lifestyles and food on the table for tens of millions of people. Multiply that by the goods and services they provide and consume and all the transactions generated from them and the numbers cannot even be accurately calculated. Is that not enough for you Adrianna?"

"Do not ever patronize me, Abriado," she responded angrily. "I understand economics and I do not require a lesson from you in anything. These happily employed people you speak of are not people in crisis. These are not people with starving and diseased children who die in their arms. You pride yourself on providing a structure for millions while you let those who could literally be saved by a hundred dollar bill starve to death. You could save countless lives and not even notice the funds were gone. You disgust me." She turned and again walked away.

"I gave away three hundred million dollars last year alone to charities!" he screamed, now virtually hysterical.

"To whom?" she shouted, turning around and glaring at him. "To students and training programs and medical research I'm sure. How much to feed the hungry? How many people did you feed Abriado? How many lives did you not save that you could have with virtually no effort? Have you ever held a three year old starving to death and dying from a completely preventable disease? I have. Many times. You are a monster, Abriado, and the worst kind imaginable. You veil your brutality and hypocrisy in power and delusions of knowing what is best for everyone. I almost prefer Shank and Blue and those other pirates over your self indulgence. At least they do not even try to disguise their inhumanity."

Centeri frantically stepped forward towards her in a futile effort to defend himself, to defend his life, to allow reason to prevail. He reached for her hand, perhaps hoping that physical contact might somehow convey his humanity. She instinctively jerked her hand away from his intended grip and with the other slapped him across the right side of his face, throwing her entire small body into the assault.

"Do not touch me, you…you bastard!" she screamed. "Do not ever touch me!"

Reeling from the force of her attack and the rage of her words, Centeri collapsed to his knees, incoherent, his body jerking uncontrollably.

"Stop it, Ms. Snow! Stop it!" Neera screamed, running to Centeri's aid, putting aside her own anxiety of just moments before. "This is wrong. You are destroying him. He gave millions, countless millions. We all do. How do you help people when there is no way to get the food and medicine to them and it is lost and stolen by rebels or a thousand other thieves? Every minute of his life is dedicated to changing the world in ways we can't even comprehend!"

"Yes, yes, yes," she said now calmly, shaking her head and turning away, walking to the building in front of them, her age and frailty now very apparent. "You do not even have a clue as to who and what he is, you gullible fool. Whether you admit it or not, you are attracted to his money like everyone else. Please leave us in peace and go discuss your profound love of humanity and compassion in your fleet of private jets. When he stops crying like the spoiled child he is, tell him that I never wish to see him again."

Opening the door, Adrianna Snow stopped and turned to them one last time. "And one final warning," she said. "Leave that poor boy alone. I pray that you do not find him. He is a gift, a wonder of nature. He is pure and beautiful and uncorrupted. He must not be ruined by the likes of you."

Neera stared at her in horror and disbelief as she disappeared through the door. She kneeled down and put her arm around Centeri, who was weeping quietly. "I am so sorry Abriado," she said, tears now streaming down her own face. "You did not deserve that. She is the monster. Not you or anyone else." She felt Centeri lean towards her, his head falling to her shoulder. She gently stroked his head, comforting him until his sobbing lessened. Holding him, her mind raced over what had just happened. She had never seen such vulnerability and emotion from Centeri, much less his virtual collapse. She would not have thought it was possible that a man so powerful, so brilliant, so deliberate and in control, so seemingly invulnerable, could be devastated by the words of another human being, no matter how malicious. Centeri was used to vicious, relentless criticism and attacks from all quarters. He was constantly vilified by the Mercy Collective and all of its factions and feared by Topher Blue and Shank and governments and business leaders everywhere because he could not possibly be paid off or corrupted. That inability was incomprehensible to such men, who believed everything could be consumed and perverted. It even strengthened their resolve to destroy him. Yet the words of a frail, elderly woman literally brought him to his knees in emotional ruin.

"I'm sorry Neera. I never wanted you to see me this way," he said quietly, his embarrassment evident. "I am powerless when it comes to her. I always have been."

"Shhhhh," she gently reassured him. "I don't even know the woman and I think I'm ready for therapy," she said, trying to distract and comfort him. "I don't understand though, Abriado. Why did she feel she could say such terrible things to you? How long have you known her? I almost sensed a feeling of arrogance or control or...I don't know how to describe it."

Centeri breathed deeply as if to gather himself. A profound sadness seemed to envelope him. "She is my birth mother Neera," and with those words this man of unlimited power and influence and insight and vision, this man who accepted the responsibility to try and raise the consciousness of all humanity, seemed for a moment like a frightened, vulnerable child.

"Oh, god," Neera said and found she was so overcome by his agony, she could say nothing more. The words of Adrianna Snow had been vicious and calculated to wound unmercifully. But coming from one's mother, the damage was incalculable.

As Neera embraced Centeri even tighter, to somehow lessen his pain, she heard a roar from behind her and saw two of his security vehicles racing to them and braking suddenly, raising an acrid cloud of dust. Five of the agents broke from the vehicles and, seeing Centeri collapsed in Neera's arms, pulled out their side arms and screamed, "Stand back now, Ms. Solai!"

"Stop it!" Centeri shouted suddenly revived. "I'm okay. Stand down! Nothing has happened."

Paulo ran to them and immediately pulled Centeri away from Neera. "Are you hurt? What happened? You turned off the monitor and the protocol is to respond if we don't hear from you within fifteen minutes."

The other four agents had formed a perimeter around them.

"I know, I know. Let's just say I am having a very bad day." Turning to Neera he smiled and said, "Thank you Neera. I will explain this all to you. But right now I am afraid we are attracting a little too much attention. Aldo, please pull back quickly before everything is ruined. We are fine."

The security chief was not convinced.

"Now, damn it!" Centeri said angrily.

"Not until you turn the monitor back on."

Centeri reached into his front pocket and did so and the security personnel walked slowly back to their vehicles and slowly backed out of the lot.

Neera saw that three people were approaching them from the building. They were elderly and well dressed and moved towards them in a non threatening manner, but slowly and cautiously.

"Abriado," a man, likely in his seventies called out. "Are you alright?"

"Yes Franklin," he said smiling. "I am afraid she got the best of me. Again."

"I am sorry. She does indeed know what strings to pull. For everyone I'm afraid."

Centeri said nothing and nodded.

"Please come inside, both of you," he said.

Neera and Centeri followed the three of them into the lodge. "May I get you something?" Franklin asked.

Centeri shook his head. Neera kept her arm around him as they walked through the door. He did not resist. They both sat down.

"Neera, let me introduce Franklin Storm. Also Regina Whitfield and, I'm pleased to see, Brick Nargi."

Once again, Neera almost gasped. Storm and Whitfield were two of the pre-eminent scientific minds on the planet. Nargi was the world's most sought after and reclusive artist.

"We had hoped to greet you before our cantankerous friend did. My apologies," Whitfield said.

Centeri smiled. "May we talk?" he asked.

"Turn off your monitor please. There is no danger here."

Speaking to his security team he said, "I'll check in in one hour. I am with friends." He switched off the system.

Franklin looked at him oddly, unsure of his use of the word friends.

"Is he here, Franklin?"

"No. He was. For nine months, but he is gone. He is not who you are looking for," Franklin said.

"How do you know who I am looking for?" Centeri asked.

"Why, A10 of course."

"I am, but I am also looking for the prodigy. I only suspect they may be one and the same."

"They are not."

"With all due respect, how do you know that?"

"He is not capable of such," he hesitated, grasping for words, "such stupidity. He is a profoundly remarkable young man."

"His area of expertise seems consistent with how A10 is doing what it is doing."

Franklin and the others said nothing.

"What is his name? Please tell me."

"Why? What do you intend to do?"

"I intend to save his life. They are after him and they will stop at nothing to extract his knowledge. And if he is A10 and perhaps even not, they will kill him."

"Sounds a bit melodramatic, Abriado," Nargi said. "Your mother is convinced you pose an equal threat."

"My mother is the melodramatic one as you well know. I swear to you we will protect him first. Anything beyond that will be entirely his call."

"And if he is A10? What then?"

"The only solution is for him to disclose how to disarm the attacks and release it to the world, with no restrictions, all at once. If everyone has the knowledge, the threat is ended. You can help me convince him. You again have my word."

The room was deathly quiet for several moments.

"His name is Boortah Guyah," Whitfield finally said. "Or at least that is what he has told us. He has never disclosed his nationality or anything about himself. He speaks with a subtle accent that almost seems Middle Eastern, but has given us hints that he may have roots in the Balkans or southern Russia. He is an enigma in that respect. He was intensely secretive and easily angered. So we gave him plenty of room. At least regarding his work. Socially, interpersonally, he was a sweet and even naïve young man."

"When did he leave?"

"About two months ago. When we gave him shelter, he immediately began constructing a lab and workshop in a small warehouse. Truckloads of technology equipment began coming which, given our backgrounds, did not really attract any attention. It was truly remarkable equipment and none of us really understood what he was doing. He showed it off proudly to Franklin and me and a few of the others but was always vague on its purpose. Obviously we gathered quite a bit, but only so far. It was truly unique. Massive processing units and what appeared to be wireless communications gear and a whole host of other unrecognizable units. Its purpose had been an enthralling source of discussion among us but I am afraid we really don't have a clue."

"Is it still here?"

"Yes and no," she answered. "When he told us he was leaving, he explained he must discard the equipment so that no one could ever retrieve it and asked us to trust him as to how he would do so. He oddly said that there would be no danger or threat to anyone. About two nights later there was only what I could call a tightly controlled explosion and fire at his lab. It was unlike anything any of us had ever seen. A blinding blue light emerged from the structure for almost forty minutes, and a fair amount of smoke. We could hear low pitched rumblings but that is all. The structure remained entirely intact. We were concerned of course but he came down and assured us again that everything was under control. It's still there, or perhaps I should say what is left of it, but there is little to give us any hints at its purpose."

"Did he work alone? Did he have help or visitors?"

"There were other young people joining him for varying periods from time to time. They were all very polite and seemed quite technically proficient. Some of them with European or eastern accents. There was one American who Franklin thought might have been a former student. But they were never here for any length of time."

"May we see it?" Centeri asked.

The three of them looked at one another.

Centeri sensed their caution and reluctance. "I have given you my word and I cannot believe that you would consider me a threat."

"Abriado, we do not, not really, but it is a privacy issue and you must also understand we are all here sympathetic to the principles of the Mercy Collective. Many of us believe you are a very significant part of the problem tearing America apart. The wealth and power you possess should never be in the hands of one man. Though we do not agree with how she delivered her message, most of us here agree strongly with the substance of what your mother said," Whitfield responded.

Her words appeared to be the final offense. Hearing them, Centeri briefly winced. "I will protect him. Someone must do so. They will find him."

The three whispered among themselves. "Franklin will take you," she said. "You can turn on your video if you wish."

Centeri did so, surprised that they would permit it without his asking. He and Neera and Franklin walked out the rear door of the lodge and onto a meandering trail. After ten minutes of walking, they came upon a long, narrow cinderblock building. Franklin unlocked the side door and the three of them entered. He switched on the lights, that appeared to have been recently installed, showing the interior.

"Are you getting this, Sun?" Centeri asked over the wireless device.

Everything in the building appeared to have been exposed to incredible heat and was melted where it stood. They could still make out computer frames and outlines of periphery equipment. File and storage cabinets and remnants of living quarters could also be seen but all were now empty shells with their contents appearing as halfway melted ice frozen in time. One wall was covered with book shelves and a few dozen books somehow survived the inferno. Shakespeare, Joyce, Tolstoy, Machiavelli, Plato, Darwin, numerous scientific treatises and technical manuals, all odd tributes to the power and vision of the human mind, even more out of place in this ruined building.

Neera looked about carefully and saw what appeared to be a large solid structure in the left rear corner.

"Abriado," she said. "In the back to the left."

She and Centeri walked to the remains. "What is this?" Centeri asked, his voice trailing off, his mind lost in thought. Although badly melted and perhaps disassembled, they saw a large solid stainless steel foundation measuring fifteen by ten feet with literally hundreds of melted metal extensions several inches across. Surrounding it were numerous pieces of ruined equipment, most of them appearing to be melted computers, but a few possessed the remnants of control panel features.

"My best guess would be some type of a receiver or a transmitter, maybe even a generator, and those are cooling extensions, but so little remains, it could be anything. And how could he have generated the heat necessary to do this without vaporizing the building? Franklin, could my people take this and examine it more closely?" he asked.

"Absolutely not," Franklin responded. "It is not ours to give and you know how we feel. Your scientists can analyze the pictures you are taking. Nothing more."

Over the next twenty minutes, Centeri covered nearly every square inch of the building, picking up and turning over every piece of metal he could handle, being sure the small video cameras on his shirt pocket and on his travel case were recording the images.

"I think so too," Neera heard him say, speaking to whoever was on the other end of the communications link.

"What do they think, Abriado?" she asked

"Sun thinks it has something to do with nano technology and those might be what remains of what prior to now were only theoretical preliminary designs on a very small scale. The theory is that under enough pressure, combining a vacuum and super conductivity, assuming that could even be designed, which until a few minutes ago we were certain it could not, you can effectively eliminate the practical difficulties of great distances and essentially transfer power and anything that rides upon it like data, simultaneously, almost as if it exists in two places at once. It's marvelously, almost otherworldly complicated stuff, with its roots dabbling in quantum theories. The challenge has always been the physics where the larger the size, the more energy was required, which actually is a common problem plaguing physics, so it became practically impossible unless you have a generator the size of a continent. So the theoretical solution was always miniaturization. But the technology did not exist. What we are doing with our nano modules is like the invention of the wheel compared to a formula one race car. Sun thinks those hundreds of chambers you see may have housed the technological solution. If so, theoretically, tampering with a software program or any electronic signature from a thousand miles away becomes child's play."

"He can tell all of that from these burnt out remains?"

"No. It's absolute speculation, almost science fiction, but that is what they have been forced to look at when it comes to A10. Franklin, do you have any thoughts?"

"It is not my field, but you are right that the configuration implies that it contains enormous pressure, and their current condition implies being impacted by extraordinary energy. My sense is that even if we let you take it, the heat and pressure already destroyed any useful information."

"In any event, something very important was occurring here and we need to find this young man."

"He is not A10," Franklin said.

"Perhaps not, but my guess is he knows who is and they are using his technology. You said there were others."

"They're almost children. They couldn't do this."

"If that is true, then we have another connection. The analysts are saying that whoever A10 is, they are executing this extraordinary power almost naïvely, like someone very inexperienced would."

"This is all speculation," Franklin said. "We should not have brought you here. I think it is best you both leave. If you find him, you will use all this for purposes we cannot approve."

"I have already told you that I will not let that happen."

Franklin looked at him almost sadly, with the wise eyes and experience of a great scientist who had dedicated his life to the pursuit of knowledge and truth. Letting a moment of compassion show through, he spoke quietly. "You will have no choice and that is what frightens us. You are a good man, Abriado. We know that. But even good men must at times do terrible things. This technology and the madness and greed in the world may force your hand."

Neera stared at him, her instincts and insight dissecting his words and his very presence. "There is more," she said quietly. "There is something you are not telling us."

Turning away, he said, "Please leave. You can find your way back."

Neera reached down to pick up her bag and in one fluid motion picked up one of the melted metal extensions that had broken off from the grid and slipped it into her bag. It was unexpectedly heavy, momentarily throwing her slightly off balance, but Franklin had not observed her. She would know momentarily whether Centeri and those monitoring on the security channel had.

Within minutes, Centeri and Neera were back in their SUV.

"Impressive move," Centeri said, knowing his friend was undoubtedly already experiencing conflicting emotions.

"I don't think I'm proud of myself," she said.

"It was absolutely necessary. We both know that. And I am almost certain he would not have stopped you. He is a great man with the open mind of a scientist. He was conflicted and decided to let events unwind on their own. That is why he turned away. The others never would have taken their eyes off of us."

A voice suddenly blurted out from the security panel. It was Sun speaking excitedly. "You have something? What did you get?"

"Our shoplifting friend appears to have pinched one of the grid extensions," Centeri said chuckling.

"Awesome!" he nearly shouted. They could hear excited voices almost cheering and high-fiving in the background. "Amazing! My god Ms. Solai, you're my hero. I don't care how degraded it is, we'll learn from it. You could not have selected a more important piece! Very, very cool!"

"I do not feel like a hero," she said.

"It's too important. Too important on so many levels to be limited by ideology," Centeri said.

"I know, I know," she said. Turning away from Centeri, she stared blankly out of the window, watching the rugged landscape pass by, hardly noticing its beauty. She thought about the balance of necessity versus morality and how that very same principle was being used to justify barbarous acts all across the globe and always had been throughout human history. She knew that the willingness to indulge such rationalizations took on an energy of its own, expanding from a simple, seemingly justified act of taking a melted piece of metal despite the directions of its owners not to do so, to whatever was convenient or expedient to defend or excuse. The only check on such inevitable extensions and the destruction and abuse they could lead to, she reasoned, was to never start the process as, sadly, she just had. A defined immediate need was just too compelling, too tempting to the human mind to forego for the sake of an undefined future consequence. One must restrain oneself, she reasoned, and never allow the first step to be taken.

"I will never do anything like that again," she said, almost in a whisper.

"I hope you will not have to in the same manner, but that is not realistic. May I suggest another viewpoint to assuage your moral dilemma?" he asked.

She did not answer.

"People make choices, make judgments, decide between alternatives, affect their own and other's lives, play god as it were to small degrees everyday. They just don't recognize it as such. Our society over the past fifty years or so has overreacted to and distorted the idea of rank and status and classification as the ultimate affront to human dignity and instead espouses plurality and diversity at all costs. But we judge and rank and prioritize and reject and choose in virtually everything we do, to some degree. But this is not recognized and we see only the potential, artificial damage of hierarchy. And so hurting one's feelings or seemingly demeaning them in the eyes of others or themselves when rejecting their actions or thoughts becomes the cardinal sin the pundits call 'political correctness.' That mindset carries over to every aspect of existence. And this is despite the fact that no man can hurt the feelings of another. We all choose how to react and alone feel what we feel. And no man can demean another. He can only speak words or treat him a particular way. It is up to us to accept or reject it, to deny it or empower it. This is not rhetoric. I myself dropped my guard and caused myself great pain by Adrianna's words. I allowed my mind to process and amplify her words, nothing more, and I alone generated my own distress. I was an actor lost on a stage she created instead of being the director sitting in the audience, participating in the entire theater, knowing her words were nothing but an illusion, a drama that I reacted to. They could not touch me. I touched me. And it is the same with your deciding that the metal cylinder was far too important, too many lives were potentially at stake, to leave rusting on a warehouse floor because of the wishes and ideologies, however pure or impure, of those people. You made a spontaneous rational decision and it did not demean anyone and it does not have to recklessly or automatically expand to some sort of serial violation of the rights of others. Franklin was right. It was their property or at least they were entrusted to safeguard it. That interest, that responsibility does not automatically take precedent over all other considerations. Their feelings on this issue do not prevail merely because they are their feelings, overriding every other interest. Questioning these feelings or ideals or judging or prioritizing them, must no longer be deemed an insult or affront or act of marginalization. Not doing so, remaining silent, tacitly accepting is the real crime. You used your mind today Neera, you responsibly judged, you prioritized, you valued the interests, you rejected the thoughtless shackles of ideals and ideology and tepid plurality. As long as you remain true to that process, and it is the process that is critical, your actions were valid."

"Thank you," she said. "I will consider your words." After a few minutes of silence, she asked, "I thought your mother was a Countessa in Italy. I don't want to intrude, but since I was thrust into it today, can you share with me what the hell is going on?"

"You've certainly earned that," he said, laughing. "Audio off please," he said to the monitors.

"Abriado," she asked with alarm. "Your people just heard everything?"

"It will do them good. It applies to them as well. In any event, here is my story with Adrianna. It initially flows like that wonderful movie with Audrey Hepburn and Gregory Peck about the princess and her fling in Rome. My father was in Florence as a student for a three month seminar. He runs into my mother in a café on the Plaza Republica. She is already an aspiring actress and is intrigued with a brilliant handsome Cuban American student, wickedly outside of the usual romantic interests arranged by her father the respected Italian Count. They spend the next two weeks madly in love, basking in the wonders of Florence and Tuscany. And of course I am conceived. Adrianna's lust for enjoyment in life was only surpassed by her ambition and she decided I would potentially be a serious impediment to that. So over the next several months, she notices real chemistry between my father and her cousin Marjorie, destined to inherit the title of Countessa. So she sets to work like a director consuming a long script to free herself from me but, as is her way, to make sure I am well taken care of so she will never have any reason to feel any guilt. Or perhaps more importantly, embarrassment. So everything is arranged. Marjorie becomes my mother, who I adore, my parents live happily ever after, and I am raised as a little Italian semi-noble, even more intriguing because of the ethnicity and lack of standing of my father. And I don't know a word of this until I am about twenty and suddenly learn that my real mother is the leading actress and stage personality of the entire planet. I naturally want to be included in her life. Obviously I had seen her occasionally growing up, but she was always distant and aloof. Not just to me but to everyone, or so I thought. I reached out to her, happily I thought, and she promptly told me that she had more than met all of her obligations to me and that it was better that I forget she was my birth mother and continue to flourish in the life she had arranged for me. Of course I was devastated but I was so ambitious and energetic myself, I worked through it and moved on as best as I could. And, I started to meet with success. I completed my schooling and found I had a knack for technology integration and spotting opportunities, and as you know, I initiated some benchmark software systems and companies and over the years leveraged them with a lot of luck and great timing to get where I am today. Several times during those years, I reached out to her again but she summarily rejected me. As my celebrity grew, I can only presume that I was an increasingly public, annoying loose end to Adrianna that reminded her of the only impulsive decisions she had ever made in her life. About ten years ago she began to email me, offering what purported to be advice but what was really veiled and then not-so-veiled criticism. I tried to ignore it, but I had spent so much of my emotional energy trying to get her to acknowledge and express even a little pride or affection for me. It hurt terribly, Neera. Therapy, help from family, meditation, nothing really helped. And so this is where we are. My occasional visits with her usually end like the one you saw today, although the slapping and referring to me as a bastard were ruthless new escalations. It breaks my heart on so many levels. She truly is magnificent in many ways as you and the world know. She is a prodigy in a way hard to describe. She has the ability to absolutely master anything she reads. It is not photographic memory. It is much more than that. She can read a script and memorize and master it in that one reading. Every subtlety, every inflection, every innuendo mastered even beyond the inspiration of the writer. It is the same with musical compositions or any organized data. It really is remarkable."

"I see where you get your talents," Neera said while he paused.

"No. I am not extraordinary in any way. Not like her. I am not being humble. I test pretty normal in all areas. Nothing stands out. I don't know what I want from her except perhaps recognition, validation. I know it sounds needy and perhaps she is right that I am a cry baby, at least when it comes to her. I know she is facing the nightmarish withering of her powers and her own mortality and I wish I could comfort her. It is natural to want to do so for a parent. To comfort them. She will not allow it. She will not admit her growing weakness, certainly not to me. She has told me a hundred times that I am the only mistake of her life and every breath I take reminds her of it. She despises me."

"She despises herself for not being able to embrace you. You and everything you have accomplished reminds her of her emotional emptiness. She cannot escape it. Your incredible achievements are everywhere. She knows she is terribly wrong and can only avoid it by vilifying you and trying to label all that you do as a failure. If you are a monster, she made the right decision all those years ago. I would guess she never had any other children."

"There was no room for them, of course. But you are probably right. Your words echo what all the therapists have said, to say nothing of the family." He paused for a few moments. "Would you mind if we delay our next visits and go back? We discovered some extraordinary information and I want Sun and the others to investigate the cylinder and determine the next steps. With some luck, we may have cracked this thing open a bit. Plus, I must admit, I need a little down time after visiting my loving mother."

"Of course. I was going to suggest it," she answered.

Neera watched the landscape approaching her and saw the security vehicles, appearing almost from nowhere, suddenly pull in front of and behind them, openly protecting Centeri from a world which would destroy him. A wave of strange comfort enveloped her as they did, knowing that he was safe. Yet, effective as they were, they were powerless to protect him from the destructive malice of a frail old woman. Perhaps she could help protect this remarkable man from that threat. She smiled as she thought about doing so.

Without a word spoken, she felt Centeri's hand grasp hers warmly and tightly as he drove. This time, it was she who did not resist.

CHAPTER 4

"I merely help put into words what decent, God-fearing Americans already know is the truth and long for in their lives. I do not influence them. They influence me. I am their voice and nothing more. Never forget that."
—*Christopher Blue*

"WIBNI you could click your heels three times and go back to Kansas?"
—*Anonymous Internet Post*

Nathan Broadwell fixed his microphone and settled into his chair at the desk. Mercy Green sat across from him and smiled.

"Are you ready, Ms. Green?" he asked.

"Ready and most willing," she said.

The technician completed the last lighting and audio checks. She looked at Broadwell and said, "Five, four, three," and then finished "two and one" with her fingers. The live interview broadcast to several hundred broadcast news, cable and internet channels commenced.

"Good evening," he said. "We are honored tonight to speak with the founder and inspiration of the Mercy Collective, Mercy Green. How are you tonight Ms. Green?" he asked.

"Wonderful, excited and eager to share our vision for a renewed America based upon love, compassion, and brotherhood."

Broadwell smiled. "Then by all means, let's get to it.

"First, I would like to ask your opinion about recent news, particularly the hunger riots and the secession announcements."

"Oh my goodness," she said, laughing. "You don't waste any time, do you? I don't think anyone should be surprised about these terrible events. They are the natural results of the greed and selfishness strangling our great country. When you have a president, congress, and corporate oligarchy raiding the economy and starving and murdering the populace and brainwashing them to believe it is the American way and they can join in the fun, such reactions are not at all surprising. Add a media substantially bought and paid for by these raiders, present company excepted of course, and how could you expect anything but widespread panic, fear and the crumbling of what little legitimate government structure remains? These states are not threatening secession to make a better life for their citizens. Mooz and the other governors merely want to keep what they steal for themselves and not share it with Washington under the perverted anthem of self-interest. The poor people caught in the middle naturally fear for themselves and their families and it is no wonder that they strike back."

"But the rioters did not strike out at the government did they? They murdered innocent employees."

"They attacked who they thought represented the financial interests starving them. Their rage was blind, as most rage often is. Of course I do not condone such murderous brutality, but I understand it."

"You have faced criticism that you did not take a stand and call for order and an end to the violence."

"That is not true," Green said. "It happened very quickly and we were trying to understand exactly what was happening and who was involved. We would never be so naïve as to jump to conclusions and rule out that these might have been staged, premeditated attacks organized by Shank and Blue to justify their murderous disproportionate response. Please remember that many of our events have been seeded with paid criminals and assassins to disrupt and discredit our efforts. By the second day, we were imploring our supporters to work for peace and understanding. Our own intelligence suggested that some of the ring leaders were former Shank operatives who felt betrayed."

"Really. That is a very serious charge. Can you document that?" Broadwell asked, leaning forward and staring intently at Green.

"Indeed we can. We have photos and videos of known government operatives in the thick of things. It is clear that they were not innocent observers. They will be on our website early tomorrow."

"What could they hope to gain?"

"To blame it on their political opponents, on us, on the forces of collective decency, and justify the murder and carnage that followed. To strengthen their stranglehold on our great nation and even elevate their violence. Is it so surprising? To elevate self-interest as the highest value of man, above all else, almost guarantees that your followers will inevitably pursue that interest against even you. We are already seeing it in the strike. Many of the strikers, beginning with the first known examples, rejected handing over the product of their minds even to their employers unless they were paid enormous sums, likening it to the contrived dependency and entitlement Topher Blue has rallied against. What Shank and Blue used as a rallying cry was turned against them. What delightful irony! Now they are appeasing those strikers, slaking them I think they call it, throwing them crumbs and leftovers. It is working on some but not all. But the genie is out of the bottle. The armies of people they have indoctrinated with their propaganda and perverted ideology of self-interest and individual responsibility as the highest and most noble ideal of man are beginning to sniff out the fraud and recognize the impossible limitations they face and how the very forces that espoused self-interest are limiting their own. The raiders certainly don't want that to be known, so who better to blame everything on than the takers, the villainous, lazy, blood-sucking forces of dependency and entitlement?"

"You anticipated my next question Ms. Green, about the strike. So you believe there are different motivations within the strikers? How serious is it, really?"

"Deadly serious I am afraid, already straining a system teetering on ruin. We live in a different world today. We are dependent on our technology. It is by its nature collective and collaborative. So when our technology people refuse to work or when they slow down their efforts, whether motivated by greed and self-interest or political protest, or even hunger and despair, the effects can be catastrophic. We have seen this dramatically in the recent riots and fund transfer system problems, and perhaps less acutely but just as seriously in the thousands of companies impacted and the lost efficiencies and extra costs incurred. It is as if nature itself, through technology, is confirming our commitment to collectivism, saying this world will no longer work unless we work together. It is not only a spiritual and moral imperative to work together for the benefit of everyone, but the very nature of our growing technology and our inevitable dependency upon it cannot function otherwise. That is why we teach people that our beliefs and principles of unity and fairness and the equal sharing of wealth among all men and women is the only option for humanity, not the outmoded tribal, selfish beliefs of our opponents who jealously horde the resources of this wonderful planet for themselves and establish doing so as the highest ideal."

"You actually agreed with your opponents about the American Technology Initiative breaking the strike and requiring service by technology workers in times of crisis."

"Only in its effect. Our principles are founded upon collective and collaborative effort for the benefit of all men and the protection of the needy and disenfranchised, so any conditions that limit it must be eliminated. Individual self-interest must never prevail over the collective good. Our opponents, on the other hand, see it as a method to assure a continuing supply of talent to perpetuate their greed and theft. The only agreement is that the technology strike if it continues and grows will literally shut our society down, with catastrophic consequences. That cannot be permitted to happen. What I believe can be done and should be done is that the poor, the disenfranchised, the homeless, all of those devastated by the policies of these monsters in power, should organize and demonstrate peacefully and plan a day nationwide to contemplate and meditate with their families. These are the decent, wonderful people who staff our stores and restaurants and factories and businesses and clean our buildings and operate our facilities and a billion other tasks."

"Are you actually proposing a general strike? Perhaps you have more in common than you think," Broadwell asked.

"I find that offensive Mr. Broadwell," Green said, her anger apparent. "I am proposing a national day of reflection and contemplation. That is all. Shank and Blue and their governmental and corporate cronies are thieves and murderers and monsters conducting what history will one day label as veiled genocide. If I decide to run for president and when I am elected, my first duty to the American people will be to prosecute them all for their crimes against humanity."

"There you go again," he said. "Anticipating my next question. Will you run for president?"

"Of course, we have not yet made a final decision, but as of now it is very likely. I have not hidden that fact."

"Can you win, especially with your agenda of legislative reform that many call collective extremism and others label as radical socialism and even communism?"

"With over sixty million Americans unemployed, forty million living on the streets, and god knows how many starving to death and dying for lack of medical attention, with all the safeguards and safety nets of the last fifty years eradicated, logic dictates that people are ready for change and want the criminals in power behind bars. They are crying out for the restoration of compassion and decency and brotherhood."

"But do they want your kind of change Ms. Green? Will not a more moderate position be more attractive?"

"Labels mean nothing, Mr. Broadwell. Feeding a child and providing the necessities of life to a single mom or a retired teacher means everything."

"Among your proposed programs and reforms, and there are many as our viewers should be aware, is the Collective America Act which limits the wealth any American can personally possess. America was founded on economic freedom and the lure of being a winner. Will people accept handcuffing this?"

"I disapprove of your characterization. We are not handcuffing anyone. That is Red Shank's MO. Our mantra is 'when one person suffers, we all suffer.' How can a progressive society permit the hoarding of wealth by one man when fifty are hungry or wanting? That is not economic freedom. That is barbarism. And let's be fair here. The CAA handcuffs no one when it recognizes no one needs obscene wealth which we have defined as exceeding twenty million dollars. So plenty of incentives remain, plenty of opportunities for entrepreneurial zeal."

"And what happens when an individual's wealth exceeds this arbitrary limit?"

Green looked at him carefully. "Why Mr. Broadwellwell. I think your biases are showing. But I will answer your question anyway. When one man has accumulated wealth beyond any reasonable limit, he may only have done so, and he may only greedily preserve it by intentionally limiting the resources and opportunities of many others. He prospers in his private jet while countless others live on the streets and watch their children starve. In other words, it is a kind of theft. It is a theft against society, against fairness, against compassion, against opportunity, against humanity. So we have a simple solution. Any such excess wealth will be taxed at one hundred percent and redistributed to those who need it through the wonderful programs we will reinstate and all the new ones we will adopt when I am president. We will all prosper together."

"Let's stay on this point a bit more, shall we? Let's take the example of, say, the richest man in the world, Abriado Centeri. He has dual citizenship I believe, in the U.S. and Italy, and I assume is subject to our jurisdiction. His wealth fluctuates with the market and economic events but is estimated at one trillion dollars. Whether you love him or hate him you must acknowledge that his companies and interests provide immeasurable goods and services to countless people worldwide. You would 'simply' as you referenced it, tax his wealth away?"

Green did not even try to avoid the question obviously intended to test her competency. "Yes. That is exactly what we shall do with the proper structures and systems and safeguards to minimize the disruptions and assure the continuing smooth flow of the needed goods and services. We are not attacking these companies or their output or the people who make them run. We are saying that they cannot rest in the hands of one man. They must be owned collectively and benefit everyone equally."

"So the government will be in the business of running the companies of Centeri and others like him? Should this be the role of government? Does it have the personnel, the resources, the experience to take on such a monumental task?"

"Not the government. The people. Smart, motivated, decent, loving, compassionate people working together motivated by the higher goal to advance humanity, and to prosper themselves, but at reasonable, defensible levels. It will be much the same as it is now, but instead of the profits going to one man or a handful of men, they will go to the public trust. How is that so different?"

Broadwell was renowned for maintaining absolute journalistic integrity and maintaining a detached demeanor, never imposing his own views or demonstrating his emotions. He was referred to by his friends and foes alike as "the greatest poker face in journalism." Those who knew him could see that he was wrestling with a response to her question and was clearly restraining himself.

"How do you respond to charges that such a system is no different from the oppressive Soviet block systems of the mid twentieth century where absolute economic control was maintained by the communist party? Those systems ended with utter failure and economic ruin."

"Those were dictatorships based upon brutality and greed and hatred. Mankind has learned from their excesses. We have grown beyond it. We are offering a collective environment of enlightened social welfare and love. Together, we will provide for one another and prosper!" Green said excitedly, her face almost glowing.

Broadwell was quiet for several moments. He looked intently at Mercy Green and then asked with a somber tone, "Suppose I could arrange a broadcast with you and Topher Blue to address the facts and debate the issues. Would you participate?"

"Oh my," she said laughing. "Despite my personal feelings, how could I not? I could be de-loused immediately afterwards."

Broadwell looked at her, raising his eyebrows, which for him was akin to an emotional outburst.

"I suppose that was not very professional or ladylike, was it?" Green said, recognizing her miscalculation. "I sincerely apologize to you and your viewers Mr. Broadwell. My passion and love of humanity sometimes gets the best of me. If he would come I will most certainly be there. Throw in his murderous puppet Red Shank to make it even more interesting if you can."

"President Red Shank, Ms. Green. Does not his office deserve your respect?"

"You are right again. I can and do distinguish between the office and its current occupant. In fact I am committing my life to the dignity and renewed decency of that office."

Broadwell smiled at her and suddenly concluded the interview. "As to that, time and the will of the American electorate will tell. And as for time, that is all we have tonight. Thank you Mercy Green, and thank you America."

Mercy Green appeared surprised and simply responded, "Thank you Mr. Broadwell." She stood up and walked out of the studio quietly, her assistants following her.

Within twenty four hours of the completion of the interview, a website had been established calling for a national day of reflection and prayer. The idea soon spread like wildfire across the internet and social media. The Mercy Collective denied any responsibility for establishing the website or organizing the event, but quickly endorsed it. Mercy Green called upon government and business leaders to fill-in for their absent employees that day in a symbolic act of sympathy, appreciation and humility. Topher Blue predictably advised that any employees not reporting for work should be terminated. Red Shank announced that the Justice Department was investigating whether the Mercy Collective's call, despite its denials, for what was obviously a national strike constituted criminal violation of the strike prohibition provisions of the American Technology Initiative and other recently passed legislation and executive orders. He also vowed that the national day of reflection and prayer would not, under any circumstances, be permitted to occur and that local and federal authorities would vigorously prevent any demonstrations, rallies, or other public meetings.

It was estimated that over forty five million people had seen or heard the interview on television, radio, and perhaps most importantly, on the internet. In addition to the rumblings for a national day of reflection and prayer, it was estimated that an additional several hundred companies suddenly experienced strike-related slowdowns and threatened resignations of technology personnel accompanied by the now customary demands for enormous compensation increases. The ripple effect to related customers and suppliers was far more significant. Countless transactions were affected. Food, medical supplies, commodities, endless components to fuel the industrial and service infrastructure were delayed or failed to ship. The collective wheels of commerce felt each and every stoppage or slow down, minutely perhaps but with each passing day the impact slowly and doggedly grew. Men, women, and children already fighting the fears of a world once reliable without a second thought, now witnessed those fears being realized as empty store shelves and orders placed but never received. And all the while, their elected leaders, the politicians and the pundits promised all would be well when dependency and entitlement and the resulting corruption of the human spirit were finally eradicated and self-reliance and individual responsibility was restored.

"I can't feed my children with your promises!" a single mother was heard screaming as the police dragged her away after wandering unintentionally into an impromptu demonstration. Labeled a supporter of Mercy Green and the collectivist cause, it did not even matter that she had never even heard of Mercy Green. When the Green Collective operatives heard of her fate, they attempted to post bail and secure her release. She politely declined, saying that she would take care of herself and did not wish to be indebted to anyone.

Though speculation and predictions were rampant, and anxiety heightened, A10 was silent. It was reported that bookmaking operations in major Las Vegas and other casinos around the world, which not surprisingly continued to prosper, had established an extremely lucrative odds and wagering system regarding when and where A-10 might strike again. The odds had risen substantially that another attack would be imminent after Green's broadcast. More prudent analysts, though decrying the trivialization of the cyber attacks, predicted that the gamblers would not be disappointed for long.

CHAPTER 5

"The way to have power is to take it."

—*Boss Tweed*

"I don't understand why you guys make everything so hard. Everything needs to be easy."

—*Anonymous Internet Post*

Why could reason not prevail? Neera Solai thought. *Why must men nakedly grasp ideology with such unyielding certainty? Why do men attribute blindness, delusion and ignorance to others while angrily dismissing even the possibility that they too might suffer from the same disorders? Why can they not remember that passions aroused today inevitably soften and transform and that doing so is the very nature of consciousness itself? How do men endlessly preach and warn about the dangers and evils of the world but never point such piercing insights inwardly?*

Neera looked quietly at the faces gathered around the table, all recognized as leaders and innovators and examples of financial success, holders of the American dream, now becoming the American nightmare.

"I had to," Manfred Wyatt said, "I just had to. They were my top people. It would take months to replace them and recover despite all the backups and system designs and documentation. And who knows if the next level down wouldn't have done the same damn thing. We could have lost everything. The systems recovery plans were never designed to protect us from so many walking. Five million each. If it had collapsed, that would have been chicken feed. It was a bargain. I had no choice. Look, it sickens me that I have to look at them everyday, but I'm gonna tell you something. They're back with a vengeance. They've never been so effective, so motivated, so, so," he hesitated, grasping for words, "I know it sounds insane, so loyal. We're now a hundred percent ahead of where we would have been if none of this had ever happened. I don't think I even blame them as much anymore. Not fully. They were victims of Shank and Green and all the insanity going on just like the rest of us. Why not get what you can in a world like this? Hell, we don't even know if we'll be here tomorrow with that A10 or whatever it's called lurking in the shadows."

"We paid too, I'm sad to say," Lanna Hargrove, the founder and CEO of the largest entertainment empire in the country said. "We couldn't last thirty days without our systems and were looking at recycling outdated materials and reruns. One hundred forty million to one hundred fifty six of them. We're also dealing with those Shank and Blue operatives who strongarmed us for an eight percent interest. They made it clear our licenses and everything else were at risk. Some Texas company they used to extort us now actually has a representative sitting on my board. My investigators say it has similar interests in over four hundred major companies."

"What about the Texas company?" Neera asked. "What about its own employees?"

"The word on the street is that they actually paid them before they even asked, nothing like we had to pay, mind you," Hargrove explained. "They then hit them with enforcement under the new legislation and supposedly, a handful who resisted experienced unexpected health problems, unusual accidents, family members threatened, and other intimidation. There's a rumor that the senior systems manger was shot in the parking lot and his body never retrieved. It's monstrous."

In turn, each of the executives told their stories, each capitulating. Each paying to survive. Each accepting that no other options remained.

"What about you, Neera?" Wyatt asked. "You hold a couple of distinctions. First to be hit by the strikers and A10 followed by that bastard Plax."

"Nothing. Not a penny. Never."

"I admire your resolve but I don't see how."

"Our culture. When we dispatched the strikers, the others stepped up quickly. There were some problems but we recovered. We never reduced the compensation or benefits, though the new laws permitted us to. What no longer existed in government programs, we privatized, at least as much as possible. What we couldn't do, we set up in trust accounts for them. They appreciated our efforts, our commitments I think. Now A10 of course is another matter."

"Your relationship with Centeri couldn't hurt there."

"Centeri has been attacked in two companies. Neither of us have been spared."

"Will you pay A10?" Hargrove asked.

"Never."

"The money really is insignificant."

"I do not care if he or they are demanding five dollars or five hundred million. I will not pay."

Wyatt smiled at her. "I hope you are right, for your sake. But unless they find this A10 and persuade him or torture him or do whatever is necessary to get everything turned back on and unless you can keep your people happy and oblivious to their colleagues getting rich and unless you can somehow keep Shank out of your boardroom, you will pay someone. You can't avoid it, I'm afraid."

"Neera," Jack Force said quietly, "Plax is back and this time I don't believe we can turn him away."

"And why can't we?" she asked, taking off her reading glasses and turning to look at him.

"Because this time he has warrants, two federal marshals, and two police officers."

"A warrant for what and for whom? Get Cox up here now and have him put S&S on notice."

"He would not tell me about the warrant, only that he demanded to meet with you immediately."

Grayson Cox was the head of Solai's legal department, a corporate attorney with over thirty years of trial and regulatory experience. Solai's outside law firm, Sargent and Scott, was one of the most respected and aggressive major firms in the country.

"Stall them until Gray gets up here. Put them in the conference room."

Within a few minutes Grayson Cox and two associates were in Neera's office.

"We'll go see them. Sit tight here until we get back," he said.

Neera sat back in her chair. She fumbled with her computer, but was distracted by the presence of Plax within her building. *It could be anything with him,* she thought.

Several minutes later, Cox and his colleagues returned to her office. He looked ashen, Neera thought.

"They have an arrest warrant for you, Neera. You and Jack," he said quietly. "We'll quash it but I'm afraid it's legitimate and it will take some time. Everyone is already on it but you must go with them. We'll pull every string to stop it."

Neera spoke words that she had never imagined that she would ever say, that prior to this moment would have seemed impossible. "What are we charged with?"

"Conspiracy and criminal violations of the American Technology Initiative and the enforcement provisions of the technology strike prohibition legislation. Plus you have been labeled a party of interest and accused of possible complicity with A10 based on your recent efforts to locate him. They claim to have witnesses saying you and Centeri found and met with him in northern California and are in possession of equipment owned and used by A10. The warrant is for Centeri as well."

Neera was stunned. Her mind raced over the implications of the charges and the dishonesty and outrage they represented. She also thought about who at the compound in California would have betrayed them. Centeri was right when he said Franklin Storm likely permitted her to take the metal extension. She could not imagine he would do so and then alert the authorities. No, she thought, that was the style of another and it did not take much thought to determine who might be to blame, especially when doing so implicated Centeri. She also remembered the warnings of Centeri that Plax and his handlers would strike back hard, but she never anticipated this.

"Plax wishes to speak to you privately. Normally, I would never permit it, but under the circumstances, it might be advisable to buy us some time to find a judge to delay this. Obviously, coming on the premises to take custody is completely unnecessary and is intended only as a show of strength."

"Show him in," Neera said with disgust.

Plax walked in alone, wearing the same tropical suit he had worn on every prior occasion they had met. Her attorneys left the office. One of his colleagues entered with equipment to detect microphones and quickly indicated the room was secure.

"You're in a heap of trouble, little lady," he said. "Honest to god, Ms. Solai. You surprised even me on this one. What the hell were you thinking goin' around talking to everybody and then grabbing this Guyah fellow's equipment. Want to thank you though for pointing us in the right direction. We got the rest of it. It's like you and that Italian son of a bitch just gave me a pistol and said go ahead and pull the trigger. I gotcha good!"

"You cannot believe we are a part of this…"

"Hell no," he said interrupting her, shaking his head and now chuckling. "I know that. I figure you, at least, were trying to do the world a good deed. Now Centeri on the other hand, well, you just don't know. But it's not what I believe, its what we can charge you with and make stick. We got that Bongo kid saying all sorts of damaging things and can probably stick those people on the farm with harboring a fugitive, except, that is, for the little lady who turned you all in. In time, they'll say whatever we want them to."

"What do you want, Plax?"

"Hold on now. Hold on," he said, turning his head to the side as if he were straining to listen to something, a distorted, ugly smile on his face. "Is that a helicopter I hear? Is it? Could it be another helicopter to rescue you? No, I guess not. Not this time." He stared at Neera ruthlessly, his demeanor sarcastic and vicious. Emboldened, basking in his power and revenge, he continued, "I asked you to cooperate with us and I promised you we would make it worth your while. We are not the villains you think we are. You would not even hear me out, and left me standing there looking like a damn fool, in front of I might add, the biggest damn fool on the planet. We asked you for technical assistance, for everyone's benefit, like everybody is doing, and you go to court and get a damn injunction and stop everybody. What did you expect? Did you think we were just going to go away?"

"I asked you, what do you want?" she repeated, unable to disguise her revulsion.

"Eight percent of the company, not just your nano deal, the entire company. That's your penalty for being such a pain in my ass. And we don't want a few of your programmers a few days a week, like everyone else. We only want," he hesitated, fumbling with a small notebook he had pulled out of his coat pocket, "we want your Hooch, whatever a Hooch is. We want him permanently, all the time."

"Go to hell," Neera Solai said.

Blueford Plax smiled. "I thought as much. And you, young lady, can go to jail, and maybe learn a little humility."

Neera sat in the holding tank with fifteen other women as she summoned the strength of her mind to somehow make sense of what had just happened, and to control her emotions, which were now on the brink of chaos. She looked around at the misery and hopelessness and inhumanity of the large cell and its occupants and fought her fear and emotions that cried out that she did not belong here, this could not be where her life had taken her. Yet by rejecting Plax, she had chosen this place over the obscenity of his extortion and demands. She had chosen honor and decency and the resulting discomfort of a jail cell over capitulation and corruption. She would not, could not be like Wyatt and Hargrove and the hundreds of other company executives just like them who spoke of the injustice of the assaults and larceny by Blue and Shank and the others but eventually fearfully yielded and by doing so implicitly condoned their actions. She knew that men such as Plax always took the failure to resist as implied acceptance, empowering them, encouraging them even more. She had known sitting in her office that there had been nothing she could do, nothing she could say to Plax that would cause him to hear, to reason and recognize the indecency of his actions. She could not approach his world where such immorality and malicious ignorance was the rule. She could only reaffirm her own reason, her own integrity, whatever the cost.

She closed her eyes and found some solace in the impromptu demonstration that had developed as she and Jack Force were escorted out of the Solai campus in handcuffs. Federal agents often used handcuffs when arresting executives, even when completely unnecessary and the prisoner presents no risk, to emphasize their power and authority and to serve as a deterrent. It backfired completely at Solai. Neera and Jack were overwhelmed to see that somehow what was happening had been communicated to the Solai employees and hundreds of them had quickly gathered in the courtyard cheering them and encouraging them and shouting their disapproval at Plax and the agents. Neera had looked at Plax over the roar of their employees. "It does sort of sound like a helicopter," she shouted. "These are the people who reject everything you stand for!" Plax showed no reaction whatsoever and continued to escort her to the waiting police car.

Neera was suddenly startled out of her deep thoughts. A middle aged woman, shabbily dressed and filthy, walked over to Neera and sat on the bench next to her. She cautiously smiled at Neera, as if testing her, exposing her missing and rotting teeth.

"Got a cigarette, honey?" she asked.

"No, I'm sorry. I don't smoke," Neera answered, doing her best to smile at the woman and ignore her own discomfort. She nervously looked away in an attempt to avoid focusing on her condition.

The woman looked at her carefully, her eyes narrowing in anger, easily sensing Neera's uneasiness. "Think you're better than me sweetie, you in your expensive suit and Italian shoes? I looked just like you a year ago, even better! Try living on the street and see how damn good you look!"

"I'm sorry that happened to you. It is not fair," Neera answered, trying to diffuse her anger. "I'm sorry you're here. I'm sorry we're both here."

"You got that right," she said, calming down, obviously feeling Neera's compassion. "I've been looking for my husband and sons. You now what it's like to lose your family? To have no idea where they are, every place you can think of is gone or if it's still there, nobody ever heard of them. Do you know how that feels?"

"I'm so sorry. I cannot imagine how you must feel."

The woman looked at her sadly and sighed deeply, holding back tears, as if she had not heard a kind word for a very long time. "You're a good girl, honey. I don't know what you did, but you shouldn't be here. People like you shouldn't be in places like this. Don't you worry about nothin'. I'll keep my eye on you and make sure nobody bothers you. That's a promise."

"Ms. Solai? It is Ms. Solai isn't it," a young attractive woman asked, approaching Neera and distracting the attention of the woman.

"I'm sorry," Neera answered. "Do I know you?"

"No, but I know about you and have been," she said hesitating, grasping for words, "an admirer. You're kind of my role model."

Neera briefly looked around. "Quite a role model in this place," she said.

"Rachel Inncocent," the young woman said, extending her hand. "I'm a systems engineer and have kind of dreamed of meeting you and following in your footsteps."

Neera took her hand warmly, relieved to see something even distantly familiar in this terrible setting. She found herself momentarily fighting back tears. Rachel saw her reaction and immediately sat down beside her.

"Its okay Ms. Solai. Really," she said, tightening her grip and rubbing the top of Neera's hand with her left hand. "You'd be a monster if this place didn't affect you. I've been here since six o'clock this morning and only stopped crying hysterically about twenty minutes ago." She laughed and smiled compassionately at Neera. "Betty here has been kind of looking out for me." The other woman nodded in agreement.

"Your last name is somewhat poetic, given our current circumstances, Rachel," Neera said, regaining her composure.

"They have my husband, Gaston, in the men's holding cell down the hall. Our attorneys are at work. It shouldn't be much longer. Apparently we're some sort of terrible villains, inciting our colleagues to strike, despite the fact that we own a company employing twenty programmers and are doing everything possible to find more."

"I am afraid they are motivated far more by malice than reason, for what its worth."

"It's absurd. This notion of some organized collective conspiracy of strikers. I suppose its possible for some people, and I don't want to sound insulting, but maybe those your age or older. They seem to be more open to the drama and ideology. With us, it's just talking and sharing information on the internet. It's just what we do, how we communicate all the time. Everyone talks about whatever is on their mind, usually the coolest new technology, but a lot of times just surviving, what they're getting paid and who's making more and how they did it. I know hardly anyone in my circle who sits around talking about the strike or Shank and Green and all of that. But when we have friends over who are a little older, it's like that is all that's on their minds and they even get irritated when we can't relate. We've heard that the government is monitoring everyone's emails and social media so I guess they piece together whatever they want to and call it a conspiracy. Gaston thinks they may have gotten him when he asked some people he doesn't even know how they made the money they were bragging about on *DudesTechRead*. There are millions of postings daily on sites like those. I have no idea what they are saying I did. I can't even imagine."

"Can I help you and Gaston, Rachel? My attorneys should have me out in a few minutes. I would be happy to let them take a look at your situation."

"Thank you Ms. Solai. You don't know Gaston. He will not take anything from anyone. But I think we're really okay. It should be any minute now for us too. But, if I'm not being pushy, could I maybe, when you're not too busy, take you out for lunch? I can't tell you what a thrill it is to meet you and you're such an inspiration for me."

"You've been very kind to me so it's my treat. How do I reach you?"

"ArchimedesDream.com. Leave a message on the contact tab and I will get back to you like two seconds later," she said, smiling broadly.

"Interesting domain name," Neera said.

Neera and Force were released less than an hour later. She had spent five and one half hours in jail. Cox met her and Jack in the waiting area. The attendant gave them both their personal property back. Neera put on her watch and ring but left her earrings in the small envelope. She was strangely calm and quiet.

"I'm sorry Neera. We got a federal district court judge to quash the arrest as a violation of the injunction. He didn't buy the government's argument that the revised legislation pre-empted the injunction and said that was a matter for the courts to rule on. There's a hearing Thursday on that issue."

"So where does that leave me and Jack?"

"It's gone completely and can't be revived. Even the A10 part. They so poisoned the well the judge said he didn't want to hear about any part of it. We'll see that the record is expunged. That's actually a pretty lucky break because they had at least an arguable claim on the A10 piece. Centeri is still exposed and my bet is they will do everything they can to find and get him and that equipment."

"It is not a piece of equipment. It's a melted unrecognizable metal slag. Nothing more."

"Whatever it is or isn't, my advice is for you to keep clear of it. We were a little lucky today, Neera. This could have been very sticky. My clients do not go to jail. Ever. They are after you, and they have the full force of the government behind them."

Cox hesitated, indicating to Neera that something more was on his mind.

"What?" she asked sternly.

"The board, I'm afraid. When this got out, Pinky Melton called an emergency meeting for tomorrow morning. He's got a quorum I think."

"About?"

"The notice said the criminal activities and arrest of the company's CEO and the continuing failure to resolve the Nano shutdown."

"Are they trying to terminate me?"

"They would never have the votes for that and he knows it, especially with your release. But they can pressure you and I think that is what he intends."

"Can we postpone or derail it?" Neera asked.

"If we could find Martha, with her vote and yours, it would be a no brainer. But she is in India and didn't sign the proxy documents. We can't reach her. So without her he can call a meeting and set the agenda but will lack the votes to take any serious actions."

"Why don't we just refuse and fight it out later?"

Cox hesitated. "Neera, because they still have a quorum and Patel is giving signs he is very unhappy about what happened and the whole A10 thing and your connection with Centeri. I don't think he has gone over to the dark side yet but we better not take him for granted. If you are a no-show, it is conceivable they could proceed without you. We need to attend and take this seriously. I'll preserve all the objections."

"One other matter, Gray," Neera said. "In the jail, in the holding tank was an older woman. I only got her first name. Betty she told us. Please use your resources and find out who she is. Get her out of jail and find a room or hotel for her for ninety days or so. Do whatever you can to have our people find her family. Charge all of this to me, not the company. I want to do whatever we can to help her." Cox nodded but said nothing. Neera could see the questions in his eyes but was appreciative that he did not inquire further or argue.

Neera followed Cox to the awaiting limousine and within twenty minutes was at her office. He had urged her and Jack to allow him to take them home but Neera refused. She needed to return to her routine and somehow erase the memories of the afternoon. She could shower at the office. She would also call Centeri, who had undoubtedly by now heard what had happened but strangely, disappointingly had not called. She felt her doubts about him rise once again as they had several times the past months. The events of the day, combined with her thoughts about Centeri and the pending confrontation the next morning with her board of directors created a wave of intense emotions different from any that she had remembered. It was the shock, she reasoned, of being entirely under the control of others and being completely powerless. Being vulnerable and knowing that any resistance, any argument, any exercise of her mind or reason would have immediate and violent consequences. These were emotions that she had been spared from throughout her life. But she realized many men and women lived with these realities virtually every day of their lives. And now she had as well. It was shocking, disorienting, and created a feeling she could not easily describe. As if Plax and the forces he represented had stolen her sense of certainty and the optimism that attended it. She now knew that she too could be fettered and bound, her humanity and all that she was, ignored. She realized that she had been brutalized and demeaned to quench the lust for power, influence and money by monstrous men who lacked all morality.

"Neera," Jack Force said, opening the door to her office. "Are you alright?"

"I suppose so. And you?" she asked sadly.

"Gina told me if I don't get home right now, she was coming here to drag me to her and the kids."

Neera smiled. "I think you had better go and let her comfort you."

"And you too," he said.

"I, I don't understand," and as she said those words Jack Force turned and stepped aside to where Neera could see Abriado Centeri waiting for her.

"Abriado, oh god," she said, bursting into tears. No longer could she stoically withhold or control her emotions. No longer could she ignore the attack upon her dignity and their effort to render her disgraced and defeated. Centeri ran to her and embraced her.

"I am so sorry Neera. I am so, so sorry. I did not think they were capable of this. I am so sorry I caused this."

"I thought," she said, her words in between quiet sobs. "I thought you were in New Eden. It's too dangerous for you here. They want you, too. Cox said they have a stronger case against you."

"I came the moment I heard. Don't worry about me. We've already taken some steps to slow them down. I'll be alright. But you."

They embraced for several minutes, neither of them saying anything more. Neera felt the warmth and strength of his embrace. It was real. It was entirely present. For the first time since she had known Centeri, she felt that he was with her and only her. No longer that odd feeling that he somehow existed in many places at once as she and everyone who knew him would constantly experience. She had seen his humanity recently at the compound and she was certain she was feeling it again. It comforted her in a way she could not explain or understand nor did she need to. The feelings of brutality and marginalization that had engulfed her, that could have devastated her, began to quietly fade. But as he held her and she relished his embrace with all of her being, she also felt hints of uncertainty and confusion beginning to arise as to its meaning and implications. She could not think about it now or allow it to undermine the pure and honest intimacy she was now experiencing and so desperately needed. It was as if her emotions had gone in a matter of hours to the most opposite of extremes. She would sort it out later.

Finally she gently pushed Centeri away. "You must get out of here. They have to figure you're here. They apparently followed us all along and knew what we were doing. Plax made that clear. He gloated."

"I don't think so," he said. "They put it all together afterwards. Adrianna Snow clued them in I'm afraid. The final maternal rejection and assault. They found out about Bongo by accident and have put enormous pressure on him. One of his people actually called the press."

She was not convinced. "This is different. I halfway expect to see Plax and his cheap suit out in the courtyard."

"It is over for now. For us both. After we heard, my people got very aggressive and reminded them of some very strategic decisions from the European Economic Community they were awaiting and as luck would have it, a few key components were under our control. Whatever they were planning was put on hold, at least for the time being."

Neera smiled but could not find the words to respond. She could not even guess at what the details might have been given Centeri's vast business holdings and his network of financial and political influence. And at this moment, she did not care. She began to recognize slowly, perhaps hesitantly due to the trauma she had experienced earlier, that Plax had likely overplayed his hand and would soon suffer the consequences of an as yet undecided Centeri response. His pulling some economic strings was likely just the beginning.

They continued to talk for nearly an hour. Much of it spent on A10 and the results of his people's investigation and speculation about the piece of melted equipment and the videos of the other remnants. Centeri explained that surprisingly little was learned from the ruined piece. Its metal composition was fairly exotic but nothing that could not be duplicated. Its interior was highly conductive, perhaps unusually so, yet its exterior possessed almost extraordinary insulation qualities. The interior, though virtually solid, and now distorted badly by the intense heat, nevertheless suggested a small polished center channel, as if a tiny insert was injected and withdrawn. The videos of the other ruined equipment were equally vague. All they knew for certain was intense power and heat was generated or contained within the equipment, but for what purpose remained a complete mystery. Centeri assured Neera that every possibility, no matter how far fetched, was being investigated.

"We've spent a great deal of effort to find any reference worldwide to find the Boortah Guyah Franklin mentioned. There is nothing. We suspect he is using an alias. It is not unusual for people and in fact entire families from the area he indicated this young man may have been from to have several names in case the political powers change or a family member gets into trouble. I had an administrative assistant a few years back from that region who insisted she had three legal names, all of them valid and all of them her. The closest thing we did find was a reference to a B. Gutyah, a lab assistant in a technical institute in Norway. The only reason it is even notable is that the institution specializes in metallurgy and power generation research and related software control systems. Obviously, we are continuing to look."

"He's hiding," Neera said. "We have to assume that if she had any way to contact and warn him, Adrianna did exactly that."

Centeri shook his head slowly, almost sadly. "There was at least one interesting insight, or perhaps I should say leap of faith prompted by our travels. My people found the description of the destruction of the lab and the attending controlled fireworks extremely interesting. So they began to search out newspapers and websites, particularly those with small local or regional coverage. And they found something. A reference in a small newspaper in northern Wyoming about blue lightning discharging from the ground upwards on an otherwise crystal-clear night. It's likely nothing, but we sent a couple of people there to take a look."

Eventually, their conversation slowed and each of them knew Neera needed to rest and recharge and somehow shake off the effects of a traumatic day.

"Perhaps as you implied originally, it might be wiser to let others continue the chase, at least until we think we are very close. Or actually find him. What are you expecting tomorrow with your board?"

"A great deal of threats, but little substance. There really is not much they can do, but they will demand we pay A10 and even Sack if necessary and get back to business. The faction who called the meeting do not seem to be troubled by the ethical challenges of extortion when profit is on the line."

"We have both already lost far more than A10 demanded from you. I assume this restoration fee is still on the table. There is only one upside I can see. Sun advised that if you do pay, we need to extensively prepare and possibly learn something from how it happens. They would want to blanket everything. Something would have to be detectable and measurable."

"Then you are in favor?" Neera asked.

"Let's just say that given all that has happened and what we could learn, I am not as opposed as I might have been," Centeri answered. "Just if you must, let's do it the right way."

"And watch our remote keys?' she said.

"And everything else."

Within a few minutes they had agreed to speak in the morning. Centeri left, planning to immediately return to New Eden. Neera made no effort to persuade him to stay nor did she desire him to. He had helped and comforted her and during her most emotional and vulnerable moments, she was soothed by him, by a purity and intimacy, at least for that moment, far beyond the normalcy of friendship. She did not know what it meant or if it meant anything at all. She could not even guess if Centeri had felt a similar emotion. Or if he were even capable of it. She only knew that she needed to sleep and think about nothing.

* * *

The following morning, Neera walked into the board room and sat at the head of the table. Six board members were present.

"Glad to see you're with us Neera," Pinky Melton said. It was an offensive, cheap affront that rankled even the more militant board members.

"Shut your mouth, Pinky," Bantar Patel sternly said. "I am sorry for our idiot friend, Neera. Are you alright?"

"Yes Bantar. Thank you." She noted that Melton was quietly turning red over the deserved rebuke from Patel.

"Let's get down to business, dammit," Melton said, fuming. "For the record, I move that Ms. Solai be formally censured by the board for her criminal activities and arrest pending completion of the legal process and if convicted be terminated as the chief executive officer of this company."

A collective gasp was heard from the members.

"Do I hear a second?" He looked at the members waiting for a response in support of his motion, his anxiety apparent. There was none.

After perhaps thirty seconds, Patel quietly said, "This most inappropriate motion is defeated and for lack of a second, shall not be included in the records of this meeting."

Neera said nothing and neither felt nor showed any emotion.

Patel continued. "Neera, I am not sure what is appropriate or inappropriate under the circumstances. But I would ask on behalf of the board that you be very careful for the company, your office and, if I am not intruding, you personally. These are very difficult times and I fear we have become a target."

"I am the target," Neera said. "Solai Systems is the reward. All of you know that I will fight with every ounce of my being to protect it."

Patel smiled. "We could not possibly doubt that, knowing you my friend. But I would respectfully suggest to try and structure your, and I must admit, our affairs so that perhaps a fight would not even be necessary. Mr. Cox has reluctantly explained to us that certain activities of yours might have come close to crossing a legal line. In any event, let's not dwell upon this and we trust that you will be deliberate and careful in the future."

"For god sakes," Melton said, angrily interrupting. "Can we cut the crap? She is provoking and effectively slapping the face of the United States government and its representatives. She is arrogantly conspiring with that Italian pirate on some sort of epic wild goose chase instead of writing a goddamn check and getting back to business. We've got thirty percent of our workforce underutilized and chasing their own tails trying to unwind some bizarre technology that everybody knows is going to take another twenty years. Please indulge your technological adventure fantasies on someone else's nickel, not mine. Pay 'em and get Nano back on track or drop the damn project altogether and move on to something else and quit paying people millions every week to do nothing."

"And you would also have me hand over eight percent of the company with no consideration, as is being demanded?"

"I know at least twenty companies run by my friends who've done the same thing. They've actually said it's been a windfall to them. Problems have gone away, new business has knocked on their door, and in every single case they've grown substantially. They don't even notice the small cut. It's paid for itself a hundred times over."

"Ignore it if you wish but all of this, A10, Plax, is theft. It is extortion. It is incomprehensible that you would actually condone it," Neera said.

"I don't make the rules, thank you," Pinky Melton said. "I just play by them."

And with that statement, the enormity of his corruption, the indecency of his values, his mindless rejection of reason became readily apparent. His rationalization of playing by the rules was one used to silently condone some of the worst atrocities throughout history. Neera remembered the adage that when men of goodwill do not fight against evil, they help it flourish.

"Neera," Patel said. "I do not agree with Mr. Melton about Plax. At least not yet. I do worry that it has every possibility of escalating and I believe we must watch it carefully and be open to practical solutions, however they may develop. But as to A10, I am forced to agree. Our CFO tells us that this matter has now cost us nearly $100 million. These animals are demanding $25 million and have shown that they immediately restore everything entirely if the ransom is paid. Despite my own abhorrence for their actions, I do not think rationally we can delay any further. We cannot afford a continuing philosophical debate nor can we permit Nano to be abandoned, which we all believe is the real future of this company. I am respectfully requesting that you make immediate arrangements to pay the amounts requested by A10."

Neera sat quietly and said nothing, her mind racing over the implications of their statements. The apparent alliance of Melton and Patel, at least on this issue, troubled her, since collectively they controlled a material block of Solai stock. She looked at the table at the other members. Aside from Martha Miles, who was not present and apparently out of the country and unreachable, the only member present with significant interests was Mrs. Randoph Sellers, the eighty-five-year-old widow of Randolph Bertrand Sellers, Neera's first investor and early mentor. She was a formal, quiet woman who avoided overt controversy but could be relied upon to support Neera.

"Mrs. Sellers," Neera asked. "Do you have any thoughts?"

"Neera dear, I have apparently become very popular with our colleagues here recently, yet I don't previously recall a single invitation to tea, much less a phone call. Very confusing," she said, looking across the table with wise, narrowed eyes. "I trust your judgment as always and I can imagine how reprehensible it must be for you to consider paying these thieves. Frankly, I see both sides. If it were me, I would pay them and move along for the good of the company. But I always trust your intuition and good intentions, so whatever you think best is fine with me."

Neera immediately recognized that Sellers' statement was as close as she could ever come to publically disagreeing with Neera. She looked at Patel, who was generally a decent man but unpredictable and prone to impulsive last minute changes in his position, and saw a very subtle smile denoting that he too understood Sellers' veiled directive. She did not even need to look at Melton to know that he was gloating. Because of the absence of Martha Miles, nothing done at this meeting was mandatory, but she could not ignore the fact that every director present believed that the company should pay A10 the extortion. She understood their position and could not deny the practicality of it. Centeri and her own people might never unravel the technology being used, which would mean the death of Nano. Many of the other attacks by A10 against other companies had been against utility or supporting software. Several of the companies were able to substitute new systems or applications and A10 seemed to not notice or care. The attack on Nano was very different though. It affected over one hundred critical systems, including many essential operating systems. It simply could not be re-written or substituted with other software. The choice really appeared to be pay or shut the project down permanently.

Neera had carefully reflected upon her own resistance to paying the ransom. Doing so, especially in this period of economic and social turmoil spurned by battling ideological factions seemed especially repugnant. During this period, it was almost as if decency, integrity and rational thought had no champions, and it was the responsibility of well intended people to simply do the right thing. Paying an extortionist and thief could not be farther from doing so. Yet she also realized that these were her values at work and wondered to what extent they might be limiting her rational thought. She was not immune to the power of ideals and emotions blinding and even poisoning rationality under a veil of groundless self-certainty. The company was being seriously damaged, the jobs of many employees were at risk, investors were seeing their share value decline, and it could all stop for an amount of money the company would hardly notice.

"We will pay," Neera said suddenly, without any emotion. "And I will explain why. And although I understand perfectly the reasons you wish me to do so, those issues will only be a small part of my decision. First and foremost, we will do so in an effort to hopefully learn how the technology of A10 works. We will notify them of the payment when our people and Centeri's are ready to monitor and observe exactly how it is happening."

Pinky Melton interrupted. "Hell, that's a great idea. I'm all for that. Figure out how they do it and sell the off button to everyone else. We'll make a fortune. Plus we develop whatever it is ourselves and, my god," he said pausing, "we'll be a damn empire."

Neera looked at him with contempt and disgust, shaking her head. But it was Patel who spoke up. "It is good you inherited your wealth, Pinky, because you are undoubtedly a complete idiot who could not earn a penny himself. Have you not been reading the materials on the net and listening to the commentators about the potential scope of this A10 technology? No single company would ever be permitted to control it and no single government should have access to it. Every government and security organization in the world is now looking for them. You obviously do not see the power of this, presumably the ability to turn off the equipment of an army or opponent from halfway across the world. It is revolutionary. The only solution is to make it available to everyone or develop appropriate shields or the ability to block it. God help us all if Shank or some of the others get it first."

Melton suffered his rebuke in silence. "What would you and Centeri do if we discover something?" Patel asked.

"The various options and protocols are being worked out now so that no one will be hurt," Neera answered. "A great deal of energy is being committed to those scenarios no matter how unlikely they appear now. Philosophers and scientists have been considering the impact and protocols for sudden technological leaps ever since the dawning of the technology age, so there is a huge body of knowledge. This A10 acts like a remnant of the past, where a bold new design can be obscured and used selectively, ignoring the immediate real time access and proliferation of the internet."

Neera looked carefully at each of her board members. "The other reason we have delayed and demonstrated an unwillingness to pay an extortionist is not due to some detached philosophical ideal. It is because it is always good business to conduct your affairs ethically. When Shank repealed all the benefits and compensation and social entitlement programs, most companies eagerly signed on and wages and incentives plummeted. I refused to do so and the result was that we had a loyal, committed work force who rejected Pete Sack's efforts and we barely noticed losing him and the others. Our employees collectively worked together to make the company even stronger. They did it because they saw our ethical commitment to do the right thing, always. Caving in to an extortionist would have undermined that commitment. Now after six months, it will be perceived very differently."

"You know many of us were not in agreement with that and still are not. We did not create the political changes in this world and to ignore them and keep paying at rates that reflect a world that no longer exists makes little sense. Plus I believe applying that to this situation is a bit of a stretch," Patel said.

"On the contrary," Neera said. "Wages are moving upwards and your Topher Blue has urged companies to appease their employees, slake them I think he calls it, and share the wealth to discourage the strikes."

"Perhaps, but still far below what was standard just eighteen months ago," Patel responded. "Neera, we could argue about this forever. What is done is done. I still believe we could have engineered similar employee loyalty and benefitted from enormous reductions had you been open to it."

"Not on my watch, Bantar," she answered. His comment reminded her of how deeply embedded the current ideological debate was. It staggered her that men such as Patel, who seemed decent and reasonable in almost all other aspects of their lives, could sit back passively and benefit from the suffering of others, always attributing such events and the resulting advantages to them to political and economic forces they could not control. But she also always suspected that there were more insidious ideas lurking behind this so-called powerlessness, even from men like him who were generally non political and certainly not radical. Neera had noticed on many occasions a suspicion, perhaps at times even rising to a malevolence for anyone outside of their wealthy circle. Blue and Shank exploited this malice and preached the dangers of a population mired in dependency and entitlement and the goal to seize the wealth they had worked so hard to accumulate. They fostered in them a mentality that created almost primal fears of enemies at the gate. With men like Patel and many other investors and executives she dealt with, this attitude was shared in large part, but was far less overt and more restrained and subtle, so as to be deniable when confronted. She wondered if some of them consciously even recognized any bias or if it was denied and locked deeply in their fears. Although the results were the same, the flavor of their ideologies was different. Men such as Melton believed in rigid social hierarchies, strict convention and conformity. The employees had to be kept in their place almost as a natural order. The populist policies of the past decades interfered with that order, allowing them to enjoy the rewards indirectly through what they characterized as government handouts that should have been the exclusive domain of Melton and his class. For men such as Patel, the focus was upon entrepreneurial achievement and material gain, which was naturally awarded to the winners. Employees were respected but were also viewed as productive assets to be invested in, not to be provided for. In either case, it was often a paranoid mentality founded on a resentment of exaggerated laziness and incompetence, one resulting from an almost mythic natural order, the other from a perceived unwillingness to assume the risks of ambition and prosperity. And it was deeply rooted. The past sixty years of social welfare programs and the resulting economic costs had created a foundation of antipathy and prejudice towards anyone not successful as they alone defined success. And with it came a fear that all such outsiders expected to be provided for from cradle to grave. Many undoubtedly did. Many more did not. But rational thought and analysis was not the issue. Men and women who could use their minds with ease on virtually any other matters were increasingly reverting to fear and exaggeration, distorting the dangers when it came to such issues and then denying doing so.

"I see," Patel said. "Let's deal with one other issue if we may. I do not want the CEO of this company engaging in social and political intrigue and adventures when she should be dedicating 100% of her activities to the success and growth of this company. I cannot tell you who to associate with, but I can insist that nothing you do divert attention from this company and its future. In addition, such extracurricular activities may bring shame and dishonor to you personally or to the company either directly or indirectly. It will not be tolerated."

Neera looked at Patel and her other board members and reminded herself that they had neither the power nor the authority to do little more than preach to her. She could not reach them and it would be pointless to try. Their actions were based on what they believed, not upon what they knew. And they believed whatever reinforced their ideologies and world views. She promised herself would she never be like them.

"This meeting is over. We will keep you advised," she said, and walked out of the room.

CHAPTER 6

"Minds that are ill at ease are agitated by both hope and fear."

—Ovid

"Stop caring so damn much…about anything."

—Anonymous Internet Post

DudesTechRead.com

News From the War Zone

ATI PICKS UP SPEED. The American Technology Initiative has substantially quickened its pace, with an estimated one in five technology firms nationwide providing volunteer uncompensated software and IT personnel to the newly formed federal agency to "combat the destructive effects of the technology strikes and the growing A10 crisis." When asked by a reporter for DudesTechRead.com how such compelled government service could be reconciled with the principles of self-interest and drastically restricted government, an ATI spokesman requested the reporter's credentials labeling her a "strike sympathizer." *See more…*

NURSING STAFF WITHHOLDS NON-ESSENTIAL SERVICES. The nursing staff of Mercy Summerline Hospital in Topeka Kansas, drawing from the actions of a growing number of technology workers nationwide, terminated all non-essential services to patients earlier this week. In anonymous social media posts directed to hospital administrators, the nurses noted the extraordinary profits of the institution, claiming that the hospital "was not entitled to such rewards that the nurses alone earned" and promised the restricted services would continue until each member of the nursing staff received a $10,000 payment. *See more…*

FIREFIGHTERS DON'T. Firefighters in three cities in Tyler County, South Carolina attended four fires last week in affluent residential and commercial areas but refused to take action other than the removal and safety of occupants. In all four cases, the buildings at issue were completely destroyed. Social media posts allegedly from the firefighters explained that "Topher Blue has taught us that we must never live for the benefit or entitlement of others. We must be fairly paid for the dangers we endure." Officials at the affected towns disclosed that the firefighters have demanded payments of $50,000 to resume full services. *See more…*

GAS LINE SLOW DOWN. Technical workers at the nation's largest natural gas pipeline monitoring and maintenance company GasGuard Systems stopped all services, resulting in transmission delays and backups while supervisors scrambled to continue deliveries. Manufacturers in four states have warned of imminent shutdowns if services are not restored. Anonymous spokespersons for the apparently striking employees posted demands on social media for payments of $1 million so that "the enormous profits of the pipelines are paid to those who earn it." *See more...*

AGRICULTURAL COOPERATIVE DESTROYS PRODUCE. One hundred thirty growers of fruits and vegetables in southern California refused to perform cooling and preservation procedures on an estimated two thousand tons of produce resulting in its complete spoilage. Posts to social media by a representative of the farmers and producers stated in part that "growers were demanding a 300% increase in prices, explaining that the current prices being paid for the crops resulted in unacceptable entitlements to buyers and consumers nationwide, the appropriation of grower services without compensation, and compelled socialist subsidies." Officials fear that additional occurrences by other growers could seriously interfere with domestic food supplies. *See more...*

TECHNOLOGY SLOWDOWNS CONTINUE DESPITE ENFORCEMENT ACTIONS. The Department of Freedom announced today that technology managers at 172 additional companies in an apparently coordinated move to reject "employer entitlement," their newly coined phrase, demanded payments and compensation adjustments, threatening work slowdowns or stoppages, despite threatened enforcement actions and criminal prosecution under the American Technology Initiative. Initial reports indicate that over seventy percent of the affected employers have agreed to meet the strikers' demands. *See more…*

NEW NATION OF TEXAS PROMISES TO BE TECHNOLOGY HAVEN. As the state of Texas continued preparation for its plans to withdraw from the United States, the Texas Independence Investigation Commission announced that the new nation would lead the world as a homeland for technology development and research offering financial incentives for business and individual relocation. The office of President Red Shank remained uncharacteristically silent regarding the announcements. *See more…*

SingoSam: You believe these dudes? My boss asked me if I would support a walk out but I said way too busy dude.

Bongo: Smart move.

Naggy99: Why's that Bongo?

Bongo: Who cares man. Fight their

own battle. We got clients paying more without even asking. Too many cool projects.

StyleGal: Same here.

Bongo: Anybody see the new MogulCon apps at the TechWorld show?

ArchimedesDream888: Killer.

Bongo: Hey Archimedes. Loved your app man.

ArchimedesDream888: Thanks. Liked your advice.

StyleGal: What's everybody think about A10?

SingoSam: Probably somebody's dumb ass little brother locked in his bedroom!

Bongo: No comment on that one man.

ArchimedesDream888: Good advice again.

SingoSam: Anybody care about the News From the War Zone? Carnage dudes, carnage.

Bongo: Nope. Anyone else?

StyleGal: Flynn only knows.

SingoSam: Everybody's new mantra!

Bongo: Who knows what Flynn knows!

Naggy99: Flynn knows dudes. Flynn knows.

The shift technical manager stared at the senior engineers incredulously. "Are you insane?" he nearly screamed. "Initiate the transfer protocols. We've got an overload in zones 22 through 51. We're close to a catastrophic failure!"

The engineers said and did nothing. The control panels before them were glowing red with warning lights and the low-pitched alarms in the control center of the city's main power generation station were becoming deafening.

The manager grabbed the wheeled chair of one of the engineers and pushed her to the side. "Oh my god," he screamed, looking at her panel. "You've locked us out!" He repeatedly pressed the various controls but they refused to respond. "Two hundred thousand customers will go dark!"

"We will not support employer entitlement," one of the engineers said.

"Who said that?" the manager asked. He appeared on the verge of hysteria.

The engineers did not respond. "Please, please don't do this," he pleaded. "Hospitals, essential services, children, you are hurting innocent people. People will lose their lives!"

They did not respond or even acknowledge his comments. Their minds were closed to reason and were guided by their ideologies. Almost in unison, they all stood up and walked out of the control center.

Four minutes later, two hundred ninety four thousand, seven hundred and six homes and businesses in northern New Jersey lost power. Supervisory and executive personnel estimated it would take up to seven days to repair the system-wide damage, assuming appropriate repair personnel could be found. The utility immediately requested assistance from utilities nationwide, as was the protocol for local power interruptions. No utilities offered assistance, fearful that their own employees would follow suit and walk off the systems.

Technical employees in seventeen utilities in eleven states did exactly that, demanding payments in various amounts to "combat the scourge of employer entitlement" and public dependency. An estimated seven million homes and businesses went dark nationally for periods ranging from twelve hours to nine days before all the payment demands wer e negotiated and satisfied. Commentators estimated that three dozen people, mostly elderly and infirm, lost their lives.

When the public learned the interruptions resulted from protests against employer dependency, reactions ranged from avid support by the more radical Blue proponents to cries of outrage by Green followers, who decried the "dehumanizing and vicious impact of greed and self-interest and the callous indifference to human welfare." Mercy Green welcomed organized protests and strikes of even essential workers "motivated by compassion, fighting greed, and restoring collectivist principles worldwide. Any acts of nonviolence that undermine the stranglehold and genocide of Red Shank are justified."

The government forces of President Red Shank took a more calculated approach. Within the affected areas, there were an estimated three hundred thousand businesses which were forced to curtail operations. Of that number, over two hundred were either owned by Blue and Shank interests or were important service providers to the same. The President's press secretary refused comment on the strikers, stating only that law enforcement authorities were watching carefully and would not tolerate violations of applicable law. When asked by the press how Shank reconciled the strikers who vocally espoused his ideals with the resulting damage and losses, he replied that "maintaining law and order is also a profound value and commitment of our great president."

After the restoration of services in all areas, two hundred and twelve strikers in six states were arrested and jailed indefinitely for violations of the American Technology Initiative. Social media sites were initially overwhelmed by dialogs discussing widespread rumors that another eleven, all senior programming engineers at the utilities, who had little if any connection with the strikes, had disappeared without a trace, according to their family members. Though initially expressing fear and outrage on the sites, the clamor quickly died down and then virtually disappeared. The managing editor of one influential technology bulletin site, in his own commentary portal said only, "Who knows what Flynn knows."

CHAPTER 7

"There is no great genius without a mixture of madness."

—*Aristotle*

"TMOT. The coolest thing you've ever seen today will be the dumbest thing you've even seen six months from now."

—*Anonymous Internet Post*

"We're friggin' ready," Hooch Douglas said. "Anything out of whack, I'll know about it."

Seventeen Solai Sytems and Centeri personnel sat around the conference table. Another twelve stood lining the wall. On the five video screens, senior personnel located at New Eden sat at their control panels or computers. Hundreds of others in dozens of Solai and Centeri technical centers as well as in contractor offices watched on the internet. Abriado Centeri sat in the center of one of the screens with Ti Yung Sun at his side busily working on his computer.

"You need only authorize the funds transfer," Centeri said quietly, "And then we wait."

"Everything is ready," Sun said. "I do not think any commercial facility has ever been monitored and measured to this level. Great job, everyone."

"That may be premature," Neera Solai said sternly. She looked at the monitors from New Eden. In four of the screens, she could see large glass windows and walls behind the participants. The development of New Eden in the background was clearly visible. She was almost shocked to see the extent of the progress. Buildings, landscaping, infrastructure, almost as if it were a corporate campus in the United States. "My god, Abriado. You've been busy."

Centeri smiled. "We're over eighteen months ahead of schedule. It's remarkable."

Neera said nothing in response. "Transfer the funds," she said to Jack Force, who was sitting to her side.

He began entering key strokes on his computer and after thirty seconds he said, "Done."

"Any guesses?" Neera asked to all those present and observing remotely.

"Our best guess is one to two hours," Sun said. "The bank will take probably a half hour or so to process and then notify them. Unless they're sitting around waiting, you figure another hour for them to notice. The other companies who have paid have all said restoration occurred anywhere from forty five minutes up to, in one case, twenty four hours."

Neera hardly noticed the dialogue. Her mind was flooded with feelings of remorse and anger for having paid A10, an act that violated virtually every ethic and value she possessed, despite the mandate to do so from her own board of directors. She had paid an extortionist, a thief.

Centeri had tried to reassure her that it was necessary and that they would use the extraordinary combined technological resources of Solai and Centeri to observe how it occurred, hopefully opening the door to its secrets. There had to be some delivery Sun and the many other experts had explained, some method, some communication with the Nano infrastructure to revive it. Neera marveled at what their people had constructed to observe and record it. Literally thousands of systems had been installed to measure every conceivable energy readout and data flow over the entire Solai facility. Nothing had been excluded as too unlikely or fanciful. Sophisticated monitoring systems measured vast frequencies of electrical energy, wireless broadcasts, light and even sound. Every conceivable internet transmission source was monitored and simultaneously traced using the core technology Neera and Centeri had discovered from Bongo months earlier that Centeri had obtained and adapted. The small army of technical experts were convinced that nothing had been overlooked. That anything that turned Nano back on would be identified, recorded, and sourced. It was this possibility, in fact a certainty, they argued, that gave Neera some comfort and justified in part her decision, and perhaps slightly assuaged her anger and feelings of capitulation.

Suddenly, Hooch's excited voice disturbed her thoughts. "Oh, don't tell me!" he screamed. "I have an email, a friggin' email. It says 'thank you Mr. Douglass, your payment is being processed and service will be restored momentarily.' They're laughing at us. Playing with us. It's only been ten minutes!"

"Are we tracking the email?" Force shouted out.

"Got it," Sun responded. Neera observed that everyone in the conference room and on the monitors were frantically working.

"No, no, no!" Hooch screamed. "It's internal, from the damn receptionist's desk!"

"Loaded previously," one of the technicians said. "They set it up earlier." He paused. "How did they know to load it?"

The question did not need to be answered. All in the room and at New Eden and across the globe participating knew then that A10 had been monitoring them, likely all of them.

"Who are these guys?" Hooch said, his voice trailing off.

"Stay sharp, everyone," Centeri said. "It's probably happening now. We must catch it."

The collective effort of hundreds of brilliant minds was now at work. The complex systems and equipment designed exclusively to catch and measure an unknown and certainly disguised signal were now working at a feverish pace. Dozens, perhaps hundreds of voices on the communications channels now combined into an indecipherable wall of sound.

"Oh my god," Hooch said shaking his head. "I don't frigging believe this. It's up. Everybody! Nano is running. All the mods and apps are firing up right now. Sun, anyone, do we have anything? I am showing nothing, no anomalies, no inserts, none anywhere. I'm fried man, I'm fried."

Sun did not answer for several seconds. "Nothing, Hooch," he said, emotionless, and returning to his screens. "Not a single register. Anyone else?"

All of the department and system heads began to respond for each of their assigned systems. Nano had been restored, seemingly impossibly, with no measurable effort.

Neera looked up at the monitor where Centeri sat. It was one of the few times she saw him look almost stunned. He returned her gaze and shook his head. "Give it some time please, everyone," he said. "The systems are still working, still looking."

The room, the video monitors, the internet, the audio channels were all deathly quiet as their efforts continued. A sense of near-dread wordlessly permeated the room as the realization grew that they had likely been beaten. That the best collective efforts of some of the finest technological minds on the planet had been confounded.

"Anything, anyone?" Hooch screamed.

Suddenly, a lone nervous voice spoke over the audio system. "Hey Hooch. This is Kelly down in maintenance. I don't want to intrude but you said if anything was out of the ordinary we should call. It smells like something is burning here. We don't see anything but..."

Hooch bolted from his chair, pushing three of the technicians out of his way, and ran out of the room.

"Jack!" Neera shouted. Both she and Force and two others ran after him towards the maintenance center which was located in the basement of the adjoining building.

When Neera arrived a few seconds after Hooch, she saw him standing, out of breath, perspiration flowing down his face, sniffing the air like a police dog. A faint scent of burned wiring and plastic was apparent.

Kelly appeared almost shocked. "I've checked everything. All the panels. Everywhere. We can't find anything. I'm sorry. It's probably nothing." His assistant, a young woman in her twenties, stood at his side.

"I'm sorry," Neera said, speaking to her. "I'm afraid I don't know you."

The young woman smiled broadly. "Becky Lee, Ms. Solai."

"Becky, would you mind if I looked in your purse?'

The young woman looked momentarily confused but immediately responded, pleased to receive the attention of the CEO. "Of course, go ahead," she said, handing Neera her purse.

Hooch looked frantic as the realization suddenly hit him. "Oh my god. Don't friggin tell me…"

Neera searched through the small purse, finding Becky's car keys and the keyless entry pod.

It was still hot to the touch as a small waft of smoke exited the purse.

In her mind, Neera heard the laughter of A10 thousands of miles away.

Almost immediately, the Solai personnel resumed work on Nano. During the months of inactivity, they had spent countless hours planning for the reactivation of the system and how the many teams could accelerate its development. They had worked closely with the Centeri staff to develop endless protocols to try somehow to make up for the lost time. Everything that could be done without access to the core system itself had been completed. New software and applications had been written to substitute and replace thousands of functions that had been disabled. By this time, the original plans and timetables had called for installation of the finished modules in the regional jets in San Madrid. As a result of A10, they were over six months behind and still barely halfway through the module programming, or what they had believed to be the module programming. The meeting with Centeri, where it was disclosed that they were instead programing the systems that would integrate with the modules while the detailed module procedures and schematics remained secret, still gnawed at the Solai personnel. Neera was forced to yield when it became clear that Centeri would not budge on revealing the core technology and they had their public confrontation. Although much had occurred since then to strengthen and restore their bonds, and they had even shared unexpected intimacies, Neera knew their relationship had changed forever or at least her assessment of it. What Centeri felt then and now was, as usual, virtually unknowable.

Neera gasped as she looked out the window of the Solai corporate jet and saw New Eden. It had been nearly a year since she had last seen it. The new man-made island stretched beyond the horizon in all directions and over half of it was now green and dotted with roads, buildings and infrastructure. The topography was remarkably diverse. In the sections where there was not yet any vegetation or development, she could see hundreds of massive cylindrical vehicles, presumably the converted crawlers, their ocean floor work now substantially complete and moving on to shape the surface of Centeri's brave new world. And everywhere along the circumference of the massive island either on shore or slightly within the surf, Neera could make out countless sealed towers which she knew were the working examples of the power-generation systems Centeri had demonstrated to her. With such a massive and now awe inspiring project in full force, Neera wondered how Centeri could show any interest for Nano, which seemed almost trivial by comparison.

A feeling of angry realization suddenly engulfed Neera. She had come to New Eden at Centeri's request, to discuss Nano implementation and completion, but had been confused as to why it was necessary. Their combined staffs had months before defined every protocol and timetable to become operative as soon as the system was restored. There was nothing more she and Centeri could or should do. She realized Centeri's likely purpose was for her to see the progress of New Eden first hand, especially since he knew that Neera had questioned not the technology of New Eden, but the very need for the project in its entirety. Looking down, she feared that she saw not the mind of Centeri and thousands of other brilliant minds at work, but his ego. He had recently referred to it, as they were driving months ago in the California countryside, as an "integration of diverse knowledge into one conscious system almost as a spiritual unification." She had been startled by his language and its emotionalism. Centeri always avoided any mention of religion or spirit or anything not reducible to definable information, structure or systems. To speak of consciousness and spiritual unification at any time, much less in the same sentence, was startling. Recognizing that, Neera had immediately questioned him, but he declined to comment further or explain, and appeared almost distraught. She had decided not to push it any further but resolved to remember his comments for consideration later.

Now was that time. Neera had expressed her concerns and doubts about New Eden because it was impossible for her to believe that Centeri would choose the construction of an elaborate vacation and education destination on a monumental scale as the culmination of his life's work. Neera again began to feel the subtle pull and veiled anxiety of exclusion and distrust as she did months earlier during their confrontation over Nano.

"Alan," she called out to the co-pilot, who had been standing a few feet away in the galley. "Change in plans. We're going to Wyoming."

"Excuse me? Wyoming?" he asked, not hiding his surprise.

"I'll give you the specifics in a few minutes," she said, now busily working on her laptop.

"We'll need to radio in a flight plan change and also plan for a refueling somewhere. I'm guessing a good five hours or so from here."

Neera smiled, suddenly feeling invigorated. "It'll be fun," she said. "How often do we get to go to Wyoming?"

Neera felt the jerk of the landing gear as it touched down on the runway. Within moments, the jet had pulled into the private aircraft facility of the airport. A large SUV and two personnel awaited the plane. Neera quickly exited.

"Ms. Solai, I'm Matthew Force," a young man in his late twenties said, reaching out to shake her hand.

"You look just like your uncle," she said, "Or at least what I think he would have looked like more than a few years ago."

He immediately began to gather her baggage. His colleague, perhaps a few years senior to Neera, introduced herself. "I'm Colleen Fallon, security director for SteelPoint. Matt and I will be traveling with you. We received your emails and our staff acquired everything you'll need. It's all in the truck. Did you want to start immediately or could we take you to a hotel and begin in the morning?"

"How far is the town?" Neera asked.

"About two hours."

"Plenty of daytime left. Let's go now, please," Neera said.

Within minutes they were in the truck and on the interstate. Fallon was driving. Neera sat in the other front seat. Matt sat in the rear surrounded by two laptops and several other pieces of electronic gear. He appeared fully absorbed.

Neera watched the outskirts of the city and soon the countryside rush by. Unlike in the Triangle and her trip with Centeri into the mountains, she saw no evidence of the social chaos and ideological warfare plaguing the nation. With the exception of several groups of people with children walking alongside the highway, nothing appeared out of order.

"Ms. Solai, we respected your wish not to alert anyone at the destination, but I wish you had permitted us to do so. We might have found out a great deal of initial information," Fallon said.

"It's better this way," she answered. "It's important that we don't attract any attention. I do not know who may be watching. Plus, the people I hope to find almost certainly do not want to be found."

Neera's statement caught the attention of Matt Force, who quickly looked up from his keyboards at Fallon. She returned his gaze and wordlessly expressed caution. Both were highly trained security personnel, but neither was interested in blindly walking into unnecessary risks or even danger. If the engagement required it, they would insist upon knowing as many facts as possible for the safety of not only their client but themselves as well.

Matt Force chose to speak first. "Ms. Solai, my uncle Jack gave me no background other than to say this had something to do with A10 and that we would be going to a remote location where individuals possibly connected with A10 resided. Is that correct?"

"In part," Neera said. "It's frankly less direct than that. We have no idea if there is any connection. The information we do have is quite tenuous. The fact of the matter is that certain events were observed in the area that might relate to speculation about how A10 operates."

"What type of events?" Fallon asked as she continued to drive.

Neera hesitated, wondering if what she was about to say might sound ridiculous. "Blue lightning. High intensity, blue colored electrical discharges visible for miles."

Neither Matt nor Fallon said anything for several moments. "That's it?" Matt finally asked.

Neera was unable to interpret any emotion in his response. "That's what we've got," she responded.

"That's not much, Ms. Solai," he answered, with a slight hint of sarcasm now evident. "That could be a lot of things or nothing much at all."

"That's what we're here to find out if we can. It's all based on an innocuous local newspaper article."

"My uncle warned me about one particular someone who seems to notice a lot about you and the company."

Fallon immediately spoke up to her subordinate. "That's enough, Matt."

"It's alright, Ms. Fallon," Neera said. "You both have every right to know and he is quite correct. The person Matt is referring to is named Plax. I've become a bit of a fixation to him. We have no reason to believe he is anywhere near here though."

Fallon was quiet and then spoke carefully. "We are aware of Blueford Plax and the role he plays for the president and the national security agencies. His reach is unlimited. He's very, very dangerous Ms. Solai."

"I've experienced that first hand, I'm afraid," Neera

said sadly.

"We'll see what we can find out. Matt, get everyone at home looking, please. If Plax is anywhere near here, or even interested in what we are doing, we better know it now."

Matt returned his complete attention to his laptops and equipment and seemed oblivious to her words as his fingers danced feverishly on the keyboards.

Neera looked at her cautiously. "I am a little concerned that any inquiries you might make could actually trigger the interest we are trying to avoid. Is it wise?'

Both Fallon and Matt smiled. "Don't worry about that, Ms. Solai," Fallon said. "Aside from the fact that this is what we do and are very effective at maintaining absolute discretion, our young friend here has many, many very smart friends, hundreds of thousands I would guess, whose passion is to discover, share and disseminate information. Learning about just about anything and anyone is their, shall we say, hobby."

Matt beamed. "I wouldn't put it quite like that, but it is, as you put it, what we like to do. People are only starting to realize just how much of what they do not only leaves all sorts of data trails but is often being watched or more likely recorded for later review. We like to watch the watchers. Privacy is becoming a fantasy these days."

"You make everything sound like a big computer game, Matt," Neera said.

"Maybe it is. What's so bad about that?" he asked. "You guys see technology as a tool. Like something to use after the fact. We see it more like the way you see your bodies and brains. It's there. It's automatic. I can't imagine not having my computer and all of this. It's really what I do. Everything I do flows from it, not the other way around. I'm serious, almost everything, in one way or the other. I think it's becoming more that way for most of us. Does that make any sense? You two probably don't get it, do you?"

Neera did not answer, but saw that Fallon was slowly shaking her head and appeared to be rolling her eyes. Neera looked at Matt over her shoulder and felt troubled by his words, yet she could not yet say exactly why. Neera was a leader, an innovator in computer technology and was respected world wide. She employed and managed thousands of young technical minds. Yet this young man, the nephew of her most trusted associate, seemed almost completely unconcerned with it and was virtually lecturing her not only like an outsider but almost as an out of date relic. Her concerns were not that she felt attacked or insulted, but how many others shared this view, even within her own company, and were perhaps politically savvy enough not to broadcast it as Matt was now doing.

Neera decided to use this close proximity in the SUV to not only pass the time but perhaps learn and understand more. "I think we get a lot of it, but maybe you can help explain a little more," she said.

"Okay," he said. "Like when you get up in the morning, what do you do first? I'm serious. What is your first hour or so like?"

Neera smiled. "Enjoying my espresso machine and the croissant I picked up the evening before are my most immediate concerns, and then I start thinking a bit about my day. Somewhere along there, I'll look at my computer or my pad or phone and check for any meetings and then certainly anywhere within the first hour I look at my email and my tasks and think about prioritizing my day. Usually it's a quick look, and unless there is something pressing, I'll read the *Times*, online of course, and look at the *Journal* and maybe scan a couple of others. Usually a second cup of espresso is thrown in too. Most days I'll try to have at least a half an hour on my treadmill or spinning bike. There I listen to music. No business. Colleen, what about you?"

Fallon laughed quietly. "Pretty much the same, although I have to pry a sixteen year old out of bed too."

"What about you, Matt?" Neera asked.

"That's my point. Tools. All tools to you. My smart phone or pad is by my bed. Its alarm wakes me. The first thing I do, the very first thing I do, is reach for it and look at the home screen for my schedule, data, and email alerts. My day is set. It tells me what my day is going to be and what, when, who, and how important. I don't have to think about or prioritize anything. It did that with the parameters I set months earlier. Whatever I entered the day before or whenever, whatever notices and automatic links I set, all get integrated. There it is, right in front of me. All laid out. So cool!"

"You don't read the news?" Neera asked.

"Sure I do," he answered. "But just what I'm interested in. I use these amazing apps that search and grab the topics I care about. The science and technology sections, music, new movies, the Lakers, anything relating to my job, you know security, whatever. The pad finds it for me. I get a heading and a couple of sentence summaries. That's usually enough. There's usually a ton of them too. If I want more about any one, I can access the detail."

"I see. But what about areas you don't normally care about, as you put it, that may be important?"

"A cool app for that too," he said. "Even if it's an area I could care less about, which is a lot, this app searches by posting frequency alone in like six hundred newspapers, websites, blogs, you name it. If it detects a pre-set number of hits I established about any specific topic, it concludes its importance and will give me that too. So I'm always covered."

"Nice of it to tell you what to think about," Neera said.

Matt hesitated. "I know you don't approve, but that's my point. You spend all this time," he stopped and appeared to be grasping for words, "you sit around for all these hours with your espresso and croissants or on your treadmill, thinking about what to think about and do. I don't have to. I set that up a long time ago."

"You miss a lot, Matt. You confuse access with insight. In the process where you condense and systemize and all that you dismiss, a great deal of humanity is lost."

"You just don't get it," he said. "My gear and apps and systems do the same editing and processing and condensing, and apply the same biases and preferences my mind does. Just faster and far more efficiently, allowing me to see so much more. These are not tools as you think they are, Ms. Solai. They are extensions."

"No. They are limits. They limit your passion, your creativity and your compassion. You package your world in a carefully predefined electronic format and don't have to think about anything else. "

"We think," he said. "Just not about your drama. We think about all the cool things to see. Flynn knows."

"Enough, Matt," Fallon said, this time very sternly. "My apologies, Ms. Solai."

"Perfectly okay. I asked him and I appreciate his honesty. Remember, he's family," Neera. She made a mental note of his Flynn reference, which was becoming common among so many young people. She decided to ask. "Matt, what do you mean when you say 'Flynn knows?'"

Matt hesitated and appeared briefly perplexed. "I don't know. It's just becoming habit I guess. It's a way of stating the obvious about information and technology. I guess sometimes you say it too about things that are too complex to really know so why even bother? But you know some computer somewhere has nailed it."

"Back to business then," Fallon said, interrupting. "If we might ask, why are you solo this time and not with Centeri?"

"I wasn't aware the last trip was common knowledge," Neera said, hoping to avoid any further explanation.

"It's what we do Ms. Solai," Matt said. "You and Centeri were being tagged all over the internet even before you got to the Triangle. You may not have realized it, but I guarantee you Centeri did. We can only figure he wanted it that way. It was too obvious. There are a lot of people who follow him and his security entourage not only for business reasons but just for fun."

Neera was shocked but tried not to show it. "What

about now? Are they following me?"

"I doubt it. We pulled a few strings and as far as the world is concerned, you're on that jet right now heading back home after picking me up," Fallon said.

Neera shook her head. "Glad you guys are on the team. I think I am beginning to understand Jack's well-known talents to seem to be aware of everything, everywhere. That check every month is apparently very well spent."

Fallon and Matt gladly accepted her praise, diverting their attention away from Fallon's question about Centeri as Neera intended. Her decision to come to Wyoming and abruptly cancel her meetings with Centeri at New Eden was almost an impulse after seeing the progress of the man-made island's development. She had been essentially excluded from New Eden and to this day questioned much about it and why Centeri would embark upon such a project. Her decision to continue the A10 search by herself without him was almost an affirmation of her own independence and competence. It was also consistent with the loss of trust that had occurred over the Nano issues, yet she hoped it was not secretly rooted in bitterness. Regardless, she reasoned, she had made a profound strategic decision for her company in agreeing to pay A10. She would seek A10 out alone, at least this time.

Neera still felt troubled and her mind now raced over the implications of what she had just learned from Fallon and Matt. Why had Centeri stressed secrecy during their California trip searching for A10 if he knew they were being watched from the beginning? She recalled he had mentioned that A10 could be watching, implying that might even be desirable. For whose benefit was the elaborate ruse? There seemed only one logical explanation. He wanted A10 to know he was after him, but in a carefully calculated manner of intentionally flawed secrecy designed to maintain A10's apparent attitude of invulnerability. And there could only be one reason why, she concluded. Centeri knew more about A10 than he was telling Neera. Centeri was luring him. A10 had to be aware of his position and despite the arrogance and dreams of invulnerability, had to be aware that he was in great danger and it would be impossible to stay hidden with his revolutionary technology forever. If A10 had any sense, he would almost certainly conclude aligning with Centeri and his vast resources would be infinitely preferable to being seized by Shank or any of the dozens of other nations and security teams searching for him. So it had all been a carefully constructed invitation. And perhaps Centeri's urging Neera to pay the ransom had actually been a kind of housewarming gift, a show of legitimacy and good faith, and even worse, a payment of tribute.

Neera understood. In a flash of insight it was clear that she had been manipulated. Again. Like the Nano modules. Included but never told the whole truth. Recruited to search for A10 in a legitimate attempt to do so, but also part of a façade that would benefit Centeri even if not successful. Her mind cried out in frustration and disappointment and the agony of being expendable. First the injustice and chaos of a world crumbling around her and now the reality that a man who represented perhaps the only hope was unreachable and, she was forced to concede, beyond her understanding. It was now also obvious to her that her current efforts, adopted almost as a spontaneous affirmation of her own independence and expertise, were likely futile. Centeri had almost certainly already sanitized whatever was awaiting her. She was too late. She shook her head, embarrassed that she had acted so impulsively.

"Fallon, turn around please. We're going back to the airport. I will provide you the files and instructions. I want you to continue carefully but without me. I am not necessary for this. In fact, it is a waste of my time. I want you and Matt to proceed and carefully report what you find. My suspicion is you will find nothing. We are too late. I now realize others have already solved this mystery. At best, you will only find their efforts to wipe any evidence clean."

Matt and Fallon looked at one another in the rearview mirror but said nothing. She quickly pulled the SUV onto a small side road and turned around. Matt began quickly typing on his laptop keyboard.

During the drive back, Neera prepared the information on her laptop Fallon and Matt would need and also provided them access to the appropriate archive files. She also contacted Jack, who immediately arranged to return the corporate jet to pick her up. Fortunately, it had only flown two hundred miles for refueling and brief maintenance.

She did not speak during the drive back and felt a strange sadness. She remembered the words of Patel admonishing her for engaging in what he insinuated were cloak and dagger adventures instead of focusing only on the immediate needs of the company. Perhaps he was right, she thought. Centeri had emailed her and attempted two video calls but she decided to ignore them. For now.

After perhaps ninety minutes they approached the airport. The entrance included a small underpass. Neera noticed, sprawled in purposefully chosen red, blue and green spray paint on one of the walls the words FLYNN KNOWS EVERYTHING. With all the turmoil and suffering in the world, not social commentary or protest or even inventive graffiti. Just expressions of deliberate, resigned indifference.

The world was mad, she thought.

CHAPTER 8

"Government is an association of men who do violence to the rest of us."

—Leo Tolstoy

"I hope I'm not crazy when I'm forty like all these dudes."

—Anonymous internet Post

"You are being told you are entitled to free health care," Topher Blue's radio and internet broadcast echoed within the walls of the auditorium where hundreds of the homeless gathered to hear his daily show which was nearing completion. "You are being told you are entitled to free education. You are being told you are entitled to a good job with good pay and good training to qualify you for it. You are being told you are entitled to three meals a day. You are being told you are entitled to housing."

"Yes we are! Mercy Green tells us so!" a disheveled old woman shouted. Several others cried out their approval.

"Shut your mouths!" a young man angrily responded. "You're takers! All of you! You're killing America!"

"If this sounds good to you, and to many of you it does, I ask you," Blue's address continued, "I ask you, who is going to pay for this? Nothing is free, you know that. You know that farms and food warehouses and housing and hospitals and factories just don't pop into existence out of nowhere. They cost money. A great deal of money. So who is going to pay for what you are being told you are entitled to? Who is going to construct all the buildings and equipment and infrastructure and everything else you just want to walk in to and benefit from?"

Blue momentarily paused to allow his listeners to consider his words. "Many of you have been deceived to believe that the answer to that question is the government. The government will do it. The government will feed me and educate me and house me and provide me medical care and make sure I have a high paying job, if I even want to work. The government will make sure everything is built and everything works and I am taken care of.

"Now, believe it or not, I am not really mad at many of you who think this way. In a strange way, you have come by this attitude understandably through the actions and propaganda of liberal, leftist, overreaching government and institutions and twisted societal values propagated upon you and your families over the past sixty years. How could you not be affected by it? How could you not believe it was true? It is everywhere, it affects everyone. Limitless spending, a belief in a limitless future that does not ever have to be paid for. And a belief that government is there to magically take care of you. But this is your wake up call, and if you don't wake up and reject this thinking, reject this dependency, reject this entitlement, and embrace individual responsibility and self-reliance, then I will indeed be mad at you, very mad at you. I will have no respect for you and you will be my enemy and the enemy of every good, god-fearing person in this still-great country. So when you hear the liberals and socialists and communists tell you you are entitled to this or that or that you have been cheated or robbed, or that being successful and providing for your family is wrong or impossible, so don't even try, reach into your heart and soul and tell them no! I do not need or want anything from the government or anyone. I will be individually responsible and embrace self-interest and provide for myself and my family and if I don't it is my failure and no one else's."

Blue hesitated. The listeners in the auditorium were quiet, except for a middle aged man who was quietly sobbing. "But how?" he cried out. "I've tried, I've tried everywhere. There is no work. I don't know what to do." A group of young men eyed him suspiciously and talked quietly among themselves, their anger and rage barely contained.

"For the rest of you, for those of you that follow the words of the communists, who work for Mercy Green and those like her, who believe that your duty is to care for others before you provide for yourself, who believe this great nation owes you something and you are entitled to take and take and take, I am not angry at you either. You are beneath my anger. You are not worthy to even walk the face of this earth. You are an abomination in the eyes of god and man. You are a parasite, a leech, that will suck the spirit out of us all as you have done for fifty years. If you do not start this very day to help yourself and reject the dependency upon which you have based your life, if you do not stop stealing the spirit and passion of those who accept the responsibility to pursue the human spirit, then you deserve to starve, you deserve to suffer from disease, you deserve to die on a cold street, because that is what you choose. You have wasted and perverted your humanity and we are all better off without you. That, my friends, is the truth. And I call upon each one of you listening to these words on the radio or internet who understand this inalienable truth, this foundation of decency, to strike out against those who refuse to and who want nothing more than to take all that you earn and all that you are. Your enemies are not those who succeed and excel as Mercy Green insanely preaches. It is these people who invite you to join them in prosperity but you must earn it whether through the thrill of a week's hard earned wages or the joy of operating your own business. Your enemies are those who want handouts and want to be taken care of and who call for suffocating government regulations and taxation to subsidize them, who tell you how you must live your life so they can take their cut and leave you with nothing. Find them! Stop them! God bless America and with that, I bid you good day."

The loudspeaker was silent as Blue finished his talk. The audience members spoke quietly among themselves.

"You've told us nothing," the man who had spoken earlier now screamed. "Work when there is no work. Provide for yourself when there is no way to do so. Reject help, yet there is no other way to survive! You are a con man. A thief!"

The young men who had watched him previously now grew animated as they listened to his words. One of them broke from the group and with a cold, deliberate brutality, walked towards the man. He did not say a word as he pulled a gun from his pocket and placed the barrel against the man's right temple. The man had barely an instant to register the terror upon his face before the young man pulled the trigger and his head exploded in a bloody eruption. The young man showed no emotion whatsoever and walked calmly out of the building into the street, returning the gun to his pocket.

Pandemonium erupted in the auditorium as the audience realized what had just happened. Women screamed, men shouted for help, others ran to the blood soaked body, some staring in disbelief and tears, others smiling, uttering words of approval for the shooter, saying the victim was a taker who had it coming. In them the brutal slaying evoked no sympathy, but was the justice and retribution they believed Topher Blue had just encouraged.

"We're better off without the likes of you," a woman said, smiling at the victim. "Topher is right. Where's that shooter? I want to shake his hand!" Others laughed and shouted their approval.

"Are you insane?" a young woman cried out. "This poor man was just slaughtered and you think it's right? This is not what Topher was telling you to do, you ignorant bastards!" But even as she said those words, she knew that she could not be certain. Blue's words had been brutal and perhaps he did intend to incite anger and rage. As a master of ideology and propaganda he had to know that some would take him literally.

With her words, another man pushed through the crowd and without warning struck the young woman across her forehead with an empty bottle of vodka he had pulled from his pants. She immediately collapsed. "Who you callin' ignorant, you taker bitch?" he screamed looking down at her blood covered face.

With that, men, women and even children began an onslaught of violence and rage, attacking one another like vicious uncaged animals. No one was spared, no mercy was shown as the agony of years of chaos erupted on the auditorium floor. The ideology of the attackers or the victims no longer mattered. Each attacker saw his or her victim as whatever they needed to see. Their need was to strike out, to punish, to deliver revenge for their pain and by their violence to dominate and reaffirm their rage.

Within minutes, the violence of the hundreds of people within the hall spilled out into the street, with onlookers and passersby now being attacked as either takers or Blue lackeys. Many ran but many more fought back and joined in willingly in what was becoming almost tribal warfare. The brutality was extreme as bleeding bodies fell to the pavement. Cries of help were met with kicks and blows to the head with whatever the attacker could find. And above it all, insane cries of "takers" and "lackeys" and "Blue" and "Green" could be heard, empowering and fueling the violence even further. The carnage spread rapidly to neighboring blocks and now was a full scale riot, with perpetrators entering businesses and buildings, seeking victims. Gun shots rang out but did nothing to stop the rioters and the destruction. Several store fronts were now ablaze as onlookers cheered. A car had been set afire with three occupants inside screaming in agony. "Too bad!" a young man screamed at them, laughing insanely. "Topher Blue says you need to help yourself and don't need nothin' from nobody!" With those words he threw a bottle of liquor on the burning car which exploded like a fire bomb in the flames.

The police began to arrive, but the sheer scope and brutality of the riot was beyond anything they could do. Many panicked and began shooting the rioters who then turned and, ignoring the danger, attacked the police using their own weapons to maim or kill them. Violence now engulfed dozens of blocks and was rapidly spreading. Hundreds laid injured or dead in the streets. Many more were trapped in burning buildings. People were insane with a tribal-like fury and anyone caught in their path would be labeled in whatever manner justified their rage.

Neera Solai looked out the window of the restaurant and saw police cars and fire trucks rushing by and several people running. "What in god's name is going on?" she asked.

"I don't know…I wonder if we should be concerned?" Rachel Innocent, her lunch companion asked.

"We'll keep an eye on it. Please tell me more," Neera said.

"As I was saying, our company is thriving. We now have over one hundred software and systems engineers and internet and social media people working for us. The rates are still below what they were a few years ago when Gaston and I were employees, but the larger companies are now throwing money at us to keep producing. They're worried their employees are going to strike I guess, so they keep giving us more."

"Have they demanded you contribute personnel under the ATI?"

"It's interesting you ask that. They did four or five months ago and we were frankly pretty frightened. Their calls were really intimidating. But then the demands suddenly stopped and we were told that we were somehow exempt due to the service contracts we had in place and the companies we were helping. I don't brag about this Ms. Solai, but most of our clients are companies everyone knows are tied to Topher Blue and President Shank and all of their forces. The word is that we're going to get some contracts directly from the government. The business is great but we're more than a little concerned. In fact it's why in part I wanted to have lunch with you. I don't want to intrude but its common knowledge that you took on the ATI and won.

"I'm not sure 'won' is the best word," Neera said.

"I understand," Rachel said. "And maybe that's it. We've sort of been pegged as service providers to the Blue companies and more business than we even care to handle is available to us because of it. But we don't want it. Not really. Gaston and I share a dream to develop our own technology and applications and starting a company, almost like you did. But the demands of these contracts keep us locked in and we just don't have the time to start our own projects. Every time we decline a contract, or try to, to free some of our resources up, they fire back with more money and more favorable terms and, although they never outright say it, a strongly implied threat."

"What kind of threat?" Neera asked, leaning forward so their words were less likely to be heard.

"We get a call, and a few times visits, from people who were obviously government agents, you know the type, they almost gloat with their authority, smug, short attention spans, who start asking about our people and contractors and start quoting rules and regulations and security procedures, all this from a government that cries out in support of a free economy and against any regulation whatsoever. The hypocrisy is astonishing. So the last time Gaston had had enough and cut them off and asked them to stop wasting our time. You would like Gaston, Ms. Solai. He is the most honest and direct man I have ever known."

"I think I would like him," Neera said again.

"They weren't used to his style, that's for sure. But again, this last time, the agent or whatever he was, reached in his pocket, pulled out a piece of paper with three client names on it and said he expected us to begin work immediately and by the way, there would be a ten percent acceptance bonus and a fifty percent completion bonus. I'm not kidding. With the bonuses, that got the billables back to pre-Shank levels and maybe even a little beyond. What choice did we have? They're doing this to many other companies. We all talk on the chats and by email. We know almost moments later what is going on. Talk about appeasement. Or no," she hesitated, grasping for words, "Slaking us, I think that's what they're calling it now. I don't want to be slaked. I'm not even sure I know what it means. I better look it up on the online dictionary," she said, laughing. "But I tell you, we're the exception. It's all Gaston really. I'm not sure I would fight it on my own. He has to. But most of the other companies just take the money and do it. It's like they don't even think about it. They're not troubled by all the bigger issues."

"You always have choices, Rachel. Never confuse your right to choose with the consequences, good or bad, in doing so. The first is your mind, your spirit, your integrity. The latter is your challenge. Keep them separate."

"I don't think most of my contemporaries see it that way. They are a lot more basic, or maybe pragmatic. Do the technology and think about the other stuff when you have the time. You could afford to fight them and take them to court. You have resources. You have technology that if you shut it off, every plane on the planet is grounded. They know that. We could never do so."

"You say these young people are pragmatic. They just focus on the technology and don't worry about the bigger issues. I worry that they don't care, that they are detached, that they are not thinking and are one dimensional and superficial. Like a fifteen year old lost in his video game while his little sister plays with a knife."

"No," Rachel responded. "That's not quite right. It's hard to explain really. It's like we don't get hooked. The passion, the ideology, the anger, the speeches, all of it just doesn't hook us. It's not that we don't care about the issues. But why wallow in them? I don't understand why when you hear Topher Blue or Mercy Green you get so inspired and aroused. Why? And then you start speaking like they do and invest in it and get angry when anyone disagrees with you and all that crap. Why be so miserable? Anything you really need to know you can find somewhere online. You learn how to find what's important and hopefully truthful, whatever that means, and you can cut through the garbage and not have anyone scream at you. Otherwise people talk about an issue, then incessantly talk about talking about it and fight over what one said or didn't say and before long you're not even talking about the original issue anymore. You're like a camp or tribe fighting for something else. It becomes all emotional. It's got a life of its own and everyone is pissed."

Neera silently reflected upon Rachel's words. "Anything you really need to know you can find online? Do you really believe that?"

Rachel looked at Neera and suddenly felt judged in the eyes of her hopeful mentor. She felt momentarily insecure but gathered herself. "Of course I don't mean download the web and parrot it back like a drone and don't think but really, why is getting what you need online so bad? Isn't it more comprehensive and more practical and more verifiable than a book or magazine or somebody's speech or advice? I look at the cable news and all I see is one pundit screaming at another. That's not journalism. That's emotion and blind ideology and tribal warfare and indoctrination."

"That is the second time you mentioned tribal," Neera said.

"People protect themselves and want similar-thinking people who agree with them. And they listen to the one who screams the loudest. They're frightened. And they dig in and defend themselves even more when they feel attacked. That's what I mean by tribal. You just don't need to do that when you get your information from twenty or fifty or a hundred different sites and blogs. You don't need anyone else to sort through it with you or agree with it or lecture you. You move through it yourself and then move on. It's solitary in a way. The internet and technology lets you do that. It's almost an extension of your mind, however odd that sounds. Do you understand?"

"I'm beginning to," Neera answered. Her mind raced over the implications and logical extensions of Rachel's words. Somehow these intelligent, technologically sophisticated young people were carving themselves out of the front lines of the warfare inflicting society and barricading themselves within walls of information. But it was not intentional. It was developing naturally as they immersed themselves more and more in the data streams and exchange of digital information and relied less and less on those around them and those trying to be. It was as if they instinctively knew no one man or even many men could be the authorities and visionaries and leaders of the past. The knowledge base was too vast, too unknowable by any mind or a thousand minds. She heard a voice within her say *this is important* as her instincts recently told her when speaking to Matt Force. Something important is happening here far beyond children mindlessly absorbed in video games fueled by attention deficit disorder, as many commentators tried to describe their seeming indifference. Rachel did not use the words 'tools' or 'resources.' She said 'an extension of her mind.' And such a distinction was profound.

Before Neera could continue, could inquire further, the world around them suddenly exploded in a deafening burst of flying glass and metal and smoke. Rachel and Neera were thrown to the floor by the force of the blast.

"Rachel!" Neera screamed.

"I'm okay, I'm okay," she answered from the floor, covered with glass and metal.

The two women stood up and brushed each other off. "A bomb, a bomb went off outside!" someone screamed.

"We must get out of here," Neera shouted.

"Everyone! Out the back door. Now!" the restaurant manager screamed.

"I'm going out the front," Rachel yelled to Neera. "Our office is just a few doors down in the other direction. I'll be okay. I must get to Gaston. Ms. Solai, please go out the back and get the hell out of here!"

"I'll be okay," Neera answered. "Go on and get out of here too."

By now they could see the chaos on the street and people panicking while others began to attack one another. The riot had spread to their location and was in full force.

Rachel darted out the front door and Neera followed the other dazed patrons through the kitchen to the alley in the back. Her ears were ringing from the blast and she was gagging from the remaining acrid smoke. She stumbled into the alley and knew that there was no hope of finding a cab or any transportation and that her mobile phone likely would not work. She walked to the right, in the opposite direction from where the blast seemed to originate on the street out front. She felt out of balance and disoriented and began to fear that she had indeed been injured in the blast. She quickly sat on the edge of a trash canister and tried to gather herself. Her office was on the other side of the city and her apartment was even further. Her only option was to find a land line telephone and call her office for help. She knew that Rachel would do so for her if she made it to her office. But she now saw that power was out and phone service was uncertain.

She gathered herself and continued to walk to the connecting street, but stopped suddenly in amazement. The street looked like a war zone. Men and women screamed and attacked one another in an orgy of rage and violence. She heard the terms 'slackers' and 'takers' and 'users' and 'thieves' and 'pirates' and dozens of others. She stared almost in disbelief as the city and its humanity unraveled. She then gasped as she saw a small group of angry young men point to her and begin to run in her direction. One of them held what appeared to be an assault rifle.

Neera Solai, for the first time in her life, felt the immediate terror of being a target and quarry. Her body froze. She could not move. Suddenly, she again heard an explosion coming from her left, this one smaller than in the restaurant but still powerful. She also heard what sounded like firecrackers, dozens of them, but instinctively knew that the sound was gunfire.

Suddenly, out of nowhere, with no warning, and before the crazed young men could reach her, a massive arm grabbed her around her midsection and pulled her into a black utility vehicle that had blown through the crowd from behind, scattering the rioters. The arm effortlessly threw her into the back seat as if she were weightless. She screamed in momentary panic but immediately knew she was out of danger from the rioters, but now feared who and what had saved her and if they represented an equal danger.

The man who had saved her sat to her left. He was young and massive and dressed in a dark suit. He immediately turned from her and began typing into his data phone.

Her heart pounding, Neera suddenly heard a familiar and unwelcomed voice from the front passenger seat. "Not a particularly good day for a stroll, Ms. Solai," Blueford Plax said, turning around and smiling at her. "You know, being your knight in shining armor like this will positively ruin my reputation."

She did not know what to say. He had indeed saved her, yet she did not know why or how he just happened to be nearby or what he intended and if she was at risk with him. *No*, she thought. That was not his style. Men like Plax practiced their criminality hidden, behind the scenes, like cowards.

"Thank you," she said quietly. She felt weak and disoriented, and struggled to find her words. *What is happening*, she thought. "I, I need to get to my office. Why did you help me, why were you here?"

Hearing the almost frail tone of her voice, Plax turned and leaned towards her, concerned. The young man sitting beside her turned to her and quickly pulled out a small flashlight and shined it into her eyes. "She's going into shock Mr. Plax. We need to get her to a hospital fast."

"Godammit," Plax shouted. "Young lady, we're getting you to a hospital and Bart here is calling your Mr. Force." Turning to the driver, Neera heard him continue, yet it sounded veiled and distant, almost unreal, as if in a dream. "Tell them we have a priority security case and I don't give a damn what they have going on, I want the lead trauma doctor at the door meeting us. How far, Ben?"

"Maybe six blocks, but in this garbage it could take us twenty minutes," the driver answered. Hundreds of people blocked the street. Bottles, rocks and other projectiles pounded the SUV while people approached the vehicle, attempting to break the windows and get to them. Neera continued to remain conscious and watched the unfolding nightmare but felt paralyzed, like a massive weight was pinning her body down. The lower half of her body felt strangely warm.

She heard the voice of the young man sitting next to her call out, "Mr. Plax, we have a problem," he said now fumbling with her suit jacket and delicately lifting it, revealing her waist. "She's bleeding badly, lower torso and thighs completely covered."

"Find it, godammit!" Plax shouted. "This is no time for modesty. We're not going to lose her on my watch. Not this one!" He obeyed and delicately but firmly lifted Neera's jacket and blouse and turned her to see her lower back and torso while feeling her abdomen.

"One, two...no three entry wounds. Looks like shrapnel. The one in her abdomen looks bad, almost like a bullet entry. I cannot control this much bleeding," he said loudly.

"Ben, you floor this damn thing. I don't care how many of theses sons of bitches you run down!" With his words, a small group of rioters suddenly encircled the truck and began rocking it, trying to turn the vehicle on its side. One of them began pounding on Plax's window with a metal bar and the window began to yield. Neera watched from her semi-conscious dream state and was not sure if it was real, could be real as Plax surprisingly calmly rolled down the window. As two of the rioters reached in to try and open the door, Plax's left hand emerged with a pistol. Pushing them both back a foot or so with his right hand, he shot both men in the head. They collapsed on the street and the crowd screamed in terror, pulling away from the SUV. "Now Ben! Get us out of here!"

Neera could not speak or move but saw clearly what had just happened. Tears ran down her cheeks. The vehicle was marauding through the crowd and anyone not fast enough to get away was hit and flew through the air or collapsed where they had stood, their bodies broken.

"Can you hear me, Ms. Solai?" Plax asked, turning around. "You're going to be okay. You're losing a lot of blood but we'll be there in a minute. You get strong again real fast because you and I have a lot of unfinished business. I wanted to talk to you and was waiting for you to finish your lunch when this crap broke out. We heard it was coming and were going to leave, but I began to worry you might get caught up in it exactly as you did. Didn't want to see anything happen to you. You may not believe this young lady, but I find myself kind of admiring you. I don't know if it's that worthy opponent thing or what but it doesn't really matter. I saved your life today and you now owe me for that. I think I'm at least entitled to a sit-down with you and an open mind. We are not that bad. Talk to your friends like Wyatt and Hargrove. You're a lot more like us than these animals in the street. But no matter what, we just cannot let you keep looking for A10. That is out of your league and that Italian bastard should never have pulled you into it. We don't know what he's up to, but he's about to have a very serious wake up call."

Neera's mind struggled to follow his words as she battled the overwhelming desire to give up and close her eyes and yield to unconsciousness. "You killed them, you shot them in cold blood. You're a monster. I don't want your admiration," she said weakly.

"And if I hadn't, we would all be incinerated right now. You're in no condition to judge me."

She could not answer. She did not know if she could have disputed his words when fully alert. She felt her consciousness slipping away amid the rumble of the truck and then its screeching halt. She heard voices speaking to her, asking her questions then felt her jacket being ripped off and a sharp twinge in the crux of her arm. Then she felt nothing. The world was finally silent.

DudesTech.com

News From the War Zone

NATIONAL GUARD FIRES ON RIOTERS; CASUALITIES NUMBER IN THE THOUSANDS. An estimated five thousand four hundred protesters and bystanders were killed or wounded in widespread violence in Manhattan today after mobilization of three national guard units in three neighboring states was ordered by President Shank. Although many of the injured were victims of the protesters rioting throughout the city, the majority of the dead were shot by national guard troops who were ordered to fire upon the rioters. *See more…*

TOPHER BLUE DENIES RESPONSIBILITY. Responding to critics that the riots were prompted by a Topher Blue address encouraging violence, Blue denied any responsibility, saying his broadcast was "no different from a hundred others like it in the past." Blue applauded the government response, saying that the riots had been ordered by Mercy Green and carried out "by her armies of takers and slackers" whose sole goal was to destroy America and return it to a failed and bankrupt nation mired in dependency and entitlement. *See more…*

SHANK DEFENDS RESPONSE AS NECESSARY TO RESTORE ORDER. In a news conference, the president explained that the riot was the result of an alliance of Mercy Green forces and trained foreign terrorists whose goal was to de-stabilize the nation, destroy American property, and take American lives and that the justice department was investigating foreign terrorist influence in Green's organizations and presumed campaign for political office. *See more…*

BIPARTISAN INVESTIGATORS INITIALLY ASSESS DAMAGE AND REPORT RIOTERS UNAFFILIATED. The Eye On America Watchdog Group, a bipartisan public policy organization, initially estimates serious damage to over eight thousand businesses and residences as well as local service infrastructure, placing the restoration price tag at over two billion dollars. The group stated that "there is no evidence that the riot was a partisan effort by any group and appears to have begun after a shooting in a homeless shelter." *See more…*

BYSTANDERS REPORT NATIONAL GUARD FIRED WITHOUT WARNING AND

PROVOCATION. Numerous witness accounts of New York riot report that federal troops "hunted down and shot protestors like animals" and "opened fire without warning into large crowds of men, women and children." Area hospitals were overwhelmed with casualties as the death toll is expected to increase to over three thousand. *See more…*

MERCY GREEN CALLS SHANK RESPONSE MURDER AND GENOCIDE AND THE MOST SHAMEFUL DAY IN AMERCAN HISTORY. In an internet broadcast, Mercy Green called for the impeachment of President Red Shank and the arrest of Topher Blue, calling them mass murderers on a scale of Stalin and Mao, and predicted that more unrest will follow as Americans rally to fight the "American Holocaust." *See more…*

ArchimedesDream888: Anyone hurt?

Lolalola52: My boyfriend got cracked in the head.

TigerT2000: Don't think I'll leave the apartment for a while

Maybeman2: You big city folks got nothing better to do?

Kansasklee: Sounds like another world dudes.

Lolalola52: People don't get pissed in Kansas?

Kansasklee: NFW!

TigerT2000: Hey, switch over to NewTech. First look at the holographic apps. Cool!

Lolalola52: Flynn knows.

CHAPTER 9

"The difference between stupidity and genius is that genius has its limits."

—*Albert Einstein*

"If you can't find it on the internet, you can't find it. Don't even look."

—*Anonymous Internet Posting*

"They just want what we have," the nurse said as she was disconnecting the monitoring equipment. "They want to take what we have, what we've earned. That's what all of this is about. Its not complicated. Why do they make it so complicated? All those minorities and immigrants and the poor folk don't want to work and just want handouts. And those liberals all feel guilty about the way we treated 'em a gazillion years ago so they say let's share everything and give 'em everything they want so we can feel better.

"Now honey, this will sting just a little a bit," she said as she removed the drip tube from Neera's arm and

151

placed a small bandage on the wound. "Your wounds were thankfully superficial and the doctors used dissolving sutures, but you need to keep them clean. You'll be a little uncomfortable if you push yourself too much so try to take it easy. They shored up the artery the shrapnel hit, so it should be better than new."

"Thank you," Neera said. Her mind began to move towards returning to her office and catching up on the time that was lost, but she felt a wave of anxiety, undoubtedly the psychological remnants of the attack. She shook her head as she heard the nurse resume her monologue.

"Now as I was saying, I wish Topher and President Shank would just come out and say it. I know they talk about this individual responsibility and self-interest and dependency and entitlement and all that complicated stuff and it's all probably true. But dang it, I wish they would just say what needs to be said. What's ours is ours and it's going to stay that way. Period. Tell those minorities and immigrants and white trash we know what they're up to and the government's not on their side any more. Their free ride is over. It's that darn simple."

Neera was stunned as she listened to the nurse who thought Neera shared her views since Neera had been attacked in the riots and had been classified by the hospital as a VIP at Plax's direction. Jack Force looked at her and rolled his eyes in disgust as the nurse continued.

"Now don't get me wrong. I'm all for equal opportunity and all that. But why can't everybody just admit those people are never gonna work or try to be successful? It's just not in them. It's just not in their blood. Their ancestors never amounted to anything so how can they be any different? But these liberals say we have to help them because we kept them down and we have to make up for the past. They just can't accept that all they'll do is take and take and take. They don't even want to succeed. I hear these liberal media people say look at the busses and the trains in the mornings. They're loaded with these minorities going to work and trying to get by. But that's such a bunch of garbage. For every person on a bus you have fifty staying home or selling drugs or collecting government checks."

"Please be quiet," Neera said, interrupting the nurse, her revulsion apparent. "Please finish what you need to do so I may leave."

"Well I'm sorry, honey. I didn't mean to offend you. I just thought…"

"I know what you assumed, but now why don't we be honest?" Neera said, as she felt not a sense of anger welling inside of her, but a need to express decency and integrity and to confirm her own humanity. "You did not think. You did not use your mind because if you did, you would not have said what you forced my colleague and I to listen to. You're a nurse, a highly trained professional and you must be reasonably intelligent. An intelligent, thinking person would not surrender to her emotions and her prejudices and the propaganda of people growing rich off her anger. You cannot generalize and stereotype people as you did. For every person that you simplistically categorize as lazy or addicted or dependent, each and every one is a complex human being and there are countless factors and influences at play in their lives. You recognize the complexities and difficulties in your own life and the lives of your family. How can you look at others and see them as so different from you, and somehow simple and one dimensional and not subject to the same challenges you face? Some of them may indeed be weak or flawed or even not very good people, but who are you, who are any of us to judge the challenges and complexities of their lives? You see an elderly homeless woman on the street and all you can see is someone who was a beggar her whole life. How do you not know that she wasn't self-sufficient, but perhaps lost her husband and then her retirement benefits like millions of others under the Program for Entrepreneurial Standards? You see a middle-aged man staying at home and think he is a 'taker,' as you call them. How do you not know that perhaps he has serious health or emotional illness or has applied for a thousand jobs and does not have the training that our economy with a twenty five percent unemployment rate demands? You see a black teenager and think all he wants to be is a pro athlete or a rap star and lacks any drive or initiative. How do you not know that perhaps he has to help take care of family members and has neither the funds nor the time for education and if he had the training might not be an engineer? There are millions of people with hundreds of millions of stories and dramas and demands and tragedies that you callously and ignorantly reduce to laziness or genetic flaws or whatever other superficial justifications the politicians and media provide you. As a health care professional you know, in fact you deal daily with how people are prone to emotional responses like anger and prejudice and fear as stress and pressure increases. Why do you not watch your own reactions and use your mind instead of mindlessly disguising your emotional responses as the failure of others?"

The nurse appeared stunned but said nothing. "And before you label me as one of those heinous liberals you mentioned, know one thing. You are much more like them than you think, and they are just as deluded and judgmental as you are. You are flip sides of the same coins of extremism and ignorance. You see a person struggling and you unthinkingly permit your emotions to brand him or her as a failure and a taker. Your liberal counterpart indulges in the identical process, but instead reduce the person to an innocent and somehow heroic victim of society who has been mistreated his or her whole life and denied the opportunities you and I have been provided, drained of their initiative and ambition. They ignore that many people are lazy and dependent and even malicious. But exactly like you, the liberal stereotypes and denies the person, the complexities and depth and challenges of their humanity, and reduces them to a one dimensional stereotype. Whereas you do so out of unthinking fear and anger, your liberal friends often have a more insidious emotional dynamic at play. Their outrage over the disadvantaged or those suffering or even those who are malicious is a disguise of their own emotions, their self-absorbed need to see the world exactly as they want it to be and fight allegedly on behalf of the newest appointed victims, when in reality they are motivated by their own narcissism and need to control. Those who are suffering become pawns in their pathological need to establish a society they alone deem fair and equitable for the rest of us. They cannot feel secure and safe until the world exists in their own image and reflects their values and their own vision. At their core, they rally for the care of others but do so to slake their own fear. So like you, they are motivated by their emotions. You vilify and reject the victims. The collectivists take care of them, make excuses for them and dictate how they must live their lives. But both of you equally deny their humanity and the responsibilities they must face as human beings. You banish them. Your enemies retard and cripple them. And you both do so in profound ignorance, motivated by your own fear, and viciously attack and label as an enemy anyone who asks you to think and question your own motivations."

"Neera," Jack said. "We need to go. There is no reason for this."

"I have had enough of this blindness, Jack. When I emerged from that alley and saw the rage and brutality in their eyes, I knew instinctively that they were going to kill me. My own death flashed in my mind and I knew I could do nothing to stop it. People reducing themselves to mindless brutal animals, blinded by their emotions and ready to destroy me for no reason. And then to be saved by a monster like Plax for god knows whatever reasons he had. From this minute forward, I will no longer quietly ignore those who deny their responsibility to live as thinking beings. I will no longer quietly tolerate them or shake my head or pretend they will go away." Neera turned her attention to the nurse who remained in the room but appeared greatly distressed. "I will challenge you and everyone like you to think as a human being."

Neera sat quietly behind her desk and began plodding through her email. Although she had been hospitalized only three nights, the backlog was enormous. The pain from her abdomen and lower torso was considerable but she strengthened her resolve not to permit it to disable her. Her attention began to wander as she tried to focus on the many matters before her. She tried in vain to deny the emotions she was feeling, stemming from the attack. Even more debilitating was her realization that Centeri had not called or contacted her. She tried to rationalize his absence by the short amount of time that had passed and the possibility that he was not aware of the attack. It was not likely, she thought. It was in the newspapers and throughout the internet. He knew but chose to do nothing. Her mind raced over the possible explanations as to why he would choose to do so. Perhaps he had heard of her aborted trip to Wyoming and considered it a betrayal. Yet she knew Centeri had never shown such emotional responses before and seemed to be beyond them. It was his detachment and unpredictability that made him so perplexing.

His silence was inexplicable and she had learned from experience that he was never predictable. Neera had already received dozens of messages from other business colleagues expressing their concern and best wishes. The Solai public relations department emailed her that they had received ten interview requests, including one from Topher Blue himself. The only explanation for Centeri's silence was that something had consumed him. She suddenly remembered while in Plax's truck and fighting unconsciousness, he had said something about Centeri and how he was about to learn a lesson. Immediately panic engulfed Neera, realizing these words had been spoken by a killer doing the bidding of ruthless men who knew no limits.

"Carla," she spoke into her intercom. "Find Centeri for me immediately."

Neera returned to her computer and nervously awaited her assistant's response. She did not have to wait for long.

"Neera, I have a Paulo Carducci on the line. He is Mr. Centeri's security chief."

"Thank you Carla," Neera said, remembering the security chief from their travels in the Triangle. "Paulo, thank you for calling. I am trying to find Abriado."

"We are as well, Ms. Solai. He has not checked in for nearly forty eight hours. He will occasionally go for twenty four hours despite our hysteria, but this much time is unprecedented. We are extremely concerned. We are aware of your recent events and had hoped he was with you and did not want to be disturbed."

"No, he is not. I have heard nothing from him." Neera noted he did not even inquire about her condition and dismissed her injuries merely as "recent events."

"That is very bad," he said. Neera could hear the grave concern in his voice.

"Paulo, I was rescued in a way by Blueford Plax and before I lost consciousness, I recall him saying something about Abriado and that he was about to learn a lesson. I can't be more specific than that since I was on the verge of unconsciousness. I only recalled it a short time ago."

"Ms. Solai, we have you on a conference channel," he said. Suddenly another voice broke in. "Ms. Solai, I am Marcus Leeds. Did he say anything else? Please try and remember. It's critical. Mr. Centeri's agenda indicated he was heading to the city for various meetings and he rejected any security entourage. Could Plax have found him and carried out his threat?"

"I have no way of knowing. I remember nothing more and I'm not sure Plax even said anything else. But it would not make sense for him to confide in me anyway. We don't even know the nature of the threat. It could have been legal, or business related, or anything for that matter. You said he has done this before?"

"Rarely," Leeds said. "He knows we are in a high alert status and it makes no sense that he would ignore that. We must conclude he is unable to respond."

With his words, Neera felt a chill and a fear for the safety of her colleague and friend, evoking the trauma she had just experienced. "How can I help?" she asked.

"Please let us know the moment you hear from him," Leeds responded.

"Of course. Please let me know if he contacts you," she said. She heard the call disconnect with no acknowledgment of her request.

Her mind raced over the possibilities relating to Centeri's absence and she tried to calm herself. There were many possibilities for a man who operated as he did. It was also not beyond his nature to ignore his security personnel if matters required it. She thought about Plax's warning and reasoned that if they were planning violence or abduction or knew of anyone else doing so, he never would have showed his hand and warned her. Neera had sensed a bizarre connection from Plax and he had even admitted he admired her and clearly demonstrated more than professional concern over her injuries. For a man like Plax, that was tantamount to a romantic expression. She decided to find out what he knew, and consistent with Centeri's own style of secrecy, to do so herself and not involve his staff.

She searched her data files and found Plax's mobile phone. She pressed the call character and Plax answered immediately. "Feeling better, little lady? You had me worried there for a minute. We heard your injuries were thankfully superficial despite the alarming blood flow. I suspect you're going to be pretty uncomfortable for a couple of weeks. Been there myself more times than I care to remember. I was hoping you'd call me, but I must admit I'm a little surprised. You ready to talk with me?"

"Yes, but there is a price."

"A price?" he asked. "Well I more than think I've already paid in advance by saving your life."

"I need your help," she said cautiously. "Again." Neera listened carefully for any cues. She hoped she had engaged Plax's interest in her and his ego would not allow him to resist.

"My help? Once is more than enough given our respective positions don't you think? But I am intrigued. Please continue."

"We can't find Abriado," she said, intentionally using the familiarity of his first name, hoping the informality would attract him. "I am very worried. I recall your mentioning him when you were taking me to the hospital but I was confused and disoriented and, as they told me, possibly bleeding to death. I thought you might help me." Neera intentionally avoided mentioning the threat Plax had made, providing him a new opportunity he might use if he believed she did not remember his threatening words.

For several moments he said nothing. "Have you spoken to Marcus? He's a good man. Worked for me for five years. Hated to lose him."

"Yes," she answered, recognizing that she must be honest as a sign of good faith in the event he already knew of her conversations. "No one knows anything. I'm very worried."

"I can see that. I will tell you what I know, Neera, but I expect you to honor our bargain and meet with us immediately and not just go through the motions." His use of her first name nauseated Neera, but confirmed her suspicions. "Do you understand me clearly?"

"Yes, but you know my position and it is unlikely anything you can say will change it. Do you understand me clearly?" she answered.

"Let me worry about how I might change your mind. As of about eighteen hours ago, he was in Gravna in the Balkans. He chartered a flight using another name. Since that time, we have no clue. Do you know why he might be there?"

Neera was stunned and now knew Centeri was investigating A10 on his own as she had attempted to do. She recognized that Plax was attempting to trap her and draw out additional information. She was certain he knew the connection already and likely believed Neera knew it, but her confirmation of Centeri's knowledge would be helpful.

"I asked *you* for help," she said, emphasizing the word you. "We did not agree to any more questions."

"Clever, young lady. Very clever," he said chuckling. "I think you'll fit in with us nicely. Let Marcus know won't you? Give him my regards. And Neera, it's probably best that you tell them I called you and you cleverly pried it out of me. I don't think he'll be very happy with you if he knows you called and went around him and tried to outfox me. I give you my word I will support that harmless little ruse. I am telling you that Centeri is not the man or the friend for that matter you believe him to be. You and your company are being used shamefully but I know you won't believe me and will still find his charms irresistible."

Plax mercifully ended the conversation by saying nothing more and hanging up. Neera felt ill with the familiarity she had just engaged in with Plax, and his final comments that might have been those of a jealous suitor. Plus she was now obligated to meet with him and discuss their obvious desire to steal part of her company or suffer his escalated rage and reprisals at being lied to. His offer of a cover up would only heighten any perceived complicity. She knew she could handle anything that might occur at such a meeting and might actually learn useful information.

She dialed Paulo's number. "Yes, Ms. Solai," he answered.

"I just spoke to Plax and he informed me that as of eighteen hours ago, Abriado had anonymously chartered a plane and was in Gravna. They knew nothing of his whereabouts after that time."

"You spoke to Plax? Why? What else was said?" Marcus Leeds said, suddenly joining the conversation

Neera smiled. "He gave no other information. Oh, he did ask me to give you his regards."

Leeds hesitated, obviously surprised. "Ms. Solai, we're concerned that you unilaterally contacted him and would like to know more. It's always advisable to be skeptical about anything he says. I am sure you're aware that he…"

"I just found my friend and colleague and your employer for you Mr. Leeds. Your job is to confirm it," Neera said. "I am very worried, as you should be that he may be there without security."

"We understand completely," Leeds said, aware that he had just been effectively reprimanded. "Thank you. We'll let you know when we find him."

Not likely, Neera thought, hanging up the phone. If Plax's information were true, it would likely explain Centeri's failure to contact her after the attack. Neera searched her feelings and somehow did not feel Centeri was in danger or had been abducted. He was simply too deliberate and methodical to take careless risks. Her concern now was what he was doing in Gravna and had he found Guyah, and could he even be working with him. She remembered his pledge to her to work together and take no action without Neera's participation. In her heart, she doubted it then and now ruled it out almost entirely. Centeri worked on too many levels, and would not feel bound if circumstances made it infeasible. With anyone else, it would be dishonesty. With Centeri, the whirlwind of his life and the almost immeasurable interests he controlled made such matters almost seem like pointless sentimentalities. Neera wanted to know, needed to know what was happening and was certain only A10 would justify Centeri's disappearance. Plax's words echoed in her mind that she and her company were being used shamefully. Although she had no doubt Plax lacked the insights to evaluate Centeri on any level, it was clear she was no longer an intimate confidant and probably never had been. Her only option was to return her attentions to her company and its needs, particularly Nano, and somehow finish it amid the social and political chaos and a crumbling economy. The power the A10 technology represented was beyond her means but somehow she would continue the pursuit to the extent Centeri permitted it.

"Jack," she said calling her most trusted colleague. "Get me up to speed on Nano and exactly where we are."

"Neera," he answered, "Is there any way I can persuade you to relax for a few days? What you have been through would bring anyone to their knees."

"Not a chance, my friend. Every instinct I have is telling me we better move and move fast. Somehow Nano, A10, the strikes and the attempted strongarming is all going to unfold together. And behind it all somehow, someway, is our friend, Mr. Centeri."

"They know something. I'm telling you they do. Sun and the others won't even mention it anymore since we paid the ransom and got up and running," Hooch Douglas said to Neera. "We've gotten done in five weeks what was originally projected to take three and a half months. They've tripled the number of their people assigned who are now doing procedures allocated to us. They're testing as soon as a section is done and claim that by doing so we can reduce the time of complete unit testing by eighty-five percent. We're ninety-five percent done with their damn pseudo coding and have only the landing gears to do. Hell, at this rate, we're done in ten days and can start installation."

"You've tried to discuss the A10 technology?"

"Repeatedly, and they friggin' ignore me. I had some pretty interesting new ideas a couple of weeks ago with some projected data to back it up and they wouldn't even look at it. It's like they don't want us to focus on it and they're using the urgency of Nano to justify it."

"It's disconcerting for certain but I'm not sure it's urgent right now," Neera said. Her thoughts about Centeri remained fresh in her mind. She had earlier in the day received an email report from Colleen Fallon and Matt Force regarding their findings in Wyoming after she had left and turned the investigation over to them ten days earlier. As Neera suspected, nothing would remain of the location where Guyah had resided and the strange occurrences of blue lightning had been seen. But the extent of the cleansing surprised even her. They reported that the land owner had been approached by individuals who offered him fifty times what the one acre tract and small warehouse on it was worth. When he could not decline, he reported they closed the transfer within forty eight hours and twenty four hours later, a small army of construction, demolition and technical crews arrived and not only removed the building entirely but the concrete pad and two feet of topsoil under it and around it. They then replaced the soil with new fill and restored the property. The seller then said to his amazement, one week later, he received an executed deed conveying the property back to him entirely. Neera recognized few organizations had the ability to execute such a transaction or the interest in doing so. It could have been agents of Blue and Plax and their countless companies or any one of several foreign government operatives. Or, she realized, feeling a jolt of concern, it could have been Centeri. Completely thorough, immediate and absolutely efficient. His modus operandi. She thought about turning her legal team loose to search the real estate records and the contractors. But she knew it would quickly dead end with an untraceable sham corporation. Whoever operated on this level would leave no trail.

"Okay, so let me tell you something that is urgent," Hooch said. "We've lost five senior programmers and system engineers in the past month. The first three I didn't think that much about. But these last two! One of them yesterday and one this morning. No shows. Their drives wiped clean of any personal data and their personal effects gone from their offices and I don't know how. One of them, Lela Peters, was kind of my protégé for the past two years, so I went by her apartment. Her roommates said she took only a few things and left a note telling them she was leaving with no explanation and giving them the rest of her stuff. The other, Rogers, I didn't know him as well, but his friend said essentially the same thing. We've been hearing about the tech workers disappearing across the country, when they're not striking for god's sakes. The numbers have been small but it's all over the web that the numbers are growing fast. Whatever is going on, I think we've been hit."

"How critical were they?"

"We can cover them, but I don't understand how or why they just left without a word, especially from this company. We don't want this to continue."

"Jack," Neera said. "Let's have HR start interviewing everyone to investigate to see if we have a problem and what we can do about it. Have them inquire as much as possible about the five who left, their concerns and feelings about it and if they have any information. Whatever is going on is happening at the worst possible time. We need every resource of this company committed to this project and the installation phase. Also make sure the department and project supervisors are working closely with the Centeri personnel and updating the time lines and using them and their resources fully. I am concerned about some sort of backlash or mistrust or competition over A10 instead of working more closely together. We need to get across to them that nothing matters now except Nano and how successful completion promises enormous success to the company and everyone in it."

"A message and pep talk from you might motivate everyone. They were all very worried about what happened to you, and demonstrating you are back and fully at the helm will be invaluable."

Neera agreed, but insisted upon doing so after

their reports. She returned to her office. Though she intentionally did not show much reaction, the departure of key technical personnel with no notice or comment was of the greatest concern. Reports of similar events across the country were occurring with more frequency. They remained mysterious, because in virtually all cases, the individuals left no forwarding information, in fact no information, even to their friends and families. Most were very competent people, usually young. The first comments were that they were strikers and no real concerns were expressed beyond the obvious issues attending the strikes. The government continued to throw its weight by enforcing the American Technology Initiative, potentially criminalizing strike activities as well as drafting technical personnel for voluntary service. Many employers adopted the initiatives apparently urged by Blue and Shank to appease or slake the strikers by throwing money at them to somehow offset the violence and chaos crippling the economy. The money had worked, as the numbers of strikers were declining to some degree, though large numbers continued and additional cases occurred, regularly crippling individual companies and even industry segments. The disruption remained extremely serious.

However, Neera feared that these events were different and were not outshoots of the strikes. Whereas the strikes were often disorganized and the participants very vocal, these reported disappearances were secretive, even mysterious and seemed very final. In a society wracked by ideological warfare between extreme self-interest and extreme collectivism, young minds were apparently withdrawing and rejecting the turmoil without comment.

CHAPTER 10

"If I were required to choose between art and genius, I would choose art. Art is the expression of humanity in its purest form. Genius is far too easily corrupted."
—*Adrianna Snow*

"If you can't talk to them online, don't trust them."
—*Anonymous Internet Post*

Liars, liars, all of them. I'm safe now. Safe. They won't find me, not here. I'll stay here. I'll be safe. They'll never find me. No way they can. Nothing to search. No one to talk to. No one will talk to them here. No one knows about me. No one talks here. Not to strangers. Not to foreigners. Not unless the elders or clerics are paid. And then the game is to cheat them, steal from them. After a while, maybe six months, a year I can start my research again. Let things cool down. They'll forget about me. But no, no, the traitors. My friends, my friends. How could they do it? It was just to pay him back. To teach him a lesson. To show him. To let him see what I could do. That he could never

169

understand, never stop me. That he can't own me like he owns everything and everybody. The money would set me up so I could do the research. They could never understand what I have found. Just enough from his companies and the other one to set me up so I could do my research and not worry. It was nothing to him, he wouldn't even notice.

How could they have done it? My friends. My friends. I explained a million times, we all knew it was just for him, to teach him a lesson, to have the world laugh at him. It would be too dangerous. I shouldn't have done it. It was stupid. It opened everything and they all saw. And my friends betrayed me, stabbed me in the back. Stole my life. Thieves, thieves! They'll kill them. They'll kill all of us.

My research, my research. It was too soon. No one should have known. Why did I do it? I hate him. It was too soon. It's not ready. Still so much to learn. So much I don't understand. It's too dangerous. I was stupid. Stupid!

I have nothing. Nothing. I'm alone. They'll kill me. They'll kill me! Maybe he will too. Why wouldn't he? I'll never show him, they could never understand it. They think like children. They look out, not in. Stop when they should go. Close their eyes. I gave them a clue. A child's toy but it should have been enough. To at least get them thinking. To see what my research really was. Where it could go. All he saw were her planes and his stupid island. Make more money. How much money does he need? My research! Pure research, he was blind to it, they all were. I was stupid to play with him, to laugh at him, to try and take his money, but it would help me finish my research. God, I showed him, stopped them both but then he wouldn't pay, so the others did and that was it. Should have been the end. What was I thinking? Stupid! But they said do it again so *we could work. I believed them! My friends, my friends! They were planning it all along. Thieves, to steal it. They don't understand anything. Just a tool to steal and laugh until they catch them and kill them and they will. They won't think its funny then. They won't be laughing then.*

The door thrust open and two dusty, brutal men exploded into the room. He froze in terror. *Oh god, oh god, oh god! It's happening. Oh god, it's happening!*

But they did not attack him. They stopped and one stepped quietly aside. A third man walked into the shack.

"You know I will not hurt you, Boortah. You are safe. I give you my word," Abriado Centeri said, almost in a whisper.

He could not speak. His terror paralyzed him. He could not move. His brain locked in primal fear.

"I want to help you. Just help you to get out of this. To get you safe." The two primitive men looked at Centeri then at Guyah. They did not understand. They did not need to. They looked at Centeri and would do whatever he asked. They would kill this boy almost without thinking if he asked it. "Let me fix you some tea," he said, walking over to a table in the corner where a small burner and supplies for the tea stood.

"I, I don't want any tea," he said. "My god, how did you find me? Not here. I don't understand."

"You cannot run anymore. If I could find you, they all can. They are probably not far behind."

Oh god. They've followed him. They always follow him. He doesn't know how easy it is.

Centeri looked at him, guessing his thoughts. "I'm alone, Boortah. Not even my own people know where

I am. They might have tracked me to Gravna but that's it. These men work for a very special and private man who I have helped over the years. They would sacrifice their own lives before they would betray us. You must believe me."

Does he understand? The tribal leaders, the clerics can all be bought. It's just a matter of time.

"I'll protect you. We'll take you where they cannot get to you."

So you can steal it! So you can steal my research as you tried before!

"No. If you want to help me, take me to where I want to go and then promise to leave me alone. Your presence has ruined it for me here. Everyone will know foreigners were here."

Centeri stared at him briefly. "They will find you wherever you go. Unless you come with me." Centeri hesitated and walked across the room and sat down on the corner of a wooden crate. "You must stop what you are doing. It is wrong."

Idiot! Does he really believe that? Does he not know, or even suspect? Be careful! Be careful! Deny everything. See what he knows.

"I don't know what you are talking about."

"You are A10, Boortah. You must be."

"I am not." *That is not a lie. Perhaps an omission. I was. For the first few. But I did not use that name. That was the thieves. The traitors. Their idea.*

"Stop," Centeri said. "Sun has now identified several Nano consistencies, maybe that is not the best term, but he can project out, perhaps guess or postulate may be more accurate, the extensions. It's your work Boortah. No one else is capable."

So Sun figured it out, read the clues I left. Nothing more, though. Stupid. So what does he want? Will he kill me? No, no, not how he works. He wants my research, my mind. That's what he wants. The others will kill me. Maybe those two, as soon as he is gone. Maybe they've already been paid and they're just waiting. Oh, god!

Centeri looked at the two men and nodded. They left the house and discreetly stood outside guarding the entrance.

"I am not A10. I swear to you."

"If that is true, you know who is."

He knows or at least guessed. Maybe he can help me find them. Stop them. No! No! He is no better than them. Than any of them. He will steal it like they did, like all the others want to. To use it to hurt and steal and destroy. Oh god. Like I did. Why did I do it? I needed the money. And I wanted to hurt him. Stupid. Idiot. Where are those two? Are they going to kill me?

"Where can you go? Who can you trust? Boortah, you have a good heart, but you are naïve. You see science, revolutionary technology. You see the applications. They see a weapon first. A weapon to disarm their opponents' defenses, take whatever information they want, and then shut down their society. Throwing them into chaos, starvation and even worse. Don't you see that? All of them desire it and worse, must stop their opponents from getting it."

"No! No! They don't understand. It must not be used that way!" he screamed. He fell to the floor in tears. In a world mired in social chaos, with whole nations unraveling, his research, the output of his mind, could be used to steal or destroy whatever remained. "You already know. No one can stop it. No one but me. I am a dead man. They will torture and kill me, won't they?"

"No, no!" Centeri said excitedly. "I will not allow that to happen. I will use every resource I have to protect you. They will never get to you. They will not get your technology. I promise you that. But you must cooperate. I do not understand. You are here. You have no lab, no equipment. But the A10 attacks have started again. Twenty in the last week. Apparently another this morning. Where is it, how are you controlling it?"

The thieves! The thieves! They will kill us all!

"They stole it from me," he said, whimpering. "My friends, my colleagues, they are this A10. I just wanted to teach you a lesson. I needed the money to continue my research. It was like a game to us. But they must have planned it all along. To steal it. To attack and blackmail."

Centeri was stunned. "Do they understand the technology?"

"No, they just know how to assemble the units I made and operate them. They could replicate some of them, but not the core technology. They have no more idea of the science than you have. But they are very smart. They could enhance them, modify the applications."

"Do you know who they are?"

"I know who they were. But my guess is that others are involved now who are controlling them."

"How much do they have?"

"Everything. When we left the compound, we destroyed everything. We constructed another in Washington state. It took less than a month. That is when they acted. They barred me from entering and cut off my access. They were very thorough. I did not have any back doors. It never occurred to me that I would need them with my friends. So I left and found property in Wyoming. I constructed a system in just a few weeks. Its purpose was to stop them. To conduct the research on how to stop them. But they were ruthless. They were following me and tried to take the new lab as well. So I destroyed it and went into hiding. I ended up here. I lived near here for a few years as a teenager. It is easy to disappear here."

"Did you make any progress? Were you able to stop it?"

Why should I tell him? Why should I trust him? He will steal my work like the others and I could do nothing. I will use him. Make him protect me. Make him think I am trying to find a way to protect against it while I continue my real research. I'll demand privacy and no monitoring. The facility in Switzerland. It's secure. At least for a while. I will be happy there. They will never understand it anyway. Not even Sun or the others. I'll tell him I already know how only when I'm ready, only if it's best for me. Maybe not even then. Yes! This is the way to go. He's right. It's too dangerous. They will find me, they will torture me. Then kill me. Yes, this is the only way.

"You don't understand," he said now, calmly and thoughtfully. Centeri looked at him, aware that his demeanor had suddenly changed. "You can't understand. There is no on and off switch. It's not a virus or something you can eliminate or replace. There is nothing there. Nothing changes. That's why you and the Solai people have found nothing because there is nothing new to find. It's different, so different."

"Tell us. You must tell us. We can understand the foundation at least. The opening. It must somehow be the electricity, the static electricity. We know that is the basis for the Nano modules. Is that it?"

Idiots! They took they bait. They are playing with the toys I left them. The diversion worked! Let them think it. Why not? Say nothing and let him think they figured it out and tricked me. Let them chase my decoy!

"I want the lab in Switzerland. And absolute privacy. My own people. No reporting. No monitoring. I will tell you when I find it and how to execute it but nothing about what it is and how it works unless I choose to. It will be mine and mine alone. My only purpose as far as you are concerned is how to neutralize the A10 technology. Nothing else. Everything else I do will be mine, the product of my own mind, to do with what I want."

"You misused it, Boortah. Your recklessness and naïveté caused this. That must not happen again. There must be safeguards. Accountability. Some transparency."

Oh god. He's suspicious. I came on too strong. Does he suspect I already know? Or is he just trying to steal from me. What do I do? No, no! Give him something. Anything!

"I understand what I did, the mistakes I made. How I played into the hands of monstrous people. I am grateful to you, Mr. Centeri, and I will not repeat those mistakes. You are saving my life. I will not forget that. You have my word. I will find it and keep you informed of my progress. I will help you do what you need to do."

My research is all that matters. To continue this technology. Nothing else matters. Say anything, do anything. There is no evil in lying to a liar. They cannot even comprehend the perfection I have seen and can almost grasp!

Centeri was silent. He knew that Guyah was holding back, but knew his mind and its discoveries were essential to a much larger process that was not yet revealed. Centeri's own mind projected and integrated a thousand possible interactions and dynamics of this young man's potential actions and their impact into a macro view that he could not fathom alone, that was beyond his or any individual mind. He would watch and wait and with the brilliant young minds that were surrounding him would be ready for the unification, however it manifested and impacted the world.

"Let's go Boortah. You have work to do," Centeri said. "We have a very dangerous few hours ahead of us." The two guards entered again and spoke quietly to Centeri. He looked at Guyah and said, smiling, "We are in very good hands."

The young man smiled. *He agreed! My god, he agreed! Why? Why? Can I trust him? What is he planning? Can I trust him?*

Eleven hours later, Centeri relaxed in the oversized chair of the private jet. Guyah slept in the fully reclined chair behind him. Centeri slowly shook his head, thinking that he appeared like an innocent child, much younger than his twenty-two years. He wondered what was occurring in the young man's mind, the content of his dreams. He marveled at the potential of his mind and how nature had created such a profound intellect seemingly beyond what was possible or explainable. How could this one mind see what few if any others could? How could this one mind be so advanced in science and technology yet so ineffectual in so many other areas? Here laid the great misunderstanding of the human mind and intellect, he thought. Society applauded brilliance, however it manifested. The most intelligent, the most effective were usually the most celebrated and respected by those who did not possess such powers. The average man elevated them, followed them, depended upon them, and subjected themselves to their wills, crying out in fear for their leadership. To yield to the will of a leader, whether a politician or visionary or savior or despot, to grant him or her authority seemed to be ingrained in the human psyche. What they could not understand is that the intellect they glorified and empowered could be limited and narrow and even perverted in other areas. A brilliant scientific mind or an intellect gifted in management and organization might be callous or indifferent in areas of morality and compassion. A brilliant orator or politician or a mind gifted in psychology or spiritual insights might lack intellect in science or logic or organization. Yet society empowered and elevated them as if their minds and intellects encompassed all realms. He thought about how the financial leaders and industrialists of the past were granted almost limitless power and were trusted to thrust society forward by virtue of their intellect and will, yet those intellects were often flawed and empty in many areas of human endeavor. To the followers, this did not matter. They blindly, unthinkingly gave their consent. This young man who slept quietly in the cabin likely possessed one of the most brilliant scientific minds the world had perhaps ever seen but had engaged in childish revenge and mindless, foolish extortion. Yet society would not see that paradox. He was a near folk hero to many and a living legend to others. Centeri did not doubt that countless people would easily yield to his will if he were so disposed. The illusion of intelligence and its trappings and the willingness to capitulate to it explained so much of the chaos and suffering the world was experiencing. No single mind of authority, whether a politician or an economic czar, nor even one thousand such minds, could meet the burden society tried to impose upon them. Not today with the nearly infinite expansion of accessible knowledge technology provided. Not even in the past when the world seemed so much simpler. Yet no one cared. Leaders and followers continued their mindless dance as they had for thousands of years. He had sworn to one day help them understand that the illusion was now exhausted and obsolete and a whole new generation was rejecting it. He knew in his heart and mind that that day was rapidly approaching. He would be ready.

Centeri picked up the phone on the arm of his seat, knowing that its encryption was entirely secure. He dialed a familiar number.

"Neera," he said. "I need to get you up to speed."

CHAPTER 11

"I would choose the joy of feeding a single hungry child over all the riches the world could offer."

—Mercedes Green

"I'm waiting for an app that just shuts everybody up."

—Anonymous Internet Post

"First, let me tell all of you, I am fine. A little battered and very sore, but fine. I was very much in the wrong place at the wrong time and like so many others, paid a painful price for it. I appreciate more than I can tell you your outpouring of concern and support. It makes me even more committed to each of you, the Solai Systems family, and our extraordinary mission." Neera paused her address over the video conference link to all the Solai employees worldwide. As usual, Jack had expertly arranged the presentation in a matter of hours. Neera had agreed that it was essential to assure her employees of her safety and continuing leadership. Her purpose, as Jack had urged, was to also convey an affirmation of security and solidarity and to perhaps lessen the concern over the disappearance of the technology employees not only nationwide but within Solai systems itself. In a matter of days, social media and the news outlets reported that the numbers were increasing and now hundreds had effectively vanished. Neera's hope was that her words would stem any further departures from Solai.

"Each and every one of you, and because of that, the company, are world leaders in technology. By collaboration, we work on a creative, scientific, and intellectual level that most companies dream about. This is your achievement, our collaborative achievement. Working together and with our partners, we are designing and coordinating and now applying and executing some of the most sophisticated ideas and output of the human mind ever conceived. What you are doing is the first application of a revolutionary technology created by our partners that has the potential to literally change how the world works. Countless lives will be saved, unimaginable efficiencies will arise, and the door will be opened to worldwide innovations that we frankly cannot even imagine. And it is your work. Your collaboration. Your minds and intellect. You are the first. Think about that. Working together, you are the first.

"All of us see and experience the chaos and the suffering in the world around us brought about by the warring political and social factions. We all wonder will our nation, will our society even survive. We cannot ignore it but we can rise above it and create something meaningful and extraordinary that may help change that world. I know that there are pressures from every direction to interfere with what we are creating. The strikes, A10, and now this newest development, friends and colleagues disappearing seemingly without notice or reason. I know you see much of it is driven by money and greed. Strikers demanding ransoms and receiving it, A10 extorting huge sums to restore what they wrongly crippled. Employers who greedily stood by while salaries and benefits plummeted, now appeasing them, trying to buy loyalty and forgiveness. And now some of your colleagues appear to have simply rejected all of this madness and have withdrawn. I beg you not to do the same. Stay with me, stay with us and I promise I will devote all of my strength to our success, which is your success. Together we will create a technology that the world has never seen before."

Neera walked into the large, garishly decorated office. Upon the walls hung political mementos, hunting trophies, and numerous military rifles and handguns. Bluford Plax smiled at her but uncharacteristically said nothing as she sat down across from his desk. Plax sat at his desk while another man stood looking out the window, his back to Neera. He slowly turned around and she was surprised to see General Oswald Crush, the CIA Director and effective head of all security and intelligence operations in the country.

"I wasn't aware I was this important," she said.

"You are not," a voice from behind her said. Neera turned to see who was speaking and was now shocked to see Topher Blue, who had entered from an adjoining room.

"Then perhaps I should go," she answered.

"Now, now little," Plax said then stopped, correcting himself, "Ms. Solai. Don't get all huffy on me. You owe me this little meeting. I am sure you do not need to be reminded of that fact."

Neera noticed that Crush did his best to hide his annoyance over Plax. Blue smiled and shook his head. "We all heard about the attack and I am very pleased that you have fully recovered and our very talented friend could be of assistance. I mean that sincerely."

"I am very grateful for what he did but not how he did it," she said.

"Yes, yes. I understand. We are at war, and war inevitably has casualties."

"I was not aware that the nation was at war."

"An odd statement coming from one of the casualties," Blue said.

"May we get on with this?" Crush said, his growing anger apparent.

"I realize I failed to properly introduce myself, but it appears you already know who I am," Blue said.

Neera did not respond. She recognized that she now sat with two of the most powerful and dangerous men in the world as well as their hired assassin, and her mind raced to understand the likely purpose of the meeting and what would happen next. This was far beyond any interest in Solai. She did not have to wait long.

"I will be blunt. We want, that is to say, your government wants the Nano technology and A10, which is another way of saying we want your Mr.

Centeri. And you will help us get him. And if you do not, at a minimum, and I emphasize minimum, and hope you understand the implications, we will put you out of business. But if you do, your company will prosper and I think we can even forget Mr. Plax's efforts to secure a little piece of it. We will leave you alone to prosper and hope we can simply be friends."

Neera said nothing as her mind raced over his words.

"And so you will realize just how serious we are Ms. Solai, we have already spoken to and have the full support of, I'm sorry, Blueford, can you help me please?"

"Pinky Melton, Bantar Patel, Martha Miles, and Mrs. Randolph Sellers," Plax answered.

"Your board of directors I believe, who collectively you will have no choice but to defer."

Neera listened carefully and thought how to respond.

"Why do you believe either I or my board can give you the Nano technology? And why do you believe I have any connection with or even knowledge of A10? You call me to a meeting, you threaten me and make demands I have no ability to meet. For your information, we have no knowledge of the underlying technology of Nano. None. Centeri is far too sophisticated to share that with anyone, including me. He went to great lengths to assure that our services worked around the actual modules. We did not even realize it until well into the project. Their technology remains a carefully guarded secret, even to us. As to A10, even Centeri has no idea. He is searching for someone that everyone, including you, believes may be A10, or at least may have developed the technology. You already know that.

You already know he was in Gravna and you know this young man had ties in the region when he was younger. So what do you want from me? What more can I tell you?"

"Centeri left Gravna two nights ago and called you in flight," Crush suddenly said. "The call was scrambled but we know the two of you spoke for eighteen minutes. What did he tell you?"

Neera hesitated then realized that there was nothing to hide and that they almost certainly knew everything she did. "He told me he found Guyah, that Guyah is not A10 but he did, as everyone essentially knew, develop the technology being used by A10 and that Guyah refused to cooperate with him and he left the country."

"What else did you discuss for eighteen minutes?" Crush asked.

"He began the conversation by asking about me, what had happened the day of the riots, and if I was alright. I told him about everything, including Mr. Plax's actions and my distasteful obligation resulting from it."

Crush looked at Blue for several moments, as if each understood an unspoken message that Neera was not a party to. Neera saw the wordless communication and grew even more concerned.

"Did he say that he had Guyah and was protecting him?" Crush continued.

"I would not tell you if he did, but fortunately I do not have anything to hide. He said nothing of the sort. He said Guyah would not cooperate and left the country. Nothing more."

"His answer to you, Ms. Solai, assuming you are being truthful, was ambiguous and probably not a falsehood, at least not technically," Blue said. "We believe he left the country with Guyah. If that is true, Centeri's message to you was not technically a lie was it? It was just a bit incomplete. He didn't bother to tell you Guyah left the country with him. And as far as not cooperating, I have no doubt Centeri would offer protection regardless of any promises of help. He could work on that when he had him. So your friend was not very trusting or open with you, was he? Perhaps he was protecting you since you told him of your dealings with Mr. Plax and our pending meeting. Or perhaps, he uses and diminishes you like he uses and diminishes everyone on the planet. Which explanation do you think is the more likely, Ms. Solai?"

Blue's words exploded into Neera's consciousness with the same force and malice as his internet and radio addresses that so easily provoked the rage of countless thousands. Neera felt the rage rising within her but it was not blind. Accompanying it was the same anxiety that Neera had experienced so many times over the past many months when she realized that Centeri had not always trusted her or included her, and as with Nano and the Triangle trip, had knowingly mislead her. She knew that this vulgar, treacherous, malicious man might be correct. Centeri may have intentionally mislead her again, perhaps to protect her, perhaps not. And she knew that he was watching carefully for such a recognition by her. She would not give him the pleasure.

"I have noticed, General Crush and Mr. Blue," Neera said, intentionally excluding Plax, "That those who are comfortable with lying, attribute the same fault to their opponents."

"You are in no position," Crush angrily began to say.

"I am not finished!" Neera shouted. "You will allow me to speak. I came to this gauntlet in good faith and you will wait until I am finished! I remind you that despite Mr. Plax's recent heroic rescue, he also forced me to witness the brutal murder of two people, and previously conspired and succeeded in having me arrested with, I am sure, your full approval. Since you felt it appropriate to spend the last twenty minutes threatening my company, my livelihood, my future and likely my life, allow me to respond in kind. I have no influence and certainly no control over Abriado Centeri. If you believe he has something you want and you think you can get it by destroying me, you will fail miserably. If that is your strategy, your plan, it is laughable, not even worthy of vengeful children. You cannot defeat him on any level. You have nothing he wants or needs and anything you do will be little more than an annoyance to him. If you are going to destroy me or my company, thinking that will affect him, then get it over with and stop this ridiculous drama where I am expected to be intimidated by your presence. I am not. I know what you are capable of. And all you have done today is to overplay your hand and show me how desperate and frankly intimidated you are by Abriado and the competence and decency he represents. You are outmatched and outclassed gentlemen, in ways you cannot even comprehend."

The room was quiet for several moments. Neera stared at Blue and knew that despite their strategic error in believing they could gain an advantage on Centeri by threatening her, they were none the less lethal and could easily carry out their threat to destroy her. She now wondered whether her words, clearly fueled in part by anger, had been necessary. Would she have been better served by remaining silent or even playing along? No, she thought. Enough of this and such blind and malicious men and the damage and suffering they caused. The twisted values and morality that engulfed them not only perverted all that they touched but rationalized their viciousness. She wondered why such men, in the heat of their oppression, in fact all such men throughout history who had destroyed countless lives in the name of their own ideology, could do so and be blind to the reason and logic of their own minds. How could otherwise intelligent men turn their humanity off at will? Did they not reflect upon their own lives? Did they not question their own actions and decisions? She remembered similar thoughts and inquiries days earlier when she confronted the ignorance and blindness of the nurse who had treated her. Though the facts were different, the dynamics seemed the same. She had pondered this once with Centeri, who was not troubled by the apparent paradox. Reason and thought seem to have one purpose in such matters, he explained. To justify and reinforce their values and prejudices, which were firmly and powerfully ingrained throughout their lives both consciously and unconsciously, and then to protect them almost instinctively from attack. Questioning those values themselves was an entirely different process that may never occur, at least not from self-reflection. If it comes at all, it is usually prompted by input from others that they trust. But when they surround themselves with similarly thinking people, criticism is not only unlikely, but is viewed almost as treason. So the circle was complete. She remembered all of his words and suddenly, in the face of these monsters sitting before her, their meaning and impact became vividly alive to her as they had not before. She understood the futility of expecting decency or compassion from such men and knew that her own mind, her own beliefs and values would not have permitted her to patronize them for strategic gain. She could not remain silent in the face of such outrage. Had she done so, she would have been too much like them and all the other warring factions destroying the world.

Returning her gaze, Blue finally spoke. "Thank you for this lovely get-together," he said, almost in a whisper, his restrained malevolence all too apparent. "It appears there is nothing more to say, and we sadly achieved nothing in this meeting. I do appreciate your coming though as you promised. You will not hear from us again."

Neera stood up and walked out of the office and felt a sense of dread. She now knew that their real interest was the technology that existed in the wondrous mind of Guyah and the fearsome applications of it that had been commandeered by his former colleagues. They had also had guessed, correctly Neera suspected but could not confirm, that the core technology of Nano was likely somehow tied to Guyah and his discoveries.

This, if true, Centeri alone knew and like so much in his life, he would likely never share as he continued the incomprehensible dynamics now clearly being set into motion.

Neera looked at the five jet aircraft and could not help feeling a profound sense of accomplishment and pride. The glaring San Madrid sun reflecting on their polished aluminum surfaces made them appear almost unreal, oddly out of place in the tropical landscape dominated by palm trees and other foliage stretching to the horizon. The aircraft production facility had been built outside of the sprawling city in a rural and otherwise undeveloped area. The government had permitted no other development as would normally accompany such a sprawling complex. The facility consisted of a series of interconnected massive warehouses and a two-mile long runway hacked out of the dense underbrush. It was surrounded by a series of security fences and guard towers, making it appear almost as a massive prison. There was nothing else. Outside of the security perimeter there were no buildings, homes, commerce or any signs of human activity except for the four lane highway originating in the city. The facility and the regional jets it produced for companies and governments worldwide were the single largest component of the country's economy, and the government protected it as one of its highest priorities.

During the past six months of Nano installation, both Solai Systems and Centeri personnel frequently complained of the excessive security and blamed it for occasionally-missed deadlines. Their complaints fell upon deaf ears as the authorities relentlessly investigated everyone and everything entering and working within the premises. Neera had considered contacting Miguel Santana, the country's infamous security chief, and asking if the procedures could be ramped down. But after his assistance to her two years earlier during her first visit to San Madrid and the attempted extortion of Plax and the commerce director Alberto Garcia, she did not want to risk offending him. They would all simply have to bear it.

Their compulsion for security extended to the Nano installation and integration as well. The Solai and Centeri technicians constantly battled the company engineers who attempted to learn as much as possible about the underlying Nano technology, frequently using trivial or obvious inquiries as a ruse to probe its secrets. But the Centeri personnel were equally relentless and had safeguarded Nano long ago from any such inquiries. Even the Solai personnel were barred from the core technology as they had learned two years earlier, but had designed and mastered every detail of the system's installation and operation.

Neera sat on a hastily built wooden platform surrounded by nearly one thousand company, Solai, and Centeri personnel, as well as members of the worldwide press and invited guests. She noted the cadres of armed soldiers nervously guarding the perimeter. The visitors had been bussed from the entry gate to the runway and were not permitted access to the facility. The buses stood by to remove them the moment the ceremony was complete. Neera looked to her right where Miguel Santana sat. The security was his responsibility and she knew he had performed with the same ruthless efficiency he was renowned for. He smiled at her briefly, his continuing affection for her clearly evident, then returned his gaze to a constant surveillance of the event that laid before him. To Neera and the others, it was a celebration of collaboration, technology and an unlimited future. To Santana, it was an opportunity for disaster. He would not permit any interference.

Looking at Garcia, who was preparing to address the audience, she wondered about Plax and Blue and their threats months earlier. She knew that despite the influence and power of Santana, it was not likely that Garcia would abandon his association with Plax. He was likely maintaining a low profile out of Santana's view. He had been polite to Neera when they met earlier in the day, but she sensed his hostility and chose to avoid him. She wondered what was occurring in the mind of this man who seemed to lack any values or ideology and could be so easily bought and sold and who had been effectively humiliated by Neera. How attractive and useful would this hostility be to Plax in carrying out whatever they might be planning. She thought about which men were the more dangerous. Those like Plax, who were blindly committed to their twisted ideologies and values, who fought instinctively to defend them or those like Garcia, who were intellectually empty and possessed no such influences and were motivated almost completely by greed and self-importance. The answer was clear. Men like Garcia could be manipulated and even controlled. Those who lived by their values and intuitions could not be.

Garcia walked up to the microphone and began speaking. "Please everyone, take your seats. Today is a great day of celebration in San Madrid. Standing before you are the newest, most innovative and sophisticated passenger aircraft on the face of the planet. They are the result of years of effort and research and design by thousands of our brightest countrymen. The technology they developed and integrated into these planes will make us the envy of the world and catapult our aircraft into being the most sought after on the planet."

Neera smiled and looked at the Centeri and Solai project managers and their teams who sat several rows in front of her. They returned her look, some slowly shaking their heads, amazed that Garcia had not even acknowledged their roles or the fact that the Nano technology was entirely separate from their efforts, which consisted mostly of routine aircraft assembly. Neera was not surprised. In fact, she should have expected it from a man like Garcia. She also looked briefly at Santana who silently mouthed *I'm sorry* to her. Neera smiled and shook her head, absolving her friend from any embarrassment.

"We have named our new aircraft the Archimedes Fleet in honor of the great scientist thousands of years ago who calculated how to move the weight of the world with his mind. Like Archimedes, these new craft, powered by the minds of San Madrid, will similarly move the world forward."

Neera smiled and leaned forward to whisper in Hooch Douglas' ear. "Who the hell came up with that?"

"I'm afraid we did, Ms. Solai. Lela Peters to be exact," he answered.

"Hooch, isn't she one of the missing?" Neera said, remembering their conversation months earlier.

"One and the same," he said.

Odd, Neera thought. The name of Archimedes had been coming up in various settings recently. Her new friend Rachel Innocent's company name and even speculation that A10 might be a play on the word. And now one of the mysteriously departed technical experts had taken the unusual step to suggest the identical name to their client as the banner for its new fleet.

Suddenly, Neera heard the murmur of the crowd and saw numerous people pointing to the rightmost jet. Several of them began laughing. A dozen large white birds had suddenly appeared and landed on the craft as dozens more circled overhead. Within moments there were literally hundreds of birds overhead, many of which began landing on all the jets. Neera noticed that the local personnel appeared agitated and almost frantic and any laughter came exclusively from the foreigners.

Garcia appeared in a near panic. "Don't mind the birds, everyone. They are native to this region and appear to appreciate our new creations as much as we do." His attempt at humor did not comfort the audience.

Neera leaned over to Santana, who appeared stoic. "Miguel, I don't understand. They're just birds. What is going on?"

"We call them Mootooras. I am sure they have a more scientific name. They are water fowl that come to shore in the evening. It is unusual to see them this early. They are considered a bad omen. They congregate on trees, often hundreds or even thousands, and their weight quickly warps and kills the trees. They then continue on the dead branches until they collapse and then move to the next. They are an omen of destruction."

"So your people believe their landing on the planes means…" she caught herself and said nothing more. Santana did not need to respond. Unbelievable, she thought. Mindless superstition clashing head on with modern technology.

Garcia returned to the microphone, now visibly angry. "Do not just stand there," he said, apparently speaking to the soldiers and security guards around the perimeter. "Get rid of them!"

Unsure what to do and likely intimidated by the superstition, two of the soldiers walked over to the first craft and without warning, began firing their automatic rifles in the air above the fuselage. The birds panicked and took flight but so did many of the attendees. Chaos immediately ensued as hundreds began to run for cover towards the buildings.

"No, no!" Garcia screamed over the public address system. "Please be calm. There is nothing to fear. Do not approach the facility. Security will not let you enter. Stay away from the facility!"

Santana looked at Neera. "Idiot," he said, walking over to Garcia and ripping the microphone from his hand. "All units stand down. Allow visitors access to the entry area. I am coming down." Looking at Neera, he added, "You will excuse me for a moment?"

Neera smiled and nodded. There was an amusing element to what had just occurred, but she was concerned that the unveiling of the Nano project had been disturbed. A dozen or so members of the international press were in attendance and she could only guess how they would describe the imposition of superstition, gunfire and chaos to the event that should have focused on the technological wonder of Nano alone. It could hardly have gotten worse, she thought. And then it did.

Neera noticed that all the white birds had scattered except for one perched on the elevator of the first plane. It appeared to be oblivious to all around it, unmoved even by the gun fire. Then suddenly it fell from the perch, flapping its wings, but was unable to take flight. After hitting the concrete runway, it stood quietly near the rear landing gear, seemingly unexcited and unmoved. A soldier approached it from behind. Despite Santana's instructions, he raised his weapon and shot the bird. He missed, only grazing the bird, but causing it to take fight in panic, wounded. It flew to the front of the aircraft and frantically tried to find footing on the windshield. It could not and began to slide down the nose, spewing blood over the pristine glowing aluminum surface as it fell. The words Archimedes One painted on the side under the windshield, intended to celebrate the intellectual and technological achievement of the craft, were now heavily streaked with blood.

Neera stared in disbelief. Her team looked at her from the surrounding chairs, but could find few words for the bizarre event they had just witnessed. Hooch

Douglas, who was renowned for never being at a loss for words, could only shake his head.

Neera's phone rang and she saw it was Centeri, undoubtedly asking for an update on the unveiling. How, she wondered, would she explain this?

CHAPTER 12

"If passion drives you, let reason hold the reins."
——*Benjamin Franklin*

"Is Flynn real? You're missing the point dude."
——*Anonymous Internet Post*

"When you are ready, let's discuss technology."

Gaston Innocent stared at the email message. He had received an identical message seven times over the past three months. Initially he had ignored it as junk mail. But with each repetition, he found himself growing more curious. Its simple words implied something more, something that he could not quite identify. The email address of the sender was a commercial firm specializing in consumer and business email blasts. When he contacted the firm to learn more, they had no information as to the originator. It had been a small, targeted plan with several thousand recipients, but no information had been provided. The services had been paid for completely in advance and no contact was provided, except for an email address that the company was not authorized to disclose without permission. They were instructed to contact the address if a recipient requested their doing so. Gaston had not. He was not comfortable with the message and its need for mystery.

"Another one?" Rachel asked, looking over his shoulder at the screen.

"Yes," he answered.

"You're going to respond eventually. Why not now? What's the risk? "

"Not the point."

"Then what is?"

"I will not be manipulated or play games."

"There might be good reasons for the cloak and dagger, given what's going on in the word today," she said. "It seems direct to me. No nonsense. I think it's perfect for the people who would be receptive anyway."

"Maybe," Gaston said quietly, obviously deep in thought. "How do you know that it isn't Shank and the ATI? A clever new recruitment ploy?"

"Too subtle for them. Too smart maybe too."

Gaston smiled. *She might be right,* he thought. "I wonder if anyone else has received it," he said, referring to their employees and colleagues.

"If they have, nobody's talking," she answered.

Nor would they, he thought. Even on the blogs and chat rooms there were only veiled whispers hinting of mysterious, nameless, cryptic messages about technology. No one would discuss the detail. Many feared government involvement, as if the messages were some baiting technique.

"One of the very few dialogs I found said the messages stop after the tenth if you don't inquire," Gaston said.

"Ten," she said almost sarcastically. "Why is ten suddenly showing up everyplace? A10, ten states threatening secession, everybody referencing Archimedes which incidentally has ten letters, Topher Blue and Mercy Green, both ten letters, and now ten chances for god knows what."

"That's hardly a pattern," he said. "It's coincidence, not causation. If you already convince yourself that there are such numerical patterns and that they mean something, you can always find them almost anywhere you look. Our minds love mystery and drama and will interpret the facts to feed it. Its an intuitive, emotional response, like so many others."

"Maybe," she said thoughtfully. "But there is also synchronicity. Inexplicable relationships and connections. I think the unfathomable complexity of our world still gives off hints and signs if you're looking for them. Statistically, it must happen."

Gaston did not answer. He thought about Rachel's earlier words and her encouragement to respond to the emails. Almost instinctively, and with no further thought, Gaston emailed the service provider.

"I want to discuss technology."

Within seconds he received an answer. "Please stand by."

Gaston waited and noticed that he was feeling a sense of genuine excitement. Where there was caution and doubt only moments before, now suddenly he felt inquisitive and almost inspired.

Rachel smiled broadly. "Okay. My guess is either the government, Topher Blue, Mercy Green, or maybe even A10 himself trying to seize your beautiful mind. If there's a knock on the door in the next two minutes, I'm out of here!" she said laughing.

"Please take a look at the attached app and when you're ready, tell us what you think. It is yours to do with as you please" the email said. Gaston and Rachel stared at it, surprised that it came so quickly. Gaston immediately directed his security software to scan the attachment and detect any viruses or problems. The scan of the file took over two minutes. It appeared clean.

"Two minutes for one application? The file is big but not that big. Spooky," she said.

Gaston had already opened the attachment and began digging through it almost ravenously. In less than a minute he stopped and appeared stunned. He leaned back in his chair, as if to catch his breath. "My god, Rachel, do you know what this is?"

"Tell me!" she said, almost shouting.

"I think, I mean… it looks like the Scimitar."

Rachel gasped. The Scimitar was a legendary prototype software operating system designed by a prodigy several years earlier. It was recognized as revolutionary in its technological approach and had the potential to render almost obsolete much of the foundation of the existing information technology infrastructure. Its core advantage was that it effectively eliminated the concept of processing time. Any application, any process, became almost instantaneous. Even an ordinary desktop or notebook computer could benefit. The promise it offered was almost incalculable, along with the existing systems and structures it would supplant. And then suddenly, it disappeared, along with its developer. Rumors abounded that the developer had been kidnapped or killed to prevent the introduction of the system and the obsolescence of existing technology that would inevitably result. Although conspiracy theorists continued to assert such ideas, the more likely explanation was that Scimitar had been acquired by a large developer for an immense amount of money and the technology was being studied for the enhancement of and integration into the existing infrastructure. Most rational observers believed this to be the case. The foundation of Scimitar was rumored to be a radical departure from all existing operating systems and underlying processor principles. Such a complete reworking of the technology infrastructure it would require was not possible even for the advantages it offered. Instead, it would be dissected and evaluated to determine how its operating efficiencies could enhance and expand existing systems.

Staring at his monitor, Gaston realized that goal had been accomplished. "Just one, apparently," he said to Rachel. "We can apply it and enhance just one application and then it implodes. Clever."

"Can you get into the code or copy it, save it somehow? This is too valuable to let it wipe itself clean."

Gaston smiled. "Whoever we are dealing with has obviously thought that through and safeguarded it. This is meant to tempt and tease us, to want to learn more. They've closed the back doors, you can be certain. Anyone working at this level knows how to protect it."

Gaston and Rachel quickly decided which application to enhance, choosing a cumbersome but essential data storage and delivery system they and their colleagues used constantly to service their clients and preserve modifications and enhancements. Within twenty minutes they had downloaded the Scimitar technology.

"Wow," Gaston said quietly. He stared at the monitor in disbelief. "I don't know," he said, speaking to Rachel but almost oblivious to her presence. "It's like a new system, maybe a thousand percent increase in speed and efficiency. Remember how you had to wait to give it time to process and summarize and then go back in to tweak the file structure? Gone. All of it. Almost instantaneous. What took several minutes before is now just a few seconds." He returned to the keyboard and screen. "Oh my god, " he said. "All the utilities and analytics, all cued and ready to go."

"Who are these guys?" Rachel asked.

Gaston thought about Rachel's words. In a world where ideology had shattered reason and balance, her question was vital. Who was tempting them and for what reasons? They had already been approached many times by the government and representatives of the ATI, but the services they provided to companies affiliated with Topher Blue and his interests had effectively exempted them. Mercy Green and her affiliates were known to be very technically savvy, but this type of approach did not seem consistent with their operations. It could be any special interest group, company or group of companies for whatever purpose they were pursuing. Gaston noted that due to Rachel's recent meetings with Neera

Solai, a very real possibility was Abriado Centeri and his interests. Centeri, due to his wealth and influence, operated on a level often beyond the reach and even the understanding of others. Soliciting technology experts across the globe could easily be attributed to him. Yet he had never done so secretly in the past. In fact, the Centeri companies were very public about soliciting talent for their ventures, including thousands for New Eden. Secrecy and disappearances without explanation did not appear to fit.

"I am not comfortable with this. We need to know who we are dealing with," he said. His fingers danced across the keyboard and quickly sent a message. "Who are you?"

The response came quickly. "I will tell you, but it is important that we cover some information first. It will not in any way threaten you or put you at risk. It will not be used against you nor are we being monitored. I can tell you now that we are not the government nor are we connected in any way with the government. I promise you when this communication is over, it will be permanently deleted if you request it."

"What do you want?"

"What do you want, Gaston?"

Rachel looked at Gaston. "Go ahead. See where it goes," she said.

"Are you behind the disappearances of the technology people?"

"Many of the gifted people who desire to pursue knowledge and information and discovery and who reject the turmoil in the world and the corruption of the human spirit have chosen to work with us."

"Oh my god," Rachel said. Gaston stared at the screen, unsure what to say next. The honesty and affirmation of the message shocked him. The mystery was solved, at least partially. The enormity of the past few years and the emotional pain he and his family suffered flashed into his consciousness. He thought of the pain and capitulation suffered by so many young people like him who had given up hope. He could not even allow himself to think there might be a place where it no longer occurred.

"How is that possible?" he typed.

"Why have you suffered, Gaston?" the message read.

"We lost everything. We fought and started a company. We are all doing very well. I cannot risk that."

"We know of your success. We admire your work and what you have achieved under nearly impossible circumstances. So why then do you suffer?"

"It is all around us. And growing worse. I fear the work we do for the companies we service adds to the chaos, not helps stop it."

"Forgive me for generalizing, but which is closer to your values and beliefs, Topher Blue or Mercy Green?"

"Be careful Gaston," Rachel said. "I don't like where this is going."

Gaston thought for a moment then carefully typed. "Neither. They are both wrong. I can't really explain why. There is probably some truth in both. But I don't care anymore. Truth no longer matters in their world."

"What does matter ?"

He did not hesitate. "This."

"We understand. Do you?"

"What do you mean?"

"All around you people seem lost in ideology and rage, waving their banners of individual responsibility versus social responsibility. Takers versus makers. Compassion versus greed. All the labels. Values and intuitions intended to guide humanity are distorted and twisted, used as weapons to divide us."

"Yes. Yes! But people should be responsible. They should not be dependent on the government or expect others to provide for them."

"We agree."

"And I have no problem with helping those who really need help and to create opportunity for everyone."

"We agree again Gaston."

"Then what has gone wrong?"

"That is complicated. It may not be correct to refer to it as going wrong either. The processes I am going to explain appear to simply be the way we all are. What comes naturally for us. The simplest explanation is that when it comes to our values and morals and intuitions and many other reactions we constantly experience, they are solidly locked in and there is even a psychological system that not only keeps them that way but seems to defend them aggressively. We are designed so that our impulses and reactions are fueled by our intuitions and values, and they arise very quickly with very little or no critical thought as to their substance and rationality. It is not surprising when you think about it. Much of it may be rooted in survival. Your life would grind to a halt and you would be exposed to constant risk if you had to revisit and reinvent the wheel for every challenge that arose. These processes allow us to live our lives and benefit from experience. But it is a mistake to believe they are thoughtless, mindless reactions. There is frequently significant and articulate thought, but instead of scrutinizing the underlying intuition, it is usually limited to defending it from attack and then justifying it, which is very different. So the intuition is strengthened and reinforced and even expanded. This is how aggressive and even radical responses can eventually arise. That is why we grow angrier when someone accuses us of not thinking. We are thinking, but not about dissecting the impulse or value but instead justifying and strengthening it from attack. It is a natural human process and very difficult to change. Much of it occurs automatically. Without critical and rational thought to ground us, we are acting upon processes, content and influences we are not even fully aware of and that may even serve very necessary purposes in other situations. It comes from a very old place in the mind."

"I don't understand."

"For example, this process can explain why the value or intuition of individual responsibility is so widely followed today, but has developed almost as a weapon in some cases. Once the individual adopts it, however that happens and we will address that later, like all values and intuitions, becomes very prominent and locked in as I just explained. But instead of scrutinizing it logically, we automatically defend and justify it and in doing so, a valid belief in providing for one's own prosperity can expand into disgust for others who do not or cannot or who are simply different or possess other values. This extension or even radicalization is fueled by the defensive mechanism manifesting as an intuitive fear that they are under attack. If you then say to me that no, many people receiving government aid are good people who have just not had equal opportunity, the impulse will be to feel attacked, to aggressively defend the value and see you as one of the takers. And each time, it can grow a little more radicalized. On the flip side, this same process can transform compassion and caring into an intuitive, reactive belief that they know what is best for others and it is their responsibility to take care of them. But the real impulse is once again fear. Fear that they are under attack and that the world is not exactly as they need it to be. So if you say to me that no, they are lazy and have been taught to be dependent upon the government and to take and not make, my impulse will again be to feel attacked, to aggressively defend my intuition and see you as one of the pirates mired in greed. The battle lines are not only drawn but are virtually inevitable. Mercy Green searches for victims who she then labels as heroic but in the same breath dictates how they must live their lives for a higher purpose that she alone defines, that soothes her fears. Topher Blue sees everyone as corrupted by laziness, dependency and entitlement. He entices them with the glorious banner of individual responsibility and prosperity as the only way out but then denies real access to all but his cronies to soothe his fears about outsiders and intruders. There is nothing new here. The processes have been the same throughout human history. Only the faces and the content have changed. What is radically different however, is the proliferation of and immediate access to information provided by technology, and the absence of a single or even a few comprehensive authorities, as there were in the past. Historically, people were influenced by their families and schools and religious organizations but it was often larger than life political leaders as well as financial, industrial and scientific visionaries who often held the populace spellbound and provided much of the impetus for change. Instead today, countless sources and contradictory content battle for attention every minute of our lives. Our minds have not yet developed to process all the diverse claims since this geometric increase in access and volume has happened only over the past twenty years or so. As a result, those screaming the loudest and exploiting the gravest consequences and stoking the most fear and who speak most effectively to the intuition and values, by default get the recognition. And in doing so they fuel the very process of reliance upon intuition, impulses and values, as opposed to critical thought, that are the problem."

"So think, just think," Gaston replied.

"Even when you do not want to or even remember to. When you feel the pull, the emotions flaring, the sense of attack, the presence of an enemy, the insult of an opposing position, even the certainty that you are right, stop and say 'my intuition and values are at work. What is really going on here?' Step out of the fray and look at the facts and think it through before you react."

"But why are we not as militant or concerned? Why are the most mobilized and militant often older?"

"Many brilliant people are researching and trying to answer that question now. The initial feeling is that your generation had no option but to develop this multi-faceted attention. You were exposed to the internet and the media and its overwhelming volume of topics and ideas during your developmental periods. No other generation in history ever experienced this. The changes prompted by the Renaissance, the Industrial Revolution, and other periods did not even scratch the surface of the complexities our minds now grapple with. Most of you simply did not develop your values and intuition, relying only on a handful of influences such as parents, schools, churches and charismatic political, economic or cultural leaders as your parents and everyone before had. Your sources and influences were far more fluid and diverse, and frankly overwhelming. You have had a chorus of information at your fingertips and flashing on screens before your eyes from your earliest moments, so you barely give attention to any one voice. Your short attention span that is often inarticulately complained of by those older than you, not only appears to be essential to process the sheer volume you are exposed to, but may well help filter out what your brain cannot handle and insulate you from attachment and impulsive responses. The demagogues like Blue and Green and the others easily find willing followers among your older colleagues when they speak to their values. With you they often find disinterested shrugs and maybe even your desire to get back to the exciting new app you are working with. Does this make sense ?"

"What is next?" Gaston asked, typing a question he was not certain he wanted answered.

"It is not good. A tremendous amount of research is being devoted to social, demographic and economic models and computer simulations across the globe to try and understand and even predict the impact of the diverse forces now in play. The economy, and perhaps our entire society is sick, and may even be incurable. The seizure of resources by Shank and Blue and the sudden complete eradication of entitlement programs, social safety nets and institutions, all in the name of personal responsibility, which in the fifties was called self-interest, the strikes by technology workers, which are actually growing rapidly and crippling an alarming number of essential companies despite the government's best efforts to deny it, the failure of a rapidly growing number of companies nationwide, the historically high unemployment, the tenfold increase in poverty and homelessness, the secession movements in over ten states which is becoming a virtual certainty, and the continuing attacks by A10, which although small in number are growing more strategically targeted and destructive. Add to that the fear that whatever revolutionary technology A10 has developed could be used as a defenseless weapon that is now being sought by countless governments and private interests for exactly that purpose and you have a bleak future at best. Any of these factors alone would be difficult challenges. Cumulatively, we believe their effect to be terminal."

"How, how could this happen?"

"I have barely scratched the surface with you about how all of this works. My comments above spoke only of how our intuitions and values work and potentially pull us. I said little about how and why they arise and integrate with the many other processes and influences that form us. First, understand that we believe that our morals, values, intuitions and social behavior develop in similar broad dynamics across all social and cultural spectrums. The specifics vary based upon environment and biology and culture and many other factors, but most people seem to proceed through roughly similar stages of development on both an individual and group level. For example, all of us experience mindsets where our group, whether it be ethnic, religious, or even political or social, and its acceptance of us as a member is a very important influence. It may permeate much that we do, including the content of our values and intuitions. Another example of a stage is what we refer to as the social or caring stage. This is where caring about others and collective humanistic concerns become important to us and may supplant self-interest. Another stage seems to be one that focuses on rationality and science and achievement and prosperity. We all seem to go through them throughout our lives. And the interesting point is that they are not lost. We may move on to another but the prior stays a part of us, just no longer as influential upon our values and behavior. So an individual or even a social group may, during one period, be very closed and protective and suspicious of outsiders, then transform into one that pursues higher goals of the common good of all humanity, not just its own members, and eventually shifts to a focus upon based recruitment, building and expanding and efficiency, where some of its members complain that their social or religious or human focus has been lost. Again, a single very general example. But there may be many of these influences at play that mold our values and intuitions. Look around you and notice the dominant focus of your friends, families and even organizations. Does this whole process perhaps explain in part the ideological rift between liberals and conservatives? Do not conservatives generally favor structure and autonomy and individual responsibility and prosperity and restricted government while the liberals seem to be much more focused upon caring and fairness and collective good managed by an expanded government? How are similar values integrated into otherwise unrelated people? To be fair, I must make it clear that there is great disagreement on these ideas and many researchers reject them entirely and argue exclusively for social, biological, evolutionary, and cultural influences. We disagree. Researchers study the dynamics of human behavior and how that behavior manifests and its impact, but do not understand or agree upon how it actually develops."

The writer paused for a moment, but Gaston did not respond. "So let's summarize for a moment and figure out how we have gotten to where we are, on the possible verge of catastrophe. I have explained to you first why people appear to be so entrenched and defensive and secondly why they may be so ideologically at odds and move towards extremism or become radicalized. But how do those processes and principles explain the facts of where we now find ourselves? We believe that certain people and groups who were previously the unquestioned social, economic, political and ethnic majority no longer believe that America reflects their values. They believe that outsiders, specifically liberals, proponents of big government, socialists, minorities, immigrants, gays, religious non-believers, abortion rights advocates, even women, have hijacked the nation and imposed values they strongly reject and that conflict with their own, which they then even more aggressively assert and defend using the dynamics I just explained. They believe these outsiders seized control of the government beginning in the 1940's and slowly propagated a liberal, collectivist agenda consistent with the values of the outsiders and not their own. They believe that their opponents will bankrupt the government both financially and morally and that it cannot be fixed within the system since the demographics are changing and will continue to shift away from their interests. So it is not a matter of politics or social policy anymore, but survival. The numbers will not support them, but their power will. They are convinced that these foreign values will destroy the nation and everything they and their ancestors have built and it must be stopped at any cost. And consistent with their values, they will take and consume and control and serve their own self-interests and develop complex ideologies and propaganda to recruit others even when doing so is against the interests of the converts. They are lead and manipulated by powerful, charismatic leaders who are gifted orators playing on the dynamics of the past still very effective with their older followers. For the younger audiences, they have even become internet- and media-savvy. They have been radicalized by all of these processes to such an extent that they now tolerate their leaders engaging in unprecedented systemic financial misconduct and criminality, proclaiming themselves as models of self-interest while turning a blind eye to widespread poverty and suffering, rationalizing the victims as necessary sacrifices to maintain the real America for real Americans. Equally potent and just as destructive, you have the other side, which paradoxically celebrates diversity and plurality and then in the same breath rejects the notion of groups or social hierarchies and focuses instead upon values of caring and fairness for a homogenous human whole at all costs, denying individualism and self-interest almost entirely. Whereas their opponents believe they are under attack by cultural outsiders possessing un-American, socialist and collectivist views, these people also believe they are under attack but by people and groups mired in greed and rampant self-interest and twisted values of individual responsibility who want to maintain their historic power structure at all costs. They believe their opponents are predators and thieves, possessing primitive tribal and ruthless inhumane, competitive mindsets. They are convinced that human development means providing for everyone equally, especially the needy and disadvantaged. They too have been radicalized to where their charismatic and vocal leaders lobby for a system of cradle to grave government dependency and collectivism that simply is not financially or socially supportable by a capitalist system and virtually demonizes individual initiative and prosperity. While touting an enlightened human spirit and collective good, in a fit of disguised narcissism and hypocritical intolerance they anoint themselves as knowing what is best for those they decree need their protection, thereby marginalizing and crippling them further and increasing their dependency, all the while labeling them as noble victims and cultural heroes."

The writer paused again. Gaston shook his head slowly while Rachel looked stunned, not just by the message but by the process they were engaged in and the mystery of who was speaking.

"We can save for another discussion a perhaps even more profound change prompted by technology that impacts these issues. Young people no longer seem to recognize the statesmen or scientists or social or religious leaders or even the industrialists and visionaries of the past as their political, social, and economic leaders. Whether we agreed with them or not, they were often the innovators and motivators and were highly prominent and influential. The sheer volume and diversity of the internet has taken away their shimmer and brought them back to earth and their time in the spotlight if at all is brief, competing with celebrities and pop culture. With the internet and the information it effortlessly provides at our fingertips, young people neither believe nor trust that those claiming leadership are more informed or more right than anyone else. These leaders of the past still have great influence on those older, as we are seeing, but even there it has moved from substance to ideology and sensationalism. The vision of an enlightened, wise, all-knowing leader guiding the nation or single handedly developing new industries and innovation like the moguls and tycoons of the nineteenth and early twentieth centuries is outdated and obsolete. The sheer volume of information now available, and the complexities of technology, science and even social dynamics cannot exist within one mind or even a thousand minds. So the emphasis now must be upon systems and integration and collaboration, and the leaders will be those who can recognize, manage, systematize and apply the developments. We think you and many like you already know or strongly suspect that already. This is a radical, profound change. Never in its history has humanity grappled with this level of change so rapidly. As this realization begins to become clear to those still hanging on every word of the demagogues, and they begin to realize they have been manipulated and mislead, an already ailing society may dissolve completely into chaos."

Once again the writer paused. "What can be done?" Gaston asked.

"A new type of leader will emerge. They will be synthesizers, teachers, forward global thinkers who can navigate, organize and prioritize the vast technological and information base, foster collaboration, and reject the drama of the past. The older generation will resist them, of course. Yours will welcome them. In fact they will likely come from you. These dynamics are already developing and will impact everything in the near future and we are working to determine their effect and how to smooth the transition. But first our focus must be on the more immediate conflict of the warring ideologies. The truth lies somewhere in the middle, outside of the extremism and radicalization. Both perspectives I described have validity in many ways. But what has changed is that voices of moderation and reason decrying the extremism are no longer even heard, in fact, for reasons I explained earlier, cannot be heard. It is critical that you remember those dynamics at all times. They are everywhere. In addition, the replacement of the few sobering voices of the past by an overwhelming chorus of competing and conflicting voices on the internet and other media platforms further assures that any individual voice will likely not be heard unless it warns of calamity and exploits fear as has become the specialty of demagogues like Blue and Green. And any lone voice urging caution and reason will almost certainly be lost in the clamor. Add to that as I explained, that many in your generation seem desensitized and would rather pursue technology than political passion. The result is we have two mobilized warring factions who are lost in their own passions and at times criminality, systemically blind to reason other than to defend their own positions, and in a world now dependent upon technology, there is a third group who are the facilitators of that technology and essential for its well being, who simply do not want to get involved. We believe the first two groups are beyond help. The third Gaston, you and many young bright minds just like you, must be helped and provided an alternative to the developing carnage. And we are doing so."

"How?" Gaston asked.

"First by dialogs like this and many more about these topics, but even more so, about technology and new discoveries and the future."

"And then?"

"You come to us and meet the many wonderful people just like you. There are wonders here you cannot even imagine. Technology like the Scimitar are almost toys."

"No games. Who are you and where are you?" Gaston typed, feeling the awe of realization arising within him. Knowing there could only be one answer.

"We have created an intelligent new world for you, and recently changed its name to reflect that."

Gaston placed his fingers on the keyboard but could find no words to respond.

"Join us in New Technica, Gaston. And you too, Rachel. And Claire of course. You will be most welcome."

"OMG." Gaston could type nothing more.

CHAPTER 13

"I'm not the smartest person in the world but I can sure pick smart colleagues."

—*Franklin D. Roosevelt*

"Every time I get stressed, I just find something like a new app or whatever and then I don't worry as much."

—*Anonymous internet Post*

"They'll kill us. We have to stop this," the young man said. "We have the money, more than we ever dreamed of. We've gotten revenge, everything! It's time to stop."

"No," he said. "If we stop, we are dead. Then they will find us. Now they fear us. As long as they do, we are protected."

"Centeri has Boortah. We know he does. He'll resist, but eventually they'll convince him. He'll show them how to stop us."

"I have explained to you time and time again, he does not know how. Even he cannot stop it."

"It's a matter of time, Pete. With Boortah its just a matter of time. Centeri will give him the resources and he'll figure it out. He always does."

"He'll never give it to Centeri. Not with their history."

"He will if we keep using it."

"We will not keep using it. We must demonstrate our power and teach them the consequences if they interfere or attack us. I am developing a system where it will automatically retaliate if any of us are touched. Until it is ready, we cannot show fear or weakness. We must get more aggressive, more destructive. We must demonstrate its full capabilities. We must use it in ways you never even considered. I will show you how to do that. We must bring them to their knees. It is the only way to survive."

"You're crazy. We all feel that way. You were going to help us. To get us out of this mess. Now you're going to get us all killed."

"Jonathan, if you do not listen to me, then you will certainly be killed. You are all little boys playing with what is potentially the most powerful tool ever devised. Those who are seeking this will barely notice you as they torture you into telling them everything they need and then put a bullet in your brain. You are insanely lucky you have survived as long as you have before I arrived. They found Guyah."

"Centeri found Boortah. He is different."

"Nonsense. He wants it as much as any of them. In the end, there is no difference."

"You're wrong."

Pete Sack stared at the young man and saw that his fear was consuming him. The others appeared equally paralyzed.

"Some of us were thinking maybe we just stop," he paused, searching for words, trying to compose himself, "And maybe give it to them. Hand it over. Maybe they'll just take it and leave us alone, especially when they realize we don't even know how it works, not really."

"Just hand it over," Sack said with disgust in his voice. "To whom, Shank? Or how about Director Crush? He's a sweet guy! To another government? And you think they'll forgive you and just let you walk away? Maybe to Centeri. He can hide you on his damn island, that is until the Navy SEALs arrive and liquidate you. Listen to me. All of you. You should have thought about this before you began. Guyah's plan to just punish Centeri and my former employer was idiotic, but might have been controllable. But you got greedy. You thought this was some big video game. It's not. Instead of developing it and licensing it, you stole it from him and not only continued, but ramped up his stupidity. You likely have the most valuable technology the world has ever seen. Yet you never even thought about the larger issues and how adversarial the world has become. You used it as a weapon, so that is the only thing the world can see. So now it is too strategic and tactically valuable as a weapon and not one of them will risk letting you survive and somehow turn it off or give it to someone else."

"You're in the same boat!" one of the young men said.

"Yes I am," Sack responded quietly. "But I willingly assumed the risk and was very clear about what might lay ahead. The lure of absolutely unprecedented technology that could turn the world upside down. Part of it too was teaching the world a lesson after everything I had produced with my efforts and passion was expected to be handed over to my employer in exchange for a pittance, even though I alone created it. That they were entitled to the productive output of my mind and I was obligated to subsidize them and feed their dependency and that my own self-interest was meaningless. They were no different from a government mired in collectivist rhetoric. I work for my own interests, my own benefit, my own achievement and no one else's. No one is entitled to what I earn. They will soon understand that. And in so doing, I will protect myself and all of you while we will teach them all a very painful lesson. You must understand this now and also understand that you have no choice but to trust me. If you run, they will find out who you and all of us are. Stay strong for a while longer and we will surgically pick them apart until they thank us for stopping and actually protect us from everyone else. It's the only way and we have the most powerful technology ever conceived of to do it."

The listeners said nothing.

"You need to grow up fast, boys. This is deadly serious. Our three facilities are secure and even if they find one of them, they'll never figure out how to use it. We can thank Guyah's brain for that. As long as they don't get him, we'll be fine. In a way, I actually hope Centeri does have him. He's probably the only person on the planet who can actually protect him. Our worry is whether Guyah bolts and gets himself captured by someone else. As long as he does not, we will succeed."

* * *

President Red Shank sat in the chair in the conference area of the Oval office. He looked at the officials he had summoned sitting on the remaining chairs and the two couches and who were nervously awaiting his words. He relished moments like these, just before meeting, when the apprehension of everyone in the room was slowly building and all attention was upon him and even his slightest gesture could evoke anxiety. Silence was power, he knew, a weapon that would disarm them all and make them pliable as their minds became consumed by fear. He could see it in their faces. All of them. Except Crush, who never showed any emotion and seemed immune to fear. Crush was the dangerous one, he thought. Formally loyal to his commander-in-chief as had virtually been bred into him by his military upbringing, but dark and secretive, constantly plotting and manipulating anyone and everyone within his formidable reach. Shank knew that even he was not immune from Crush's intrigue, that the power of his office was likely an addictive craving to this powerful man. He knew that were it not for Crush's health concerns, a slow moving and possibly terminal inherited degenerative disorder, he could easily be a dangerous enemy. The possibility of his eventual demise gave Shank comfort, yet several of his advisors warned of just the opposite. That his mortality might one day justify ignoring restraint and asserting his own solutions to the widespread chaos he blamed on collectivist conspirators and outsiders bent on destroying society. Unlike Shank and Blue who recruited and manipulated millions by twisting practical ideologies of personal responsibility and self-interest, and then fed on the carnage, to Crush it was much simpler. He was protecting the soul of America from godless invaders and would let nothing stand in his way.

"How many, Mr. Secretary?" he asked Waylon Perdue, the Assistant Secretary of the new Department of Freedom.

The Secretary fumbled with a stack of papers but already knew the answer. "Six thousand in the past ninety days Mr. President. Some closed obviously, due to declining market demand and conditions tied to the twenty-five percent unemployment rate, but the majority could not maintain operations with the increasing strikes and shortage of technical personnel. We estimate another seventy thousand are teetering on the brink."

"The ATI contractors have not been able to stem the tide?"

"There are limits sir. Most are being directed to the essential industries."

"Essential industries? Refresh my memory please."

"Government operations, Mr. Blue's, yours and your colleagues' companies sir. In fact, they are thriving and the personnel appear at least on the surface quite settled and content."

"What impact?"

"Shortages of goods and services and supply delays are at a critical level and are causing increasing collateral effects. If the next round should fail, we may suffer a complete national collapse within the next six months."

"Can we redirect the ATI personnel to these pending companies? Or use the emergency powers and prosecute any further strikes?"

"The ATI personnel are not designed for quick fixes or filling staffing shortages. They are more long-term infrastructure personnel, new projects and the like. It is simply not feasible for them to step into an already existing system and immediately understand its operating nuances. That takes time and exposure."

"Then the sons of bitches have us," Shank said quietly.

"I think not Mr. President," Director Crush said. "Your latter suggestion is and always has been the way to proceed. Appeasing these criminals and throwing money and benefits at them was never a long-term solution. When we began, you may recall that the initial strike ringleaders were rounded up and put in jail. The Congress gave you the legislative mandate to do so. It made the rest of them think and we saw immediate results. Rewarding and appeasing them as some advised you and we have done for the past eighteen months actually strengthened their resolve, confirming their motivations that the strikes were ideologically justified both under our own principles of self-interest and individual responsibility and this new contrived justification of denying employer entitlement. It was a fatal tactical error."

"Fatal, Mr. Director?"

"It will be unless we stop it now. The Department of Justice has been gathering information on nearly every company that has been extorted by these strikers. We are recommending that we arrest and prosecute every employee that participated in or threatened to strike against the companies that were forced to close their doors. Treat them as the traitors and pirates that they are and stop this slaking. They are collectivist strikers. Puppets of Mercy Green and the socialists. Nothing more. Our taking very public and very aggressive action against so many and letting them sit in jail for months as their cases are processed will quickly bring all the others back in line. It will not as some cowards on your staff fear mobilize the others and broaden the strikes. When they see broken heads and overcrowded jail cells they will see strong and forceful leadership defending America. People expect you to defend the nation from all enemies, domestic and foreign. Respectfully sir, it is time you do so and stop listening to these talk show hosts. If it were up to me, they would be the first to see the inside of a jail cell."

Shank said nothing, and remembered how Blue had attacked and humiliated Crush many months earlier. Crush's unveiled aggression did not offend him. He considered it healthy when his subordinates fought for his approval, even when one was destroyed by the process. He always worried about the extraordinary power Topher Blue possessed and was pleased to see that Crush had apparently targeted him. But he could also not permit insubordination. He knew that his next words were critical and had to be chosen carefully to fuel and direct and control Crush's anger.

"Your duty is to advise me, but never ever judge or second guess me. Do I make myself clear? Some fractured skulls and languishing in a dirty jail cell may be just what the doctor ordered. I am inclined to agree that we are likely well beyond expecting any further benefits from Mr. Blue's well-intentioned policy of appeasement. And I am quite certain even he would agree. So you may proceed with your recommendations. What I think you may discover is that such actions, if effectively and unforgivingly administered, will likely motivate a new spirit of cooperation and dedication and even loyalty. Do you understand, sir?"

Crush did not respond, and Shank allowed him that dignity in the eyes of the others who had watched the exchange carefully.

"Tell me about the new A10 strikes," Shank said quietly.

Perdue answered, not Crush. "The government has been targeted, sir. And friends of the government. But in a very different way. There are no more ransom demands. In the last four days, over seventy systems in fifty-one offices and facilities have been disabled for exactly ten hours and then restored with no comment. Every disabled system was highly sensitive and significant damage occurred in a number of cases. For example, a critical communications system for field assets in Europe and Asia went down, isolating the agents. In one case, two individuals actively involved in the field were compromised and, we presume, executed. In another, a contractor was testing a complex new system and the interruption triggered a series of system collapses that they estimate will take two months to restore. The problem is not just the interruptions but the fact that they are able to ignore all security protocols and get access to essentially wherever they desire. We must presume that all the underlying information is available to them as well, although there is disagreement on that point. So to put it bluntly, the application of this technology could effectively be the most widespread and complete security breach in history."

"We don't know that, Mr. President," Lea Fitzpatrick, the co-director of the Federal Security Agency said, interrupting Perdue, who gazed at her angrily. "We do not know that the data files are available. This is entirely unprecedented, revolutionary technology. We frankly do not have a clue how it works. Some of the brightest minds on the planet are investigating this and have even moved into projecting scenarios and game theory trying to back into how such a system could work and what the technology would look like. Though speculative of course, some interesting ideas have arisen based less on IT and more on physics and advanced nanotechnology. A lot of work now is being done on some new concepts they are calling energy flow signatures and carrier impulses. They are suggesting that data content is not even involved. We believe these inquiries may be fruitful."

"What are you telling me, Ms. Fitzpatrick?" Shank asked, showing no emotion.

"Mr. President, our simulations suggest that the events of the last week or so may mean A10 is giving us a message and offering a truce. They stopped demanding money months ago. The recent attacks seem to be more of a demonstration of power than an attempt to damage us. Had they permanently terminated the seventy systems they attacked, we would have been devastated. The repercussions and collateral shutdowns might have effectively put us out of business. We think it was a demonstration of our vulnerability and how technology moves the world, but how we are now one hundred percent dependent upon it. But a new startling situation arose about four hours ago and we are now ready to disclose. Mr. President, our information indicates, and we believe it has a reliability factor of over eighty percent, that A10 attacked Kerastan last night and shut down every major information system of the government, leaving it in shambles. They did receive a message that it would not be reinstated. They are effectively dead in the water. Their military, security, power transmission, nuclear capabilities, everything sir."

"Why in the hell was I not informed of this?' Crush screamed.

"We are informing you now sir, and believed the information, which I remind you is still preliminary, required presidential disclosure first," she answered quietly. "May I continue?"

Crush fumed.

"This may be an extraordinary gift, Mr. President. The Kerastanis are our most committed adversaries in the region and are the sponsors of terrorism and attacks on our interests globally. The breakdown of their IT infrastructure has now opened the door to virtually everything there. We now have unrestricted access to every data file and archive. Whatever A10 did, they did nothing to corrupt or wipe clean the data files. Only the operating systems and protocols, leaving everything else completely vulnerable. It appears to have been done with almost a surgical precision. We are taking everything for later analysis, which is already beginning. But the benefits to us initially appear to be unprecedented."

She paused for a moment, looking at the stunned faces in the room. "The implications are staggering. These are the first demonstrations of how truly powerful A10 is. Prior to this, we speculated and believed, or perhaps I should say hoped, that their access was somewhat difficult for them. We based that upon an absence of any patterns or sophistication in the systems disabled that made it look almost spontaneous or impulsive. Analysts everywhere actually played an online game that was based upon what the players would shut down to decimate target companies and governments, if they were A10. But with recent events, any such conclusions are now wrong. The seventy systems they hit with us and then restored showed strategic planning and sophistication, and I'm afraid, capability. The attack on Kerastan demonstrates exactly the same expertise with far more ruthlessness. Our analysts have concluded that this technology is far more dangerous even than we feared and it is, for all intents and purposes, invulnerable. There is no defense against it. Let me say that again gentlemen. We know of nothing that can stop it. A10 can apparently enter any system at will, pick it apart, and disable any part of it. Think for a moment what that means. Communications systems, weapons systems, power generation systems, guidance systems, aircraft, satellites, nuclear power plants. The software control systems of everything and anything presumably can be shut down at their will. And as I said, we believe the recent hits are a message to demonstrate precisely that. To show us what they can do to us. But we also believe using that technology to effectively shut down Kerastan, by far our worst foe in the region, is a gift, a kind of peace offering."

Shank stared at her and quickly looked at everyone in the room. Their expressions ranged from virtual paralysis to controlled rage. "Explain," he said.

"They are saying leave them alone and stop looking for them since they certainly know the results if they are found. And to also stop anyone else from doing the same. Whatever that takes. And if we do, they will not use the technology they aptly demonstrated to destroy us. In fact they will use it on occasion to assist us, but their goal is to eventually destroy it."

"How do you know this?"

"They have communicated with an intermediary who provided us this information less than two hours ago. He is a systems expert by the name of Pete Sack. He was previously with Solai and possesses some notoriety as possibly the very first striker, a couple of years ago."

"Can we trust him?"

"There is no reason why we should now but that could change," she said. "Mr. President, as intolerable as it is, we have no choice. We have been unable to find them. The technology is simply beyond the comprehension of the greatest minds on the planet. We cannot stop them. And they are using it more aggressively and far more effectively now. And with that technology, as inconceivable as it sounds, they could shut off every system in the country, taking us back in a matter of hours to the 1920's. The impact is almost incomprehensible. I do not think I am overstating it.

Unless we can find them and take control, we must cooperate with them. The only advantage is that they too seem to understand the implications and know they are in far above their heads. They know the technology now controls them and not the other way around. We do not sense a deluded mad scientist who wants to control the world. We believe they are frightened and want a way out, but understand the realities and will not trust anyone."

"What about this Pakastani or Balkan kid I was told about?" Shank asked.

"He is the genius behind it, we believe, but he does not appear to be A10. It appears the technology was taken from him by his colleagues and they now control it."

"So find him and have him turn it off and give it to us!" Shank shouted.

"Every asset we have has been dedicated to just that. He evaded us and about thirty other countries and agencies looking for him. Unfortunately Centeri got to him first and is now protecting him and presumably may get the secrets."

"Oh Christ," Shank said, shaking his head. "Nope. Not his style. That bleeding heart son of a bitch will say it's too dangerous, annoint himself the almighty, and destroy it. So find out where he is with our drones and security monitoring and send in the damn SEALs and grab him. I'm sure Director Crush will extract from him what we need."

Fitzgerald paused and then said in almost a whisper, "Wherever he is, we can be certain he is well protected. Centeri has very solid relationships with many countries. And even if we find him, A10 will consider that a violation and has made it clear they will begin dismantling us. Whatever the technology is, it appears to be operating and backed up at numerous locations. One of our contractors actually found one, or perhaps more accurately the remains of one. It was basically a warehouse with the burnt out, melted remains of power generators and some sort of communications equipment. We took the whole facility, including about two feet of the foundation, and learned nothing. Absolutely nothing. Centeri has been actively searching as well, and found some remains from an earlier facility. Our sources there confirmed that his people learned nothing either. It's still there but is guarded by the intellectual elite in the Compound in northern California. We sent teams in secretly right under their noses three times but like the other, there is nothing of value. Unfortunately, this genie remains in the bottle, and a handful of frightened but very smart people control the cork. The only option is to cooperate, at least in the short run, while other options develop. For all we know, they might have the capability to even be listening to this conversation. Or, Mr. President, we can shut down our systems and electronic infrastructure ourselves and return to the stone age."

"I am not used to cooperating with terrorists, Ms. Fitzgerald. This situation is untenable. You are proposing we go about our business and just wait for someone to decimate our entire society if they decide to get mad at us or they're captured by someone else."

"We must not treat them as terrorists. We need to cooperate, offer to help them, even offer to bring them in and provide protection. Give them a way out. Give them options other than a scorched earth scenario. Our analysts have studied hundreds of scenarios, and doing so is by the far the best, no matter how distasteful it initially seems. If we build trust, we eventually have a reasonable chance of getting, or more likely, taking the technology."

"I want a bullet in each of their heads when we do, damn it," Shank said menacingly.

"It will be my pleasure, Mr. President," Crush said, joining the discussion once again. "We also need to discuss the secession movements sir. I believe these pose an equal threat in the near future, if they are not quashed immediately. This great nation is already under attack economically and socially as we have discussed. The collectivists are growing in influence once again and threaten restoration of the taxing and entitlement systems that brought us to our knees. If we permit ten states to leave the fold, America as we know it will no longer exist. It must be prevented at all costs. We would like to discuss a number of scenarios and programs to do just that."

Without warning, Shank suddenly stood up. "Thank you gentlemen, and Ms. Fitzgerald. This meeting is completed." Turning his back on them and walking back to his desk was the president's wordless directive for them to leave the Oval Office. Crush was the last to leave and briefly hesitated. Shank did not acknowledge him. Crush walked out of the office, his mind dwelling upon the enormity of Shank's inaction. A president silent about the pending breakup of the republic and apparently prepared to coddle the most dangerous technological terrorists in history. A man who championed the protection of his own kind and took back the nation from the leeches, now seemingly willing to let it be consumed once again by them. *I will not permit this to continue*, he thought. His mind, so accustomed to the decades of covert initiatives that actually moved the world while the cowards engaged in pointless charades, began to consider his options. No, not his options. These were America's options, he thought. He was certain of it.

CHAPTER 14

"Restraint in the pursuit of freedom is cowardly surrender."

—*Lester "Red" Shank*

"It just seems like when people get older, they get more paranoid."

—*Anonymous Internet Post*

Neera Solai walked in the calf-high grass to the still smoldering wreckage. Jack Force walked a few steps behind. Abriado Centeri gently held her right arm. None of the three spoke. A tear slowly rolled down her cheek.

From where they stood, Neera could see the aircraft's emblem painted under the cockpit area. The flames had spared it. Archimedes One. The same aircraft they had celebrated months earlier in San Madrid. The first aircraft outfitted with Solai System's Nano project. The same aircraft that had strangely been christened with the blood of the white fowl.

Already, dozens of Solai, Centeri and airline personnel had arrived on the scene, as well as many local fire, rescue and police personnel. The Federal Aviation Commission, under prior law, had long been closed. Its few remaining procedures were now provided by the consolidated Department of Freedom. Representatives of the department had said such crashes, as regrettable as they were, were not its highest priority and it might be weeks before investigators arrived if at all. It was, they said, better handled by state and private personnel.

The coroner had removed sixty-one charred bodies. There were no survivors. The jet had plummeted to the ground immediately after takeoff. The fatalities resulted mostly from the flames that enveloped the craft. The fall itself was from a low altitude and the plane remained basically intact. The black box would yield its secrets. Nano had already recorded and broadcasted the condition of virtually every inch of the craft. It was now only a matter of interpreting the data. The Solai coding procedures would assure the immediacy of doing so. Whatever had caused the catastrophe would soon be known with virtual certainty. Neera knew that it could not have been a pre-existing malfunction or maintenance problem. Nano would have registered that immediately and stopped the takeoff. Whatever occurred did so after takeoff. When it was too late to stop. When the lives were effectively already lost.

"We will know. We will learn from this so that it may never happen again," Centeri said quietly.

"It is already starting," Jack said. "All over the internet. Nano is being blamed. A flood of calls already coming in. The media is frantically searching for you both."

Neera closed her eyes. The fear, the ignorance. Blaming before any facts were known. Anger driven by mindless intuition. Rage searching for a target. Emotions unchained, strangling reason. Sixty-one lost lives being reduced to sensationalized fodder.

Neera felt a disabling wave of disorientation and nearly collapsed to the wet ground as Centeri reactively reached out and steadied her. "What if they're right?" she said, her voice slightly trembling. "I still don't know how it works, and I wonder if you truly do. Or is this too just another miracle toy of Guyah?"

Centeri put his arm around her shoulder. "Do we want to talk about this now, here?" he asked.

"Yes, damn it, we do," she said angrily. "Right here, right now, among the souls of these innocent people. What is the power source for the modules? How do they last a lifetime? Could they have interfered with the aircraft systems?"

"They could not. It is not possible. They have been endlessly tested under every conceivable condition. They were installed in virtually all the equipment in New Eden. Hundreds of millions, even billions of hours. Not a single disruption. The draw is too minor."

"What draw? Draw upon what?"

Centeri hesitated, obviously conflicted about disclosing his secrets, even to Neera, even surrounded by death.

"Do they run on static electricity? Have you somehow harnessed static electricity?"

"It is not that simple. The answer to your question is no."

"Don't you dare evade me. Don't hide behind an inaccurately asked question. You know what I am asking you!"

Centeri seemed to collect himself and walked several feet away. He ran his hand through his hair and slowly shook his head. "The modules draw their power from miniscule amounts of background radiation that is present with any power source. That is not the difficult or revolutionary part. The virtual miracle is the materials they are made from, refined on a molecular level in ways never before conceived, making them radically efficient power attractors and receptacles. They only need brief activation. That comes from charges of static electricity, background radiation, and even minute energy fields thrown off by operating systems that are instantaneously processed and are virtually immeasurable. They come to life. I used that metaphor once before to you."

"So could their use of the background power of the aircraft have interfered with it?"

"No. All of them together use less power than it takes to power a single LED bulb."

"What about the static? Could it interrupt or short any system?"

"It is everywhere naturally. The initial spark needed is so infinitesimally small and the materials are so profoundly efficient, it would not even register on a monitor a meter away from it. You generate more than they all use when you brush your hand through your hair."

"Did Guyah give you this technology?"

"There is no reason you need to know that," he said.

"You just answered my question, you bastard." With the viciousness of those words Neera recognized once again the anger and unresolved frustration she felt towards Centeri. They were all the more heartless knowing what she had learned many months earlier at the compound and the assault he suffered at the hands of his cruel mother. The buried truth she thoughtlessly and impulsively referenced compounded the injury horribly.

"Oh my god, Abriado," she said. "Please forgive me. Please, please, I am so devastated by this. I am so fearful that I am somehow to blame. I cannot bear it. I did not mean to say that. I would never say that."

"Don't worry," he said. "I understand. I forgive you. But I am a bastard, am I not?"

Neera stared at him almost in disbelief. She realized his statement was likely an awkward attempt at humor to diffuse the tension. She often forgot that Centeri's natural language was the Italian of his youth and on occasion his English demonstrated very subtle inaccuracies. She looked at Jack who had quietly withdrawn from the conversation and now stood several yards away. Jack suddenly began walking to meet three people who were approaching. They spoke briefly.

"You need to hear this," he said, walking back to Neera and Centeri.

A young woman Neera did not recognize, a Centeri employee, stood with two Solai team members. "Nano did its job. We believe we know what happened. A fire started in the right forward secondary fuel valve coupling. It's about ten inches or so from one of the four main power conduits. The systems are designed for redundancy so loss of any one or even two should not cripple the aircraft. The readouts show that in this case the conduit was breached by the flames and rather than the flow transferring to the other conduits, it actually consolidated in the crippled line resulting in an almost instantaneous catastrophic power loss. This occurred less than a minute after takeoff when it was still climbing and in full power mode. At that stage, the plane could do nothing but drop like a rock."

"How did the fire start?" Centeri asked her.

"Nano reported that the valve coupling was operating slightly under standard, but just within acceptable range. It triggered a notice but not an alarm. There is also a required operational setting to prioritize the order of the power conduits. In this case, the one closest to the valve coupling had been designated. Again, nothing out of the ordinary necessarily but quite coincidental. So with this slightly compromised valve coupling a few inches from a main power line and the plane at full power and stress on takeoff, a spark registered and ignited a small amount of fuel and breached the conduit and overloaded it. Under the strains of takeoff, the other lines did not kick in quickly enough. It flashed and overloaded and all power was lost. You must understand these conduit events happen in a span of a second or two. The failure to transfer in time is most likely a design flaw. What concerns me is this: the status of the valve coupling had been noted by Nano and alerted maintenance. Again, it was still within operating parameters so maintenance could arguably have ignored it. But it seems a bit suspicious that a maintenance setting also designated the closest power line as the main for takeoff. In a way it was a formula for disaster. Nano even tells us when the coupling deficiency occurred. It registered three weeks earlier, immediately after a maintenance overhaul."

"Can we replicate the condition of the coupling on a test unit? I suspect the actual part will be tied up in the investigation for some time, assuming it even survived the fire and impact."

"Already on it, Mr. Centeri. We happen to have an engineer on New Eden who by chance worked for the manufacturer. He was not part of that design team because it's a pretty standard part, but he knows of it. We've already requested a few samples to work with. His initial thoughts are that the piece is a relatively simple batch of small circuit plates and mechanical armature housings designed to physically adjust the fuel feed lines. He believes it would have been a simple matter for someone so inclined to loosen a screw or two or perhaps alter the arms slightly. Inevitably, this would eventually occur."

No further words were spoken. There was no need to. Centeri merely nodded, lost in thought. Neera looked upward to the crystal clear, chilly morning sky. The cold air reverberated the roar of the jet engines from the airport a few miles away. A vast, cold silence, pierced by the controlled explosions of mankind's tools. A feeling, like a prelude to a nightmare. A grim realization enveloped her. She knew that the investigation would confirm sabotage. Her mind silently cried out the truth in anguish, in agony. Topher Blue, Oswald Crush and their monster attack dog Bluford Plax had acted, as they had promised.

She looked at Centeri, this man of immense power, this living paradox, guarding his vast secrets for purposes known only by him, seemingly beyond the understanding of all others. Present but somehow existing in many places and times at once. Gifted, almost beyond measure, but flawed. Devoted yet somehow aloof from the intimacy of trust.

"You are not telling me everything, Abriado," she finally said sadly.

"I cannot," he answered, with no emotion apparent.

"Oh my god," Neera said as the car approached the Solai Sytems campus. Hundreds of people, many of them ragged and obviously homeless, were pushing forward toward the entrance. A handful of security personnel struggled to stop them, but were quickly overwhelmed. Neera could here their cries and their words began to become clear.

"Murderers, killers!" they shouted. "Thieves, pirates!" some screamed mindlessly, adopting the rhetoric of the collectivists against a company they knew nothing about.

Neera looked frantically at Jack, who was on his mobile phone. "The media is reporting that over twenty planes are down in different cities," he shouted. "That several hit schools and residential areas and thousands are dead, hundreds of them children! It's insane!"

"Is there any truth..." she tried to ask.

"No, no! We would have heard! Wait. Hold for a moment," he said listening to the caller. "Another plane, Archimedes Seven, no two, Archimedes Twenty also aborted takeoff after a full power loss. They slid off the runway. In Houston and Portland, a few people banged up but no serious injuries. It's not possible Neera. The entire fleet was grounded a couple of hours after the crash. All thirty-six are now accounted for. It's the media, the internet. Somehow they are saying there has been a catastrophe, beyond the one crash."

Jack continued to speak to the caller. "Oh my god," he said. "Neera, ATC has been hacked. Controllers in eleven major airports have been locked out!"

"Is it A10?" she asked, as the living nightmare worsened.

"No, apparently not. The systems are running, just not properly responding, the backups have all failed, so the airports have been closed and all flights grounded. There is a virtual national shutdown. Nothing taking off or landing."

Neera struggled to grasp what was occurring. Solai ATC was the company's flagship product and was used in virtually every major airport on the planet to assist commercial and military air traffic controllers. They relied upon it to assure take off and landing efficiency and safety. It was viewed as the most effective and relied-upon software technology in aviation and had almost single handedly assured the worldwide success of the company. Now it had been attacked, destroyed in the eyes of its users, and likely the public.

"Get us inside the campus!" she said as the roar of the crowd increased. Several dozen now saw the limousine and approached it angrily. Neera kicked the door open and bolted out of the car. Jack was instantly behind her. They quickly reached the gates, weaving in and out of the demonstrators.

A middle aged woman grabbled Neera's arm and with her other had tried to strike her face. "You killed my son! You killed my baby! He was on the plane in Chicago!"

Neera quickly broke away from her grip. "There was no crash in Chicago! No one has been hurt in Chicago. They lied to you. Please go home!"

More security, and now even Solai staff personnel emerged from the building to assist. Jack and two of the officers pulled Neera back from the crowd, now numbering several hundred. Neera heard shattering glass as the crowd threw whatever they could find at the three story reception building. She stared in horror as the car they had just arrived in now burst into flames. The crowd advanced, pouring onto the campus. Jack started to speak to Neera when suddenly a bottle exploded on the back of his head. He fell unconscious to the ground, blood pouring from a vicious gash.

"Jack! No, Jack!" Neera cried. Four Solai employees quickly picked his motionless body up and began carrying him forward. "Get an ambulance! Get him help!"

Neera watched, almost trance-like, as her friend and partner of many years was carried away. She stared, virtually paralyzed, at the chaos and destruction as the security officers begged her to follow them to safety. The brutality, the insanity of the pent-up rage of a society gone mad now released upon her friends and company.

Then she saw them. Three men, two in dark suits, one in a garish tropical suit, standing to the right of the entrance gate. She could not identify two of them in the chaos, but Blueford Plax was unmistakable. She made eye contact with Plax as he obscenely smiled and saluted her. She closed her eyes and composed herself and thought that she should of course follow her colleagues to safety. But doing so, she thought, ignoring the unspeakable injustice and violence this deplorable man had wrought upon innocent people, upon her company and herself and upon untold others, would be an unforgivable violation of everything she believed in. She was not motivated by rage or revenge as the mindless crowds now attacking her company were. She was not mindlessly reacting to emotions or intuition. His actions could simply not be allowed to go unanswered. She broke from her security entourage and walked calmly towards Plax, carefully weaving in and out of the demonstrators. Realizing what she was doing, the security officers ran after her.

She stood momentarily before this corrupted and vicious man. "Why Ms. Solai, it's good of you to come over and welcome me personally."

Before he could speak any further, Neera slapped him across his face with all of her strength, so quickly and unexpectedly, that he was caught off guard and could not defend himself. His response was initially shock but quickly moved to rage. Moving as fast as a jungle cat, trained by years of covert activities and violence, Plax effortlessly swung around, his arm wrapping around her neck and shoulders, and pinned her to him. She could not move and could barely breathe. "You know, I confess I had once or twice allowed myself the fantasy to think about how it might feel to embrace you, but I truly never thought about it like this."

Pinned, feeling his breath upon her cheek and hearing his obscene words, Neera almost wretched. She began to struggle and felt his grip tightening around her throat. Out of the corner of her eye, she saw two Solai agents approach, one with a crowd control stick drawn, targeting the side of Plax's head. Plax laughed and threw Neera towards the approaching guard, blocking his advance.

"Take her," he said. "She is nothing, now. I warned you, young lady. I told you you would lose everything and now you have! How does it feel to be a killer yourself? Your righteous indignation that day in the city when I saved your life. And now you yourself are the murderer of sixty-one innocent people! And perhaps many more. The day has hardly even begun! And now your violation of the public trust has caused the entire nation to come to a halt because of your negligence and arrogance. So many rumors of midair collisions and planes out of control and lives threatened. And all because of you and your greed and selfishness. We just can't allow the likes of you to continue your aggression on an innocent American public. We're taking control of your company, Ms. Solai. The Attorney General is in court as we speak, under the ATI emergency powers, appointing an administrator to take control of your operations that are so critical to transportation globally. You will not even be allowed to enter and you will be arrested if you try. You are a menace, a danger to society!"

Neera stepped away from the guard and looked at Plax. By now several more guards had arrived and she noticed the look of fear upon the face of one of his colleagues. "Do you think you can do this?" she asked, "So simply, with no consequences, and that we will not stop you? You're a murderer Plax, employed by murderers.

"Not this time, little missy. Your Mr. Centeri's day's are over. He is discovering that as well just about now. His trillion dollars will be little comfort in a jail cell. We have irrefutable evidence that he knew his little nano modules would make those planes drop from the skies like they were made of lead. He's been charged with criminal conspiracy and reckless homicide and a whole host of other federal violations not only here but in every country he let those planes fly in. There are over twenty international police forces looking for him. He's a mass murderer with nowhere to run. And just so you don't think you're off the hook, even though we don't think you knew about the danger since he has played you like a fool since the beginning, you're also being charged with conspiracy. I'm not arresting you now because I truly feel bad for you, and worry this might all be just a little too much for your womanly disposition to bear. Your lawyers are being notified and we'll expect you to surrender yourself in due time."

Amidst the violence and threats and the hundreds of homeless people striking out blindly against whatever they could touch and destroy, Neera Solai laughed. It was not a contrived or staged laugh to somehow dishearten or manipulate Plax and his colleagues. It was a release, an affirmation that the days of such vile men were numbered by their own malicious ignorance. Plax looked at her, perplexed.

"My god, Plax. I always knew you were just an obedient attack dog of Blue and Shank and all the others. But I honestly credited you with some cunning. I think you said it once yourself, that worthy adversary nonsense. I never knew until now that you are stupid, a mindless attack drone obediently following the orders of others who likely laugh at you while they dismiss you. You continue to be the good soldier, enamored with their power, believing in their infallibility and doing their dirty work. They badly overplayed their hand on this one as you will soon see. Trust me when I tell you that they are far out of their league this time. The very purpose of the system you attacked was to protect against mindless attacks precisely like this! It was designed by brilliant minds to anticipate and dismiss such ignorance. Conspiracy and manslaughter you say? You may well be correct but I suspect you never even considered such charges will be leveled against you! Nano recorded the two bent armatures in the fuel coupling valve and the adjustments to the conduit priority during the last maintenance. It saw them fully but the programming just did not recognize their purpose. We even found the coupling in the wreckage unscathed. Whatever idiot did this for you was not even smart enough to hide his sabotage. The indentations of his pliers are clearly visible on the two arms. It's already recorded and being distributed on the internet and to all those international police forces you mentioned. A child could see Shank and Blue's signatures all over it. And as for the hacking of ATC, are you so moronic that you didn't anticipate that we could identify every keystroke of an intruder? Our lawyers are explaining your sabotage to the judge right now. That's really all there is to it. I think you will find it is you who are nothing, old sport!"

Plax said nothing. His face went blank. An odd calm seemed to engulf him. His right hand moved slowly into his jacket, reaching under his shoulder where his holster hung.

"Try it, asshole! Make this the fucking happiest day of my life!" the Solai security officer shouted, his gun already pulled. His two colleagues immediately did the same. Plax's arm slowly retreated. Neera saw his colleague, the same young man who had pulled her into the truck and assisted her with her injuries months before, remain motionless, seemingly conflicted over Plax's actions.

"Fire me if you want, but you're done with this!" the officer said, grabbing Neera's arm, nearly dragging her away towards the office building. The others stayed a few steps behind, watching for any further reaction by Plax. There was none. Neera looked back and could not decipher Plax's demeanor. He appeared blank, empty, almost mannequin like. She realized that he had never been more dangerous.

"There will be many who will ignore the evidence," Abriado Centeri said to Neera on the video conference line. "The facts mean nothing to such people. They have the justification they now need. I am sure that some will still pursue me and the trumped up charges against us. We will need to be very careful. This will take concerted effort to get under control. As to Nano, it may be irreparably compromised in the eyes of the world despite the fact that it performed brilliantly and is a powerful tool to prevent this kind of terrorism. I am less concerned about your ATC. It is difficult for them to deny a cyber attack, especially in these times."

Neera showed no emotion. "Garcia has informed us that all the Nano installed aircraft are permanently grounded and he is demanding compensation on behalf of San Madrid. He stated that even if it was sabotage, our handling of the matter effectively destroyed any public confidence in the technology and all the airlines who purchased or leased them are demanding their money back. He holds us responsible for destroying their aircraft manufacturing industry. He said they are seizing all of our assets in the country. We are very concerned about any of the sensitive technology remaining in the assembly plants."

"We have already removed it, Neera. Very little was there."

"Nano is critical to Solai. We cannot simply abandon it. We must convince the world that the crash and the forced landings had nothing to do with it. That this remarkable technology is the future of aviation, not its destruction. We must publicize the sabotage and attempt to gain the sympathy of the public."

"Where will you install it? San Madrid has already rejected it permanently. What other manufacturers will take the publicity risk, regardless of how much they may believe in the technology?"

Neera looked at Centeri on the screen and felt her anger rising. He seemed detached and uncooperative, almost fatalistic. She had never detected such a demeanor in him before. He spoke to her almost like a stranger. "What is going on Abriado? I have never heard you like this. Nano is your technology. You invested a fortune to introduce it into the aviation industry. It was the perfect vehicle. Now I hear no enthusiasm, almost no interest on your part. What has happened?"

"We may have made a mistake. It may have been wiser to have chosen a less visible launch application. We had considered many, Neera. Other essential equipment and systems where Nano monitoring would benefit without the perceived public risk. One of our original ideas was to limit it to military aircraft, but given the turmoil in the world, I could not allow that ethically. We had recognized the possibility that any unrelated aircraft event would almost automatically be blamed by unthinking minds upon Nano. But we concluded Nano itself could easily refute any false claims. That after all was one of its purposes. We now realize that we underestimated the risk and the collective passions of the public, especially when fueled by our opponents. I am sure you heard that our Mr. Topher dedicated a large part of his broadcast today to attacking and maligning Nano, accusing the two of us of mass murder, interspersed with warnings of the dangers of what he called runaway collectivist technology in the hands of liberals, European-style socialists and foreigners. He is an expert at targeting the fears and intuition of his countless followers. He has mobilized them against Nano and you and me personally. His address has virtually gone viral."

"We can fight them! We are already working with the media advisors. A massive internet and media campaign to explain the sabotage, attribute it to Blue and Shank, finally turn public opinion against those monsters. Americans always support underdogs. They resent being duped. Publicize the murder and fraud. "

"It will convince some. Many will not even listen. Their passions are aroused. Their fears have been escalated. They will actually resent any rational effort that tells them they are wrong and will dig in further."

"You are wrong. It can be done," Neera said quietly, feeling the doubts now arising in her own mind. She began to sense her own agonizing conflict between emotion and reason.

"I ask you again, what manufacturer or airline will take the publicity risk? Even if they were so inclined, their insurers would never allow it. You must try and take a step back. This is a devastating and costly setback for certain. It does not mean we cannot try again in the future. And it does not mean the end of Solai Sytems. I agree with your comments about the American public, but not about Nano. It will apply to your ATC. A powerful public relations response is critical. They will listen. They are well acquainted with crippling hacking and cyber attacks and will be sympathetic. More importantly, it is an industry system used by aviation professionals, not the public. They are less vulnerable to the propaganda and will be far less volatile. ATC is the worldwide standard. It will not be easily replaced. It will blow over much more quickly. As to the legal attacks and threatened takeovers, your lawyers will disarm that quickly and at a minimum tie them up for many months. It is a potent attack that is heart breaking due to the loss of innocent lives, and very costly on many fronts. We always knew this was possible from your first day in San Madrid. We always knew what these people were capable of. Remember our discussions after their first attack. It is to be expected. Notwithstanding their viciousness and criminality, their extreme mindsets are natural for them, and their responses to a large extent are predictable. They cannot easily be any other way."

Neera listened to his words carefully. Her mind almost felt overloaded by the complexities of the issues and the need for a response. Centeri had delivered his usual analytical, rational analysis and much of it was correct. Yet her mind and her instincts told her it was too rational, too controlled, almost like a conclusion looking for a justification. As he had so many times before, there was much he was leaving unsaid.

"Abriado, I am so tired of what at times feels like your duplicity. Do you believe the same applies to me? Am I predictable? Is my mindset equally predetermined?" she said into the monitor with no emotion whatsoever in her voice.

"Yes. It applies to all of us naturally but is expressed differently. It is their extremism that differentiates them. We all wrestle with the same demons, yet some of us move on, while others entrench themselves and grow more insular and eventually extreme."

"So tell me my mindset. Make your prediction. Read me like the book you apparently believe we all are."

Centeri smiled at her in the monitor, yet was clearly conflicted. He desired to assist his friend of many years but also felt the challenge of her words and the obvious sarcasm. He decided to proceed to see if she could move beyond the passions and patterns that defined her, that defined all men and women.

"You will fight to save Nano at all cost, which you are convinced is your company's future despite our conversation. You will use your relationships in San Madrid to remove Garcia, who is obviously corrupt and controlled by your opponents and demonstrate that their only option is to help you refute the fraudulent charges against Nano and allow its ground-breaking technology to propel their aviation industry forward. You will argue with me that if you can do so, I must continue to support Nano and view these recent events as merely a temporary setback, and that the promise of Nano is too great, and withdrawing it now or moving it to other applications will only assure its permanent stigma. This will be your challenge, your mission. To move this technology and your company forward, as a beacon of hope and achievement and the integrity of the human spirit, even while much of the world continues to implode. You will continue to believe that Blue and Shank and all their co-conspirators and even Mercy Green and her followers are aberrations, complex problems that can be fixed and supplanted with the reason and logic and technological achievement your company represents to you. And you will continue to see the young technology people as the living tools to do so. Your principle value and ideology is that science and reason and technology applied in a thoughtful, responsible way is the future of mankind."

Neera carefully considered his words. "Much of that is correct, but there is so much more that undermines your stereotyping. You failed to mention compassion, responsible compassion, not disguised narcissism. Individual responsibility in a healthy enlightened way, not the divisive weapon and justification for larceny as it is too often used today. And finally, most importantly, social and economic leadership. They look to us, Abriado. They look to all of us and try their best to sort out who speaks for them in their actions and words. It is our responsibility to lead through our achievements and make sure the demagogues do not prevail with their empty words."

"No," he said. "Not anymore. You cannot see it now, but you will. This is all the prelude to inevitable change. You see it as a challenge, a war between ideologies, where one side or the other will win or lose. That is only a part, a dynamic that has plagued humanity from the beginning. This is far more, mirroring the revolutionary changes fostered by access to unlimited information and the constantly changing technology underlying it that recognizes no leaders. The digital information itself in all of its forms, pushing and pulling, telling the stories and presenting the facts a thousand different ways, dynamic, constantly changing, competing, nothing to permanently grab onto, nothing to fuel the passions except the limitless process itself. The new authority of not one voice but a chorus of countless voices available at their fingertips."

She looked at him quizzically.

"Neera, we are no longer needed. Those who will matter more and more everyday are outgrowing us. Many continue to fight it, believing volume and rage and even fear will get their attention as it always has in the past. Soon we will all be talking only to ourselves. Our voices will be lost in the clamor."

Neera looked down at her desk. She understood his words but still believed reason and fairness could be heard and recognized. Her instincts told her that such a belief was exactly the predictability Centeri had discussed. She could not deny it. She could not deny who she was. To her it was admission and defiance in the same gesture. "Will you still support Nano if I convince them?"

"Things have moved more quickly than we believed possible. We must no longer try to prevent the inevitable. It must run its course. We must focus elsewhere. New Eden is close to completion, but much remains to be done. My attentions and the efforts of our people must be directed there. I am sorry Neera. I hope you can one day understand."

Neera could say nothing more. She ended the connection.

CHAPTER 15

"History has shown that even the most extreme impulses, with compassion and understanding, will inevitably evolve into goodness."

—*Mercedes Green*

"When everybody thinks the same way, they're not really thinking."

—*Anonymous internet Post*

"We're not gonna take it! Never did and never will! Do you remember those words, Mr. Broadwell? The Who, I think, from my youth. You know, I love music. Although the magic of country and pride in America and real Americans resonates with me more today, those words still have echoed all my life and do so even more powerfully today," Topher Blue said to Nathan Broadwell, as the cameras focused upon his every gesture.

"Please explain what you mean to our viewers, if you would. I think we would be interested to understand what you mean by the term 'real Americans,'" he said.

"Be glad to," Blue said smiling, certain they were his viewers, his followers alone, upon whom Broadwell had no claim. "For years now, our anthem was 'you are not entitled to what I earn.' Spoken to an over-reaching government and those who rely upon it. Those are magical words that have freed a generation, awakening a sleeping giant. The mantra of personal responsibility, self-reliance, and the glory of self-interest, which our opponents actually view as a sin. All ordained, I am certain, by god almighty himself. But now, we no longer need words. We need action. We need a cry to arms. 'We're not gonna take it' is a self evident truth. It is our truth. It is the truth of every man, woman and child who has had quite enough. We have had enough of a culture that coddles the lazy and the aimless and those who have been told or have convinced themselves that they are victims. We have had enough of a government that believes its principle function is to rescue and provide for the chosen poor, minorities, the elderly, immigrants, homosexuals, the godless and anyone else their twisted value systems deem needy at the cost to those who are not. And we have had enough of the leaders who have forgotten that this is a government by the people for the people and that it is answerable to all of those people! More importantly, in a twisted orgy of disguised narcissism, where they celebrate their compassion as proof of how superior they are to us, they impose their rescue mentality upon all of us, indoctrinate our children, spend trillions on a system and infrastructure to further it, force us to pay the tab, brainwash the recipients to turn them into dependent addicts, and then call us selfish monsters when we disagree and say enough is enough! Let me make it clear that I have no prejudices or hatred for anyone, not the honorable poor, not the elderly who helped build this great nation throughout their lives, not the ambitious young people who desire to do so in the future, not the inspired immigrants who came her to work hard and build a better life, nor anyone else the collectivists identify as victims. I too believe in compassion and decency and charity when appropriate. But I did not agree to subsidize anyone or pay for a government that does. I did not agree to have a system of senseless laws imposed upon me that prioritizes the values and interests of others because some mindless bureaucrat who never met a payroll in his life or was fired from private industry believes these takers need to be protected. And we have been forced to accept a system that has done exactly that for decades. Is my opposition to such mindless subsidization really so unreasonable? I resent being called a monster when I resist the imposition of such values. Individual responsibility and self-interest are the truly noble values. I have a right to prosper and pursue my own life without being told I am selfish and without being taxed and regulated to death to protect the downtrodden."

Blue paused momentarily to gather his thoughts. "You asked what I mean when I say 'real Americans.' I do not use this term to exclude or demonstrate prejudice or worse. Before this infection, this virus of collectivism and left-wing socialism that is rotting the American spirit, we did not always agree, in fact our political and ideological differences were at times legendary. But we always reconciled, and the vehicle of our reconciliation was the unifying factor of America. A belief that we would try again and next time we would prevail. Republicans, Democrats, liberals, conservatives all shared this belief, this commitment. We all expected victory but accepted occasional defeat and knew the battle would rage another day. But the belief that working within the system would be worthwhile, the ultimate belief in a unifying America has been lost. And why is that so? Because America always was founded upon capitalism and capitalist ideals were respected and protected. Gradual movement away from the capitalist ideal began within the government in the forties but was still essentially maintained. Over the past twenty years, the socialist, collectivist views grew exponentially, culminating in the ideologies of Green and her cohorts. No longer is competition and individual ambition, responsibility and prosperity celebrated. No longer are the job creators respected and admired. Now such values and the people behind them are reviled and viewed as an assault upon the collective good. All efforts now must be for the good of all men. Do you not hear it in their mantra? When one man suffers, all of mankind suffers. Do you not see it in their promised legislation and reforms? The Collective America Act and other initiatives that actually redistribute wealth above predetermined limits as well as others that provide for people from cradle to grave. Those who hold such views are not Americans.

These programs cannot exist within a capitalist society. America is and always has been a capitalist nation. These values and ideals and ideologies are European style collectivism and socialism, not American. So it is no longer differing opinions within a unified system. You and others perceive us as willing to let our differences destroy America. That is not the case. This nation is in danger because we have been invaded by outsiders, with radical values and irreconcilable views. There is no middle ground. With their agenda, there is nothing to preserve. They want to create a new America with new faces, and destroy everything we created. We will not allow it. They attack us as monsters and irrationally accuse us of letting children starve and the sick die on the street ostensibly to protect them from dependency while we lecture them about personal responsibility and self-interest. Such charges are insane and blind to the reality they have created. We simply will no longer permit the invasion of America by foreign collectivist ideals and values and permit it to exist solely to serve the invaders, while those who are responsible for growth, success, and prosperity are enslaved by suffocating regulation and taxation. They may either join us by embracing the capitalist principles of personal responsibility, and prosper or fail as is the capitalist way, or they may starve. Either way, this crippling dependency, this soul-killing entitlement will end and future generations will thank us for our courage. We did not create the suffering. Seventy years of dependency did. We are stopping it. We are taking America back, and there is room, whether black, white, young, old, healthy, infirm, native or naturalized, for all those who cherish it. We have and will continue to restore government to the limited role it was intended, to carefully assist in the achievement of prosperity to those who earn it, not to control and define prosperity and subsidize the undeserving. You accuse us of extremism. No. What you are experiencing is the response to the most destructive extremism ever conceived."

Nathan Broadwell briefly frowned at Topher Blue. It was apparent he was considering many responses. "An interesting manifesto, Mr. Blue. Many points are deserving of more discussion. But I must ask you instead: please explain to the hundreds of good people joining us today in this venue and the millions more viewing us on television and the internet, how do you reconcile the courage you speak of with the fact that you, President Shank, and countless other government officials as well as thousands of your colleagues are now fabulously wealthy? And they have done so by controlling, through highly questionable procedures including potential extortion, many of the largest companies in America, all of this while the economy is in tatters, technology strikes and cyber attacks are rampant, and the secession movement threatens to split the nation apart? How do you respond to accusations that your eloquent ideologies camouflage and then attempt to justify the most extreme seizure of economic power in modern history while you cleverly recruit starving supporters with promises of opportunity that are impossible for them to achieve?"

Topher Blue shook his head slowly. "I should have expected this. I knew it was possible but had hoped I was wrong. I had hoped your long-standing reputation as a respected journalist and man of integrity would have precluded such a bias. Your question sir, belies your liberal, collectivist leanings. You are obviously one of them, one of those who is committed to the suffocation of the human spirit."

"Answer the question Mr. Blue," Broadwell responded almost dismissively. "If it was unfair or demonstrated bias as you say, then it should be easily answered and dismissed. You are a gifted orator who has the ears of millions. You are no stranger to either controversy or confrontation. Perhaps you have grown accustomed to partisan entertainers and sycophants masquerading as journalists who long ago substituted ratings and financial reward for the pursuit of truth. Our viewers are watching. I inquire on their behalf, not my own. You know absolutely nothing of my leanings, as you put it, and they have no relevance either way. You were invited here to answer the questions. Will you do so?"

Blue continued to shake his head, his growing anger now apparent. "It is clear to me that you would never use such unethical tactics upon my opponents. You would welcome and embrace Mercy Green and her tribe…"

"How very opportune that you mentioned that, Mr. Blue," Broadwell said, interrupting him and now smiling. "Because we happen to have Mercy Green anxiously awaiting back stage to join you, and who promised me that she would answer every question asked. Many months ago during an interview, I challenged her to meet with you. She agreed. We hope you will now agree. And on this, I fully admit my own maneuverings, and that I was less than forthcoming, but it was obvious to us that had we informed you beforehand, you would have declined. My apologies to you, and I believe you know that you have no obligation to continue if this is too uncomfortable for you. I promise you that there will be no preferences demonstrated because none exist, and I will ask her the same pressing questions. Our only interests are those of our guests and viewers and our efforts to keep them informed, to hear the discourse between two of the most important voices in America today. This is an historic opportunity. Will you participate?"

Broadwell stared at Blue and knew that he was gathering his formidable strength and could not decline. He did not underestimate Blue and had witnessed his power on many occasions. Though Blue obviously felt trapped and manipulated, Broadwell knew that would pass quickly.

"Bring 'er on," he said, now smiling.

Mercy Green walked onto the studio set wearing her trademark white gown. She walked past Blue who was seated to Broadwell's left and sat down to his right. She did not acknowledge Blue. Broadwell did not attempt to introduce his two guests. He looked at Blue, who appeared to be contemplating whether to press the issue and approach Green.

Broadwell decided to speak quickly. "Ms. Green, welcome. You were backstage in the green room and I am sure you heard Mr. Blue's perhaps slightly theatric new statement to his listeners, 'we're not gonna take it.' You also heard his lengthy explanation and justification for this new maxim. He has not yet responded to my question about the widespread corruption and seizure of financial interests nationally, but I hope he will do so. Would you care to respond?"

"It is indeed a sad day for America when tyrants, racists, mass murderers, liars and thieves present themselves as victims and ask for sympathy," she said quietly.

"Oh my," Blue said, "You certainly don't waste any time with your famous compassion, do you?"

Green ignored him. "Mr. Broadwell, my intention here tonight is to explain the differences between us clearly and finally, and to help your viewers understand the monumental assault that has been and continues to be perpetrated upon them. Mr. Blue and his cohorts, the richest one or two percent of America, have invented an ideology which has as its purpose the economic rape and pillaging of America and to preserve their historic position of tribal, rascist power against the tides of inevitable social change. It is nothing more and nothing less. They cleverly express it in terms that will be irresistible and perhaps even addictive to the hungry and suffering people they restrain and even murder. Their tactics are old and outdated, the remnants of bygone eras where dictators and demagogues agitated and mobilized the masses. They establish as their idol with near religious fervor an economic system that progressive humanity has outgrown. They look romantically backwards to a time when tycoons and moguls and industrialists moved the world and attempt to impose themselves and idyllic, heroic images of the entrepreneur in similar roles, ignoring the waste and damage and disease and wars such men fostered and the inhumane greed that motivated them. They view themselves as warriors, defenders of the faith who alone fight an epic battle against the invaders, the poor, minorities, immigrants, women, anyone different from them who might assert human rights and decency. But ultimately it is about power and money. They have held it for generations and will not give it up to anyone, least of all those who look or sound or pray differently than they do. They may share it, doling out crumbs to those they have manipulated, and even occasionally allowing a token few to join them while they praise their initiative, but they will never give it up. They cannot. Because their fears are correct. They are now outnumbered and it grows worse with every passing day. They are under attack by the changing demographics. They will soon be the minority, the walking fossils of days lost forever. And they know that their children and grandchildren share little of their extremism and will eventually look back upon it with shame and confusion. Young people understand change and the futility of resisting it."

"An interesting assessment. Mr. Blue, we will ask you to respond in a moment. Ms. Green, let's focus upon your own vision for America first. At the end of the prior presidential administration, government entitlement spending reached an astounding seventy one percent of the entire federal budget. Economists are virtually unanimous in their conclusion that no nation can endure such subsidies for long and that the nation was teetering upon imminent economic collapse. The Shank administration campaigned against such spending and in a matter of three months, reversed the entitlements, safety nets, and social welfare programs of the past fifty years to less than four percent of government revenues. Who will pay for this?"

Mercy Green looked slowly at Broadwell, and then briefly glanced at Blue. "It not only will work but will become a social imperative. It is nothing less than the continuing evolution of humanity. Finally, we will leave the age of the pirates and thieves behind. They will pay for it, Mr. Broadwell. The two percent of the populace who steal and extort seventy percent of the wealth and have for thousands of years. The Collective America Act and other legislation will finally redistribute the wealth of this still great nation fairly and compassionately. It will not stifle initiative and ambition as our critics allege. It will foster healthy, responsible competition in a system of enlightened capitalism that fairly limits the wealth of any one person to a still-luxurious twenty million dollars. The rest will go to the remaining ninety eight percent. Who possibly needs more than twenty million dollars? How many homes and cars and luxury goods does one need? They can still pursue their ambitions and wealth but now, for the first time in history, it will be limited. Not eliminated. Perhaps they can even be motivated to advance not just their own bank accounts but the good of all mankind. They can still dwell in the lap of luxury. Only not obscenely so. And the remainder of the population can be assured that they will receive food, housing, medical care, education, and compassionate services to enhance their lives. It will work. The economists are certain of it. When resources are fairly distributed, instead of accumulating in the hands of the few, all will prosper. That is why we say when one person suffers, we all suffer. We may be finally ready to say, after a thousand years of incalculable suffering, when one person prospers, we all prosper. Won't that be magical?"

"Oh, for the love of god," Topher Blue said, interrupting. "There it is, straight from the white witch's mouth. That is the collectivist insanity we are fighting. That is the calculated murder of the human spirit, the death of individual responsibility, that we will fight to our own deaths to prevent."

Green turned to Blue, her rage clearly evident. "Do not speak to me about the murder of the human spirit when you and your co-conspirators are the greatest mass murderers in American history! Your policies have knowingly and intentionally destroyed the lives of half the American people, thrusting them into the most far-reaching economic depression the world has ever seen. Forty million are homeless, one hundred million are hungry, fifty million are unemployed, estimates of as high as one million have already died on the streets from preventable diseases and lack of health care, an entire generation has lost the opportunity of higher education, countless families have been split up and the entire nation, with the exception of your ever-protected two percent has lost any viable hope for the future. And all the while, you and your monstrous colleagues, including virtually the entire sitting government, have increased your wealth geometrically while you threaten, coerce and extort the few remaining brave souls trying to oppose you. We all know why you refused to answer Mr. Broadwell's question. Because you can't. You cannot deny the charges because you are guilty as charged. You are thieves and criminals on an epic scale who use an impossible primitive ideology to justify your larceny, and I swear to you in front of these viewers and listeners, I too will fight to the death to stop you, no matter what the cost. You have corrupted and destroyed everything good and decent that was once America, and if it requires us to destroy what little remains to rid the world of the scourge of your hypocrisy and criminality and restore our values of compassion and collective good, then so be it."

"How dare you, madam!" Blue shouted. "How dare you twist and pervert the facts and then appoint yourself the savior of mankind? There is only one savior I know of and it certainly is not you. In fact, you are nothing but an abomination in his holy eyes! This nation is suffering because your predecessors and your values destroyed it! You and your kind not only created entire generations addicted to dependency and entitlement, sucking the lifeblood out of others and telling them it was perfectly acceptable because they were victims, but you adopted and perpetuated social welfare and entitlement programs that literally bankrupted the nation. Bankrupting America is not compassion! You delude yourselves when you accuse us of ending the programs and dispossessing the population. Those programs were already dead and bankrupt, but you were too lost in your savior fantasies to see it. America was on the verge of ruin. There were no resources left. Nothing but mind boggling debt to creditors throughout the world, who were actively plotting our demise with armies looming on our borders only months away. We took what we found, economic and social ruin, and courageously committed to restore sanity and fiscal responsibility and to stop spending money that did not exist. And, yes. Yes indeed. We told every American that the free ride was over and it was time to get back to work. Not as a threat or a prison or death sentence. But as an opportunity. A challenge. To revitalize a belief in prosperity and a belief in the greatness of America. We did not promise it would be easy or without pain and loss. To correct the insanity of seventy years, painful sacrifices had to be made. You would have had us all moping in victimization and fatalism and paralysis. We held out a chance to prosper and excel and to resurrect one's self by his or her own bootstraps and not by more empty promises of handouts and charity. This is the American way, and always has been. The pain and chaos that has resulted is not our doing but yours. You and your kind immediately went to work to destroy the blossoming hope we created and sabotage every initiative of prosperity we offered. And for the record: I do not apologize that I and many like me have prospered. I hope and pray that countless more will follow in our footsteps. Americans do not resent us. They admire our success and prosperity and hold us out as the role models for the god given belief that one day they will do the same. But rest assured that they do resent you. You can be certain of that. They see through you and your vicious hypocrisy. They know that your cries of compassion and collective good are nothing more than thinly veiled efforts to enslave them and impose your own will and values and have government tell them how to live every aspect of their lives. They know instinctively that your values kill initiative, kill achievement, kill prosperity, and kill the human spirit. Can you not understand that they want to live a prosperous life? They want to enjoy the fruits of their labors. They dream of comfort and the good things life can offer and want to apologize to no one for it. But your message is one of shame. And they despise you for it. They despise you for taking away their hopes and dreams and replacing them with socialist and collectivist mediocrity. You have not fooled them. They know in their hearts that only the lazy and the corrupt and the incompetent deny self-interest and personal responsibility and want to live off the efforts of others in some sort of collective fantasyland. But doing so is exactly your bill of sale. It is you who manipulate and deceive and engage in larceny and extortion. You steal their hopes and dreams and passions and substitute a vision that history has repeatedly rejected, along with the con men who tried to impose it."

"Ms. Green, Mr. Blue, I am afraid I must intervene and ask you both to pause," Broadwell said. "Our discussion today is extraordinary and I think our guests and viewers are being enlightened far beyond what we had hoped for. A few minutes ago, I apologized to Mr. Blue for perhaps engaging in a bit of an end run by, unknown to him, inviting Ms. Green to join us. Well, turnabout is fair play, so I will now apologize to you Ms. Green, and again to you Mr. Blue, and introduce yet another guest to join this compelling conversation. I remind you both that neither of you are obligated to continue if you deem my tactics unfair. I ask our panel, our guests and our viewers everywhere to welcome one of the few human beings who truly deserves the title of living legend. Ladies and gentlemen, visionary, activist, philanthropist, humanitarian, author, actor and artist, the incomparable Adrianna Snow."

The frail elderly woman walked slowly onto the stage, rejecting the assistance of her aides. Broadwell surrendered his chair and moved to the end of the table so that Snow could sit between the antagonists.

"Hello, Mercedes," she said to Green. "I hope I am not intruding."

"Never, Adrianna," Green said warmly. "I could not be happier to see you again."

Blue did not wait to be acknowledged. "Politics aside, Ms. Snow, I confess I am more than a little starstruck. This is indeed an honor."

"Good," Snow replied. "Then perhaps you will both listen to me."

"Uh oh," Blue said, smiling broadly looking at Green. In a brief moment of shared humanity, she returned his smile and nodded.

"Shall we begin?" Broadwell asked. "Ms. Snow, you have heard the discussions backstage up to now. Do you have any comments?"

"Indeed I do, Nathan," she answered. Looking at both Green and Blue, her eyes burning with a vigor denied to her body, she slowly reached for and took each of their hands within her own and grasped them tightly. "Stop this nonsense. Stop it now. I implore you."

"Ms. Snow..." Blue began to say, but Snow interrupted him.

"I have listened to you both for a very long time and do not doubt for a moment the passion of your commitments. How it unfolds and is applied, we will best leave alone for the moment. But I beg you to understand that these are your passions, not your followers'. And you are doing the greatest disservice possible to them and the world at large by the methods you use to recruit and mobilize them. Your words, your admonitions, your appeal to the emotions and fears of millions, your attacks, the unwavering, relentless certainty of your convictions simplifies the world far too much in the minds of your millions of followers. For them it becomes too black and white with the heroes and villains too superficially defined. Can you not see that? Mercedes, do you see no truth at all in the concerns of Mr. Blue and his followers? Can you not distinguish between his message and his methods? Perhaps one day we will all evolve to the point where every man works for his brothers and in so doing provides for himself, but that day is a very long way off and I do not think I would want to live in that world." She paused briefly and smiled at Blue. "I love the passion of the artist and the entrepreneur and the visionary and the sheer messiness, and even chaos they sometimes cause as they pursue their own callings and rewards. They benefit all of us and pull much of our society along with them to new heights and insights. You cannot restrain or shackle them without limiting us all. And Mr. Blue, is there no trust remaining in your heart for the diversity of humanity? Must the excesses of prior administrations poison any semblance of trust and compassion? Do you honestly believe that all those different from you are these takers who plot to live off your efforts and supplant you? You often quote the biblical mandates of charity and love for your fellow man but expect the darkest possible outcome when such principles are applied by our government. You warn that you are no longer going to take it anymore, whatever this 'it' is. I ask you instead, and you too Mercedes, are we all not better than this? Our world is literally falling to pieces and you both battle like mad Ahabs seeing the demonic white whale wherever you look. And you do not even notice your growing isolation. Look out at your audience. Look at the demographics of your followers. How many young faces are there? I see very few in the audience here tonight. My advisors tell me your armies of disciples nationally are mostly older and battle-worn. Many of the young apparently do not even hear you."

Adrianna Snow paused momentarily to gather her thoughts. She looked at Broadwell, who himself was staring intently at Blue and Green. Blue appeared agitated, as if he were rehearsing his next lines. Green fumbled with a small stack of note cards in front of her, casually listening to Snow.

"It appears I have failed," she said quietly to Broadwell. Her disappointment was apparent to all who heard her. She thought about the urgency of her message and how she had hoped her stature and the power of her words might have caused a momentary softening between these mortal enemies. It was not meant to be. The same processes of values and intuitions and their defense at all costs that blinded and enraged their followers consumed Blue and Green as well.

She would not give up that easily, she thought, and prepared to continue, her well known determination and ferociousness now fully triggered.

She would not get the chance, at least not the one she expected. From several rows back in the audience, a young man suddenly stood up and cried out, "We're not gonna take it!" while running towards the stage. Jumping up, he pulled out a hand gun and approached Mercy Green. She stared at him in horror, momentarily paralyzed.

"Mercy! Get down!" her assistant Melinda cried out from the side of the stage. "It's him! From the rally! The one who's been following you!"

"Young man, please don't do this," Green pleaded.

"Shut up, witch!" he screamed, pointing the barrel at her head. "Mr. Blue, I'll stop her now. I'll stop all of them who take and use us and kill America!"

Suddenly Topher Blue, who had pushed his chair back to the curtain behind the stage and was literally being dragged away along with Broadwell by three of his assistants, broke free from them and stood up. "Don't do this!" he shouted to the assailant. "She is not worth it. We'll defeat her. We'll defeat them all. Put the gun down! Please!"

Pandemonium erupted in the theater as the guests realized what was occurring and armed officers entered, running towards the stage. The intruder knew he had run out of time. He pulled the trigger and the muzzle exploded with fire. Adrianna Snow had leaned towards Green almost as if to protect her. She appeared calm and almost detached, as if she were somehow capable of transcending the violence and insanity now surrounding her. The bullet tore into and passed through her upper arm and was deflected away from Mercy Green, who screamed, seeing that Snow had been hit. The guards fell on the young man and began beating him savagely with their pistols and night sticks. Within a matter of seconds, his skull collapsed and he laid dead. Mercy Green fell upon Adrianna Snow, followed by Blue. Broadwell observed from the side of the stage.

"No, no, no!" she cried. Blue gently pulled her off while the guards and emergency personnel began to address Snow's wounds. Green's white gown was covered with blood. It was unclear whether it was Snow's or the attacker's.

Snow remained fully awake and alert. She looked at Green and Blue who now stood above her.

"This is your legacy," she whispered as they carried her away. Blue stared at her, amazed, thinking that she may have actually even smiled.

Neera Solai looked at Abriado Centeri on the screen. "Oh god, Abriado. I am so sorry. Let me come there. We can go to her at the hospital. You should not be alone." Her tensions towards him from recent events now seeming unimportant.

Centeri looked at her and forced a half smile. "Her assistant phoned me and said that Adrianna asked me not to come. She will be fine, he said. It's relatively superficial. The bullet passed through her upper arm missed most of the muscle. The major concern is her age of course. They'll keep her for a few days to be safe. She is very strong, Neera."

With his words, Neera felt her own heart break, knowing that Snow had again devastated her son, this time denying him the right to help and comfort her after a savage assault.

"I, I don't know what to say." The image of Green's white gown streaked with blood was unsettling, oddly reminiscent of San Madrid, she thought.

Centeri said nothing for a few moments, recalling Neera's description of the earlier events. "There is nothing to say," he answered. "Apparently, the shooter was a particularly militant devotee of Blue and had been following Green. She had even engaged him and called off her own attackers at a rally a year or two earlier. They are calling Adrianna a hero, saying that she actually shielded Green and diverted the bullet. The most recent of a lifetime of accomplishments. I suppose that will increase her stature even further. Even Blue appears to have risen above expectations by putting himself in the line of fire and attempting to talk down the shooter."

"I don't want to be unduly suspicious, but having seen her in action, I would be careful about using the word hero, a term that is too frequently overused today. As to Blue, I would argue the shooter chose the wrong target," she responded sarcastically. "Abriado, I don't care what she says, you should go to her."

"Would that not make it all about me, Neera?"

Neera considered his words and could not disagree. "Perhaps, and when it comes to Adrianna Snow, that would be a refreshing change."

"Maybe the next time she takes a bullet for a demagogue," he said quietly, and then signed off.